WINTER'S STORM

WINTER BLACK SERIES: BOOK EIGHT

MARY STONE

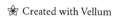

To my husband.
Thank you for taking care of our home and its many inhabitants
while I follow this silly dream of mine.

DESCRIPTION

Human webs are the deadliest...

When Ryan O'Connelly—the unwilling accomplice of a bank robber turned mass murderer—slipped out of the FBI's grasp, no one expected to hear from him again, much less of his own volition. But when he shows up at the FBI's doorstep after almost a year of successful evasion, he has information to point Special Agent Winter Black in the direction of a brutal serial killer.

As Ryan takes the team into the deep, dark web of sinister secrets, Winter receives an even more disturbing message from her brother than the last. She can feel him out there...watching, waiting.

Lucky for Winter, she isn't afraid of spiders. She's only afraid when the spider disappears.

Book seven of Mary Stone's addictive Winter Black Series, Winter's Web, exposes what goes on behind closed doors and the web of lies and deadly truths we ignore to protect the ones we love.

1

Before he stepped off the packed earth trail, Jackson Fisher cast a paranoid glance around the clearing. Though the moon was almost full, a handful of clouds had moved in to obscure all but a faint glow. Even if the sky was clear, the hiking trail he was about to leave cut through a wooded area, and the canopy of tree branches blocked out any light from the moon or stars.

In the clearing, however, Jackson was afforded a clear view of the moon's dim glow. The meager illumination was more ominous than helpful.

As he strode through the clearing, Jackson shook himself out of the thoughts. Just because he couldn't see Jaime yet didn't mean he wasn't there. Jackson needed to focus.

Outdoor meetings with Jaime in the dead of night weren't a new occurrence, but Jackson couldn't help but feel like he'd wandered onto the set of a horror film. According to Jaime, his brain worked clearest at night, and the kid *hated* cities. As far as Jaime was concerned, the more rural, the better.

Jackson had never been a fan of metropolitan areas, either, but right now he wished they'd agreed to meet at a twenty-four-hour diner. Or a damn mall. A festival with a million people pressed in on every side would have suited him better than the eerie quiet dancing on his nerves.

He should just leave, he knew, but he needed this meeting. Just because he and Jaime disagreed on their methods didn't mean Jackson could afford to cut ties with him. Jaime was a man of action, and their cause needed men like Jaime.

As a show of good faith, Jackson had reluctantly agreed to meet with Jaime at the isolated area. The kid was volatile, but he appreciated small, polite gestures.

Now, Jackson had to hope that this display of goodwill would start their dialogue off on the right track.

Slowing his breathing to a quiet rhythm, he listened to the rustle of the tree branches in the night breeze. The sound was unobtrusive, but at the same time, it might have blocked out the slight disturbance of footsteps on the grassy clearing.

A flicker of movement from a line of shrubs behind a picnic bench jerked Jackson's attention away from the edge of the forest. Despite his efforts to keep his breathing measured, he took in a sharp breath at the sudden disturbance.

He'd looked over the area behind the picnic table, and he was sure he'd spotted nothing out of the ordinary. Still, somehow, there he was. Jaime Peterson.

With both hands thrust into his pockets, Jaime walked up to stand just to the side of the wooden bench. Jackson slowed his advance but didn't let his stare waver from the shadowy figure.

In the darkness, Jaime's trademark olive drab jacket looked black. As he moved to close the distance between them, his dusty work boots made little more than a whisper of sound against the lush grass.

Truthfully, Jackson didn't want to stand any closer to the lunatic than was absolutely necessary. But he couldn't back up now. He *wouldn't* back up now. In front of Jaime Peterson, Jackson would show no weakness, no hint of anxiety, not the slightest shred of fear.

Crossing his arms, Jackson felt the reassuring weight of the forty-five he'd tucked into a holster beneath his arm. He was sure Jaime was armed, but the kid's weapon of choice tended to be a six-inch hunting knife. Jackson had only seen him brandish the blade once, back when they first met.

Back then, Jackson had been confident that Jaime shared the same goals and ideals as he did. He was sure Jaime's ties to Tyler Haldane and Kent Strickland were proof enough of his dedication.

He should have known better.

The second he saw the look in those eerie blue eyes, he should have known that Jaime Peterson wasn't like him.

Jackson had been dedicated to the cause since before Tyler Haldane and Kent Strickland had taken up arms to spread their message at the Riverside Mall in Danville, Virginia. Jackson's father and his father before him had been dedicated to the same cause as Tyler and Kent—to return the country to its glory days. The days when women knew their place and men could be men. But he should have known that Jaime was different.

Jaime wasn't dedicated to a cause. The kid was a psychopath, and he was out to advance only one cause. He served only himself. He used the guise of their mission merely to satiate his own bloodlust.

Despite the realization, Jackson had still accepted Jaime's offer to meet up at a tattered picnic table just off a quiet wooded trail. Even if Jaime served no cause aside from his own desire to kill, the kid could still be useful. He was a weapon. If Jackson found a way to point him in the direction of their adversaries, he could fire him like a Howitzer. Jaime would do the dirty work, and Jackson's hands would remain clean. When the cops came to investigate the series of brutal murders, they would wind up at Jaime's doorstep, not Jackson's.

But a weapon like Jaime Peterson was volatile on its best day, and downright treacherous on its worst. Jaime might have been a psychopath, but he wasn't stupid.

He should have known Jaime wasn't one of them.

The shadows shifted along Jaime's scruffy face as his lips curved into a smile that sent a wave of icy fear down Jackson's spine. "You came. Honestly, I wasn't sure you would."

Jackson forced a neutral expression to his face and nodded. "We're still in this fight together, brother. Just because we don't agree on everything doesn't make us enemies."

The statement was at least partly true. Hopefully, the half-truth would keep Jaime's suspicions at bay. Jackson wasn't here to mend fences with the kid. He was here to sever their relationship.

As Jaime returned the nod, the same unsettling smile remained on his lips. "I'm glad to hear that."

The ice in his voice told Jackson that he was anything *but* glad.

As much as Jackson wanted to back away four or five paces, he held his ground. "We're fighting the same fight, but we aren't fighting it the same way."

Jaime lifted an eyebrow. "So, you think that man I killed for you should have been allowed to live? He was married to a black woman. You and I both know that's unnatural."

Grating his teeth, Jackson nodded. "I know. I understand why you did it, but I don't see how we can sustain our fight by murdering civilians. We need to think bigger. We need to gather our forces, and we need to target the weaklings in our government. Not by killing them, but by usurping their power. That is how we win this fight. We cut the head from the snake, not the tail."

Jaime tilted his head to the side in what Jackson could tell was a feigned show of pensiveness. "And how, exactly, would we do that without killing them?"

Jackson opened his mouth to reply, but Jaime cut him off.

"They still have too much support. We're here to get rid of that support. We're here to finish what Tyler and Kent started. *They* weren't afraid of spilling a little blood. The only way we can get the support we need is by proving that we aren't weak. By proving that we'll do what's necessary to make sure our message reaches an audience."

Even as he racked his brain, Jackson knew he didn't have a suitable rebuttal. He couldn't say that the faces of the man and woman he'd killed haunted his dreams, even in his waking moments. He couldn't express regret or remorse.

Finally, Jackson shook his head. "I can't help you with that, Jaime. You need to fight in your way, and I need to go my way. Even if we're fighting for the same cause, we can't work together if we don't fight in the same way."

As Jaime's face went carefully blank, the clearing lapsed into silence. The distant hoot of an owl and the hushed whisper of a temperate night breeze were the only sounds as the seconds ticked away.

Parting ways with Jaime Peterson was like disarming a bomb. One wrong move, and shrapnel would rip through Jackson's body like he was made of paper mâché.

When Jaime spoke again, his voice shattered the eerie spell of quiet. "Okay."

Okay? That was it? That was all he had to say?

Before Jackson could stammer out a response, Jaime met his gaze and laughed, the sound splitting the quiet of the night. "What's that look for? You look like you've wound up in the middle of a warzone or something. What, did you think I was going to *kill* you? Jesus, Jackson." Shaking his head, Jaime pulled his hands from his pockets and rested his hands to his hips. "Stop acting so paranoid."

Jackson swallowed as his heart rate increased, adrenaline spilling into his system. The remark had been made to placate him, but he still wasn't so sure he believed anything that came out of Jaime's mouth. All he managed in response was a nod.

Jaime's smile didn't reach his eyes. A less keen observer might have missed the gradual movement as Jaime slid one hand around his back beneath his jacket, changing his stance to cover the motion. The action was slow and deliberate, but Jackson had been put on high alert as soon as the psychopath moved his hands.

"You're right." Jaime shrugged, and his hand moved a little more. "We'd be better off if we were both playing to our strengths. Yours is communicating, and mine is…well…"

In a blur of motion, the pale moonlight flashed against silver as Jaime unsheathed his favored hunting knife. By the time the blade was in Jaime's gloved hand, Jackson had only just wrapped his fingers around the grip of his forty-five.

He already knew he would be too slow to brandish the weapon, but he'd be damned if he didn't try. Jaime had brought a knife to a gun fight, and Jackson had the gun.

But the speed with which he'd produced the knife didn't seem humanly possible. Jackson wasn't out of shape, though he carried a little extra weight on his broad frame. Jaime, on the other hand, was tall and lean. And he was *fast*.

With one swift step, Jaime closed the distance between them just as Jackson pulled his forty-five free of the holster. Jackson didn't have time to so much as bring the weapon to bear when Jaime arced his arm down with the same blinding speed.

Fire ripped through Jackson's forearm as the blade tore

through muscle and tendon with a sickening wet rip. Jackson didn't remember initiating the sound, but a sharp growl of pain escaped his lips. The world was moving in slow motion, and he felt as if he was fighting his way through molasses.

He clenched his hand as tightly as he could manage, but the effort to maintain his grip on the forty-five was for naught. Though he didn't know much about human anatomy, he could only assume that Jaime had severed a tendon or damaged a muscle. Each minute movement sent a new fire rippling through Jackson's forearm, all the way up to his shoulder.

With a muffled thump, the forty-five fell to the grass.

The glint of the pale moonlight was dulled by the blood that stained the blade as Jaime retracted his arm for another blow. As Jaime brought his arm down to drive the blade into Jackson's heart, he frantically pivoted his body to the side.

Rather than pierce Jackson's heart, the hunting knife cut deep just above his collarbone. A freshly fanned fire licked at each and every nerve ending along Jackson's shoulder and chest. For a split-second, he was almost convinced that Jaime had indeed hit his heart.

As Jaime sidestepped to follow Jackson's movement, the muted light glinted off the wicked blade like it was an other-worldly weapon and not just a hunting knife. Another series of clouds had moved in to obscure the moon and stars. How fitting for what Jackson was sure were his final moments of life.

No. I won't let this psychopath win. Not tonight.

Jackson took a frantic step backward as he clasped at the newest wound with his uninjured hand. The forty-five was still on the ground, but Jackson knew better than to try to secure the weapon. The second he turned around to reach for the handgun, Jaime would seize his opportunity and jam the blade into Jackson's lung.

He needed to run. He knew he couldn't outpace Jaime for long, but as long as he could get to his car, he would be in the clear.

Spitting out a string of obscenities, Jaime stepped forward and raised the knife again.

With a sharp intake of breath, Jackson spun around on one foot and darted away from the clearing. He trudged directly into the thicket that formed the perimeter of the picnic area, but he didn't balk as the branches of a handful of shrubs scratched at his cheeks. The fire of his two stab wounds far outweighed any potential discomfort that came with a jaunt through thick vegetation.

As he emerged from the line of bushes, he increased his pace to an outright sprint. He was sure Jaime was right on his heels, but he couldn't focus on the kid's proximity right now. With one hand clamped down on the deep shoulder wound and the other rendered all but useless by a well-placed cut, Jackson had to use all his energy to keep one foot in front of the other.

Adrenaline cut through the fire of the injuries as he zigzagged around tall trees and unruly bushes. As he approached a fallen log, he realized that he had no idea where he was going. He thought he'd taken off in the direction of the gravel parking area, but now, he wasn't so sure.

For the first time since he'd started to run, Jackson dared a glance over his shoulder. Though he half-expected to see the menacing shape of Jaime's tall form, the area was still. Trees stood close to one another like a series of shadowy sentinels, but try as he might, Jackson couldn't spot so much as a hint of movement.

Despite Jaime's absence, Jackson kept his ragged breathing as quiet as he could manage. After another paranoid glance around the area, he picked his way over to hunch behind a jagged, moss-covered rock.

If he wanted to get out of these woods, he needed to get his bearings. He carried a compass whenever he went for a hike or a hunt, but he hadn't thought he'd need the device tonight. When he left his car to trudge up the trail to meet Jaime that night, he hadn't expected to wind up in the middle of a forest.

Not that he knew which direction would lead him to his car, anyway. If he'd thought to bring his compass, he'd have stopped to get his bearings, but he'd taken no such precaution. A foolish mistake. One of many mistakes he'd made that night.

After wiping the blood off one hand, Jackson reached into a back pocket for his smartphone. Though he wasn't surprised to see that he had no service in the isolated woodland, he barely managed to bite back a handful of four-letter words.

He was lost. In the middle of a forest at half-past midnight with a psychopath on his tail, Jackson was lost.

Bile stung the back of his throat as he slumped down to a low crouch, giving himself a few more moments to think. He needed to think.

As he slowed his movements and the adrenaline receded, the two knife wounds felt like those parts of his body had been permanently set ablaze. He'd heard from soldiers that the pain from a sudden injury like a gunshot was almost too much for a human's mind to process. As a result, such a traumatic injury felt more akin to a burning ember they couldn't shake.

He'd retained skepticism, but now, he suspected the stories were all true. The wounds on his arm and collarbone had taken on a life of their own. Whenever Jackson breathed or shifted in place, he stoked a fire he couldn't see.

He could deal with one situation or the other. If he was only being chased by a psychopath, he could outrun or outsmart them. If he had only been lost, he could keep walking until his phone had a signal. But he wasn't so sure he could handle both at the same time.

Plus, he was bleeding. Badly.

As he looked down at the front of his t-shirt, he watched blood seeping steadily from the burning injury on his shoulder.

How long did it take a person to bleed out? How long until hypovolemic shock settled in?

He didn't know, but if he didn't do something, one or both of those possibilities would become real. Just as he started to pull off his jacket to construct a makeshift bandage, he froze in place. The sound was faint, but he was sure he'd just heard the crackle of leaves or branches.

He kept still, and soon, his lungs ached from holding his breath. Despite the discomfort, he still didn't dare to breathe.

Something was out there. Something, or some*one*.

And that someone had a name. A mission.

Him.

When the faint snap sounded out again, the disturbance was more noticeable. It might have been a wild animal—a coyote or an opossum, maybe a raccoon. But it was just as likely that the sound had been caused by Jaime's careful footsteps.

Jackson balanced himself on one hand as he crept closer to the edge of the boulder. He inhaled slowly through his nose and blinked repeatedly against the darkness. From beneath the cover of the trees, the moonlight was even fainter than it had been in the clearing.

Each inch of movement was agony, but Jackson kept his breathing silent until he was afforded a glimpse of the same area from which he had come. In the darkness, no shadows stirred.

Jackson held the position as another surge of adrenaline

rushed through his tired body. He knew he hadn't imagined the sounds. He knew something had been there.

Clenching his jaw, he started to ease himself back to the relative shelter of the rock.

Before he settled back into his position, another crack splintered the night. A fresh dump of adrenaline surged through his body as he realized that this noise came from *behind* him.

Ignoring the newly stoked fire that ripped through his shoulder, he snapped his head around to face the source of the sound. But it didn't matter how quickly he moved. He was too late.

Even in the pitch darkness of the woods, Jackson could still make out the eerie blue shade of Jaime's eyes. As he jammed the blade through Jackson's ribs, the smiling psychopath never broke eye contact.

Clasping the hem of Jackson's shirt with one hand, Jaime leaned in closer. "You disappointed me, Jackson. You showed real promise, and then you pissed it down your leg. Just like the others."

The taste of iron spread over Jackson's tongue. "O-others?"

Jaime's laugh was more a taunt. "What, you thought you were special? Thought you were the first?" He twisted the knife smiling as Jackson screamed. "You're number three," Jaime continued, his voice as light as if he was having a conversation with the queen. "You aren't special. There are tens of thousands of racist pricks out there who'll run to my beck and call as soon as I give the word. Honestly, I've never really been sure why you idiots fixate so much on the color of someone's skin when the real problem doesn't have anything to do with it."

Jackson made a desperate attempt to swallow the blood

that bubbled up from his throat, but like everything else tonight, the effort was for naught.

With a derisive cluck of his tongue, Jaime twisted the knife, sending a fresh wave of agony through Jackson's body.

"Women." Jamie said the word as if it tasted bad. "Women are the real problem. You and your people are focused on the wrong thing, but don't worry. I'll make sure they see the error of their ways. I'll set them all straight."

As Jaime drove the blade the rest of the way into Jackson's lung, the only sound that slipped past his bloodied lips a wet gurgle.

The pain from his shoulder had dissipated, but he couldn't remember when the air had gotten so cold. As the chill rose up to greet him, Jackson's eyelids felt as if they'd been weighted down with lead.

After one more effort to take a breath, he gave up and let the darkness envelope him.

2

As William Hoult slammed the trunk closed, he glanced over to the man at his side. Jaime's blue eyes flicked back and forth before he met Will's questioning glance with a nod. Their footsteps crunched against the gravel of the circular parking lot as they made their way to the front of the car. Wordlessly, Will pried open the passenger side door and took his seat.

After adjusting the rearview mirror, Jaime fastened his seatbelt with a click. When his expectant gaze shifted over to Will, he followed suit. There was a body in the trunk of their car. Not just a body, but a body that Will had helped wrap in a tarp and carry through the woods.

For the first part of Jaime and the other man's exchange, Will had been hidden just off the walking trail. He'd been out of earshot, and the low light had made it difficult to make out either man's facial expressions. But based on the way the broad-shouldered man had held himself, Jaime was right. The man wasn't on their side, and he never had been.

But did that mean that Jaime had to kill him? Will had never seen another person die before, and he supposed he technically still hadn't. By the time Jaime had beckoned him into the woods, the other man was already dead.

As the car's engine hummed to life, Will felt Jaime's stare on the side of his face.

"What's on your mind, Will?" Jaime asked, his voice light and conversational.

Shaking his head, Will met his new friend's gaze. "I'm just wondering about that guy, I guess. What did he do?"

With a sour look, Jaime shifted the car into gear. "He was going to rat us out."

Will sucked in a sharp breath. "He was?"

Jaime nodded, but his eyes were fixed on the road. "He was. He didn't have the stomach for what we must do, and he was going to tell the cops about us. About *both* of us. He put you in danger too."

Angry now, Will cast a reflexive glance to the rear of the car. "A rat, huh? Then I don't blame you. Rats have to die."

Jaw clenched, Jaime nodded again. "That's right. I didn't want to have to kill him. I tried to talk some sense into him, but he wouldn't listen. Then, he pulled a gun on me before he tried to take off. I didn't have a choice. I had to go after him."

Though Will's pulse had picked up, he wasn't nervous because Jaime had just killed a man. He was nervous because they'd come so close to being caught before they could even put their plan into motion.

A few months earlier, Will had come across Jaime in an underground forum where likeminded men could share ideas about their vision for the future of the United States. None of Will's friends understood the peril their country faced, but Jaime had.

In Jaime, Will had finally found a confidante.

Before long, Will learned that he and Jaime lived less than two hours away from one another. They hadn't met up in person until a couple weeks ago, but Will already felt like they had become good friends. Unlike the other posters in the online forums, Jaime had a plan of action.

Jaime was determined to make a difference in the world, and in Will's mind, the only way to make a difference was to follow in Tyler Haldane and Kent Strickland's footsteps. Fortunately, Jaime agreed.

As he pulled himself from the reverie, Will cast another quick glance to Jaime's stoic face. "So, do we need to find someone else? Someone to replace that guy?" Will still didn't know the dead man's name, but he didn't care. A snitch was a snitch.

Jaime slowly shook his head. "No. We don't need to find someone. We can start this ourselves, and then they'll come to us."

Even though he still wasn't sure what exactly Jaime's plan entailed, Will nodded. "Where do we start, then? Or, well, *how* do we start?"

The question sounded at least marginally more sophisticated than simply stating that he didn't know anything about Jaime's plan. Despite their bond, Jaime had kept the details close to his vest.

Jaime's blue eyes flicked to Will and then back to the road. As he pursed his lips, he drummed gloved fingers against the steering wheel. "I can trust you, can't I, Will?"

Will nodded like the answer should have been obvious. "You know you can."

The slightest hint of a smile crept to Jaime's face. "You're right. I did know the answer to that. Okay, Will, I'm going to tell you something that I didn't even tell our friend back there." He jerked a thumb over his shoulder.

This was it. After three months, Jaime was finally about to let Will in on his vision. On his *action*.

"I helped Tyler and Kent plan for the Riverside Mall. I don't know why they decided to wear those stupid Nazi armbands, but I also know that you know that's not our mission. There is no 'master race.' God created all men equal, but *women*. Women are the real problem. If men weren't so wrapped up in their racist crusades, they'd see that women are what's ruining our society today."

Nodding, Will shifted in his seat. "How do we make them see that?"

The smile on Jaime's lips grew wider. "We finish what Tyler and Kent started. They picked the Riverside Mall for a reason. That's where the sinners and the harlots like to congregate. A mall is like a woman's drug. They go there to spend the hard-earned money of their husbands, or the money they make in their jobs. Women shouldn't be out at a place like that, and they shouldn't be spending a man's money."

"They should be at home," Will finished for him.

Jaime waved an appreciative finger at Will. "That's right. That's why Kent and Tyler went there. They knew they would be able to take out plenty of the sinners if they went to a mall. And they did. Everyone there deserved what they got, and everyone who didn't get what they deserved needs to be punished."

As the implication dawned on him, Will's eyes widened. "We have to finish what they started. We have to deal with the people who made it out, don't we?"

"We do." Jaime's voice was cold but determined.

Will scratched the side of his bearded face. "How do we find them, though? Some of them were in the news, but not all of them."

Jaime nodded his agreement. "You're right. Computers aren't exactly my strong suit, but I'm sure we can find someone who knows how to get what we're after."

"A hacker?"

"A hacker," Jamie confirmed." The smile returned, though

the evil living inside it caused the hair on Will's arms to raise. "Yes. We find their names, and then we can start our mission."

A portion of Jaime's smile made its way to Will's face. It had taken years, but Will had finally found someone who was as convicted as he was.

3

E ven with the faint drone of the voices of a group of nearby grillers, the dock that Winter Black and Autumn Trent had chosen for their early afternoon fishing expedition was quiet. Patches of trees dotted the shore of the lake, and a slight breeze cast ripples along the water's surface. The grillers were hidden from her view by a handful of tall oaks, but every now and then, she caught a glimpse of a red or blue coat or a whiff of seared meat that made her think of Noah Dalton, her boyfriend.

She smiled, just thinking of herself, of all people, actually having a boyfriend. But she did. A good one too. A man who had supported her when she didn't even deserve that support.

When Winter's phone rang, she was surprised that she was in a service area. As Autumn unfolded a canvas chair, she lifted her eyebrows. Apparently, she was surprised that they could receive a signal on their phones too.

With a shrug, Winter set down her chair and fished the smartphone out of her jacket pocket. The screen displayed the name James Bond, but she knew the caller wasn't 007.

James Bond was the codename she'd decided to use for Ryan O'Connelly.

Winter had gone through a handful of other codenames, but none had suited the conman turned FBI informant quite like the MI6 agent. Since Ryan occasionally worked undercover to glean information for the Bureau, she hadn't wanted to store his real name in her phone.

Swiping the answer key, she raised the device to one ear. "This is Agent Black."

"Afternoon, Agent Black." Though fainter than it had been a few months ago, Ryan's words were tinged with a slight Irish accent. His tone was chipper, but Winter had learned not to read into the man's pleasant moods.

Ever since he'd been absolved of jail time two and a half months ago, Ryan was usually chipper. His sister, Lillian, was planning to use the time over Christmas break to move herself and her two children from their current home in Omaha, Nebraska to Richmond. Winter suspected that after the rest of his family was within arms' length, Ryan's upbeat demeanor would be dialed up to eleven.

Winter pushed the thoughts aside. "Hey, Ryan. What's up?"

"Not much. Sorry to interrupt your Sunday, but Agent Welford and I just finished following up on that lead from Tyler and Kent's manifesto." Though barely noticeable, some of the good humor left Ryan's tone as he mentioned the neo-Nazi mass murderers who had committed a massacre less than a year earlier.

Winter set her brand-new fishing rod and tackle box down on the dock. "Did it turn up anything?"

Ryan's sigh gave her the answer before he did. "No. I'm afraid it didn't. Agent Welford said she found the kid who had been making some threatening posts on random forums, but he was just some seventeen-year-old high school student.

He lives in a rich neighborhood and goes to a private school. Agent Welford said that he figured out a way around his parent's wi-fi firewall, and then he just spiraled down the rabbit hole. Apparently, he was making those posts because he wanted to stir up trouble among the neo-Nazis."

Can't fault him for that. Winter kept the unprofessional thought to herself. "So, it's another dead end, then?"

"It is. Other than a high schooler being grounded for the rest of the decade, we didn't get much out of it. Sorry, I was hoping we'd finally find something too."

Winter swallowed a sigh. "Yeah, me too. It's all right. Thanks for letting me know."

"Take care, Agent Black."

Once the call ended, Winter permitted herself to heave out the breath she'd held back during her brief conversation with Ryan. She really needed to stop getting her hopes up. It wasn't good for her cardiovascular system.

Fishing rod in hand, Autumn took a seat in her canvas folding chair. "That didn't sound like good news."

Shaking her head, Winter unfolded her own chair and slumped down to sit. "It wasn't. It wasn't bad news, either, it was just..." she rubbed her temple, "news, I guess."

As Autumn fastened a purple rubber worm to the fish-hook, she nodded. "Another dead end, huh?"

Winter opened her tackle box and selected a similarly colored worm. "This case has been nothing *but* dead ends over the last couple months. When Ryan found Kent and Tyler's manifesto and we saw that there was a third person involved, the first thing we did was go over security camera footage and witness statements from the day of the shooting. We didn't see anyone else with a gun aside from the cops. But Kent and Tyler took over the security room, so it's hard to tell if they might have diverted the cameras from a certain area. I was talking to Agent Welford the other day, and she said they're going to circle back to the person who posted the manifesto in the first place and see if they can dig anything up that way."

"Well," Autumn rose to stand as she arched the fishing rod over one shoulder, "that's probably a good idea. Strickland's family have been about as helpful as a pack of rabid hyenas, haven't they?"

With one smooth motion, Autumn sent the line sailing out from the dock and into the rippling waters of the lake. Her emerald green eyes followed the motion until the hook plopped onto the water's surface.

Winter managed a quiet chuckle as she nodded. "That's a good comparison. If I didn't know better, I'd think Kent Strickland had been *raised* by a pack of rabid hyenas. The Haldanes are a little more cooperative, but they still haven't been able to give us anything useful."

Tucking a piece of auburn hair behind her ear, Autumn glanced over to Winter as she retook her seat. "Well, Tyler and Kent spent the summer before the shooting at Kent's father's place, didn't they?"

Winter nodded. "Yeah, it's a plot of land just outside Bowling Green. We're still looking for George Strickland, but we haven't been able to find him. He's either laying low, or he's out of the country. Bree and I went to George's house a couple weeks ago, and no one was there. The closest neighbor is something like two miles away, so they didn't notice anything weird, or anything at all."

While Winter rose to cast her own line into the lake, Autumn reached down to a cooler at her side. According to her, the only real way to fish for catfish was to sit on a dock and drink beer while they waited for their bobbers to move. By the time Winter moved back to her chair, Autumn handed her a glass bottle of beer.

They'd followed the weather for a solid two weeks in the

lookout for a day warm enough to go fishing. Though the temperature was above average for that time of year, there was still enough chill in the air to warrant a light jacket.

A silence settled over the dock, and the breeze carried with it the faint scent of roasting meat. Even in the middle of December, Virginians didn't give up on their grilling. Maybe the next time she and Autumn came to the lake, they could be the source of the mouthwatering aroma.

When Winter glanced over to make a comment about her plan to grill, Autumn's thoughtful stare was fixed on the distance. "What?" Winter asked.

Autumn's green eyes flicked to meet hers. "What, what?"

"You, right now. You look like you're in the middle of an epiphany."

With a shrug, Autumn took another long sip from her beer. "No, not an epiphany. You mentioned Bowling Green, wasn't that the high school that your brother went to? You guys found it when you were looking for him, right?"

Winter nodded. "Yeah. We talked to the principal, and she gave us photocopies of everything in his file. He was using the name Jaime Peterson. I saw the yearbook pictures, and it was definitely him." She jiggled her line, her heart sinking as she thought of her brother. "We have the same eyes as our mom. My dad had green eyes, kind of like yours."

Autumn's lips curved into a slight smile. "I got my dad's eyes, actually. Genetics are weird, but they've always been really interesting to me. Recessive traits and dominant traits, all that."

"You studied a little of that, didn't you? At least with regards to mental illnesses and that sort of thing?" Winter followed her friend's lead and took another drink of her seasonal craft beer.

As she set her bottle in the chair's cupholder, Autumn nodded. "A little. That was mostly focused on trying to decide if there's a genetic component to things like depression or schizophrenia. Which there definitely is, but the person's environment has a lot to do with it too. Someone can have a genetic predisposition to depression, but if they live a relatively stress-free life, then they might never actually have depression. It's called the diathesis stress model."

Winter returned her friend's thoughtful nod. "I remember learning about that in one of my psych classes. Do you think that had anything to do with why Cameron Arkwell turned out like he did? I mean, he lived with two upper-class parents who clearly loved one another, but he still wound up killing five women without a shred of remorse."

"Well, Nathan Arkwell admitted that he and his wife weren't ready for a kid when they had Cameron. Plus, Cameron's mother was diagnosed with bipolar disorder when he was little. If something goes wrong in those early years of development, a lot of the time, there's no turning back from it. That's not to say that it's her fault. Bipolar can be really hard to deal with, even if you have medication. But to have an undiagnosed mental illness *and* a child you're not ready for…" Autumn pursed her lips and shook her head, "that had to be really hard on all of them."

"That makes sense." Winter watched the water and began peeling the label from the bottle. "Speaking of, have you heard anything new about Nathan Arkwell's trial?"

Autumn tugged on her fishing line, though only slightly. "Last I heard, his lawyer was filing every pre-trial motion under the sun. He was trying to get all the charges thrown out at first, then he tried to have the judge move the trial location because they thought too many people would know about the crime for them to form an impartial jury. It didn't pan out, but now that they're in jury selection, the defense will probably try to stack the jury."

Winter heaved another sigh. "At least Cameron pleaded

out so we didn't have to waste our time on a trial when we knew for sure he was guilty. It's not often someone accepts a deal that involves life in prison without the possibility for parole."

Shaking her head, Autumn let out a little snort. "They do when they're trying to avoid the death penalty. No prosecutor in his right mind will give the possibility of parole to a serial killer."

With a quiet chuckle, Winter took another drink. "That's true. Well, provided Nathan Arkwell's lawyer doesn't pull any more rabbits out of his hat, that trial should be starting pretty soon."

Autumn waved a dismissive hand. "That's all provided *Nathan* doesn't plead out too."

As Winter crossed her legs, she pulled on her line to move the red and white bobber. "You're right. If he doesn't plead out, we'll probably both have to testify."

"A cross examination from an overpaid defense lawyer doesn't sound like a good time to me." Autumn followed the grumble with another drink.

Winter couldn't help her laugh. "I won't argue with you there. That reminds me, I got an email from Maddie Arkwell the other day. She got accepted to VCU to do a pre-med program."

At the update, Autumn smiled. "Good for her. Dan got his medical degree from VCU too. If she needs a letter of recommendation when she's applying to her post-grad, I could ask him."

Winter chuckled. "I doubt that kid needs any *more* connections. How's Dan, anyway? Or, I guess I should say, how are things *with* Dan?"

Autumn seemed to perk up at the mention of the chief medical examiner—the man who also happened to be her ex-fiancé. As much as Winter liked Dan Nguyen, he must have been a special type of stupid to dump someone like Autumn.

"It's good," Autumn said. "He's a good friend, and I'm really glad we can be friends. How about you and Noah? I mean, you guys always seem pretty great when I'm around, but it never hurts to ask."

Winter grinned. Even after a few months together, thoughts of Noah Dalton still brought a smile to her face.

"It's good. We've been waiting to talk to Max about it, just to make sure of everything." Winter doubted she needed to be any more certain than she already was, but they wanted to approach Max from the standpoint of an established relationship and not one that was brand-new.

"Good call." As Autumn shifted her line a little more, she nodded her approval. "Do you think you'll have to change departments or anything?"

"I doubt it. But if we do…" She shrugged. She and Noah had discussed the possibility, and they were both more than willing to make the change if the SAC dictated it was necessary. "Then we'll move. We'll still be working for the FBI, we'll just be in different areas of expertise."

With a smile, Autumn nodded. "Good for you guys. I'm happy for you."

As much as Winter wanted to blurt out a question about Autumn and SSA Aiden Parrish's obvious affinity for one another, she swallowed the remark. She didn't want to be the friend who pestered her only single friend about why she wasn't in a relationship. As the dock lapsed into silence, Winter settled back in her chair.

Even through the frustration over the lack of progress in both the investigation into Justin's whereabouts and the investigation into the identity of the third person involved in the Riverside Mall massacre, the past couple months had been relatively quiet.

But no matter the quality time Winter had been able to spend with her friends and family, a nagging sensation in the back of her mind persisted—a faint insistence that a storm was on the horizon.

Winter, Noah, and Autumn had all spent Thanksgiving at Gramma Beth and Grampa Jack's house, and unsurprisingly, Beth had taken an immediate liking to Autumn. As soon as Grampa Jack had learned that Autumn had seen every episode of *Star Trek: The Next Generation* at least three times, he'd proclaimed her his honorary granddaughter.

The three of them spent the night at the house in Fredericksburg, but before they left, Beth and Autumn had swapped secret family recipes. Autumn had given Gramma Beth her adopted parents' recipe for banana bread, and Beth had given Autumn her heavily guarded meatloaf recipe.

Winter was surprised when Beth handed over the secret recipe, but Gramma had told her that she wanted to make sure she could enjoy a good home-cooked meal even if she couldn't make it to Fredericksburg.

As soon as Noah learned that Autumn could cook Beth's meatloaf, he'd suggested that he and Winter move into Autumn's one-bedroom apartment.

At the memory, Winter snickered to herself.

Autumn glanced up from the cooler to arch an eyebrow. "What's so funny?"

"Just remembering how Noah tried to get us both to move in with you after Thanksgiving."

Autumn grinned. "My animals like you guys, so just let me know what you figure out."

Winter's grin widened. The very thought of living with Noah, sharing space with him day after day both scared and soothed her. She loved him, she knew. She loved her job. She loved her friends. She was in a good space. A calm space. Mostly.

Autumn lifted her bottle. "To figuring it out."

Winter lifted her bottle to second the toast. "To figuring it out."

Winter knew they weren't just talking about her living arrangements. Or her relationship. Or her job.

Justin. Jaime. Jekyll and Hyde?

She shivered.

Even as Winter tapped her bottle against Autumn's, the thought that they were in the midst of the calm before a tumultuous storm still lingered in the back of her mind.

4

The lack of patrons seated throughout the cozy dining area of Emmie's Bakery lent an air of exclusivity to Noah and Bree's little corner booth. Though business hours had ended earlier that afternoon, Bree Stafford and her fiancée, Shelby, had called ahead weeks ago to reserve a timeslot for a cake taste testing. Their wedding wasn't until May, but they wanted to get a head start on making all the arrangements.

When Shelby's work trip to California had been extended by a few days, Bree extended an invitation to Noah. She'd told him that she wanted her friend with the best appetite to join her for the taste test.

As Noah took his seat across from Bree, a middle-aged woman with honey-brown hair pulled back into a ponytail approached the table. Her nametag read Emily, and Noah could only assume she was the proprietor of the homey business.

With a wide smile, Emily brushed off the front of her pastel blue apron. "Nice to see you again, Bree. Where's Shelby? Could she not make it?"

Bree wasn't able to completely hide her disappointment behind the wide smile she gave the woman. "No, she had to work." She introduced the two, waiting through the greetings and hand shaking that followed. "Emily owns the bakery. Shelby and I have been coming here for years."

"Nice to meet you." Noah patted his belly. "I'm a big fan of your work."

The corners of Emily's blue eyes creased. "It's always nice to meet a fan."

Though Bree hadn't brought a cake to work in months, Noah could still recall the praises Winter had sung about the bakery's German chocolate triple decker. He would have to make a mental note of Emmie's Bakery when Winter's birthday rolled around.

"We've got all the flavors we talked about ready for me to add the frosting. First..." Emily wiggled her index finger, which was painted a pastel blue, "butterscotch, then strawberry, Italian wedding cake, good ole marble, red velvet, and last but certainly not least, lemon blueberry. Plus, I've got a few different flavors of frosting to use too."

As Emily counted off types of cake on her fingers, Noah absentmindedly patted his belly. He'd thought about skipping lunch so he would have plenty of stomach space available for tasting, but he'd lost the battle a couple hours ago when he'd ordered a basket of chicken strips from a restaurant close to his and Winter's apartment complex.

Bree offered Emily an appreciative smile. "The lemon blueberry is Shelby's favorite. She loves lemon blueberry everything."

Noah rubbed his hands together. There was too much talk, not enough eating going on. "It's a good combination. Your wedding is in May, so you'll be well into the spring season."

Raising her eyebrows, Emily nodded. "That's true."

Bree leaned back in her seat, seeming to be equally surprised and impressed with this insight. He might be a constantly hungry behemoth, but he hadn't been raised in a barn.

"I'll make sure to keep that in mind," Bree said, sounding more than a bit in awe.

Emily took a step back. "Perfect. You two get comfortable, and I'll bring out a couple glasses of water while we get those cupcakes frosted for you."

As their hostess departed, Noah tossed the napkin in his lap. Chicken strips or not, he was always ready for cake. Bree typed out a message on her phone before returning the device to her pocket as Emily set down their water.

"How has your weekend been so far?" Glancing to him, Bree took a sip from her glass.

Shrugging, Noah squeezed a slice of lemon into the water. "Can't complain. Seems like it's the first weekend I've actually had *off* since I started at the bureau. Well, no, that's not true. *Last* weekend was the first weekend I feel like I've had off. This weekend's just a bonus."

Bree spooned out a piece of ice and popped it into her mouth. "The down time is nice, even if it *is* filled with paper-work and meetings. Speaking of, have you and Winter had 'the talk' with Max yet?" She even raised her fingers to add air quotes.

As he shook his head, Noah let out a half snort, half laugh. "SAC Osbourne is a grown man. I'm sure his parents had the sex talk with him a long time ago. Besides, he's my boss. That'd be weird."

Midway through tucking a piece of curly hair behind her ear, Bree fake scowled at him. "I guess I was asking for a smartass response, wasn't I?"

Noah grinned. "You were, yeah."

"Okay, but really, have you two told him yet?"

He tapped a finger against the cool glass, already dreading the conversation. "Not yet. The plan is to do it sometime this week, maybe even tomorrow. I've actually been meaning to ask you about it. What do you think will happen? It doesn't seem like there's a real hard and fast policy on two colleagues having a relationship. At least not when they're both on the same level."

Bree nodded her understanding. "There's not, really. I've been with the FBI for about twenty years, and this is definitely not the first time I've seen something like this happen." She offered him an exaggerated wink.

"What happened with those people?"

"Not much. They just weren't partnered up on cases anymore."

Noah frowned, looking thoughtfully into his glass. "We've already been making a point not to do that. It just didn't seem like it'd be a smart idea. Conflict of interest, unprofessional, all that jazz."

"Max will appreciate that," she said. "You guys will be fine. I know Max seems like a hard-ass most of the time, but he's been married for more than thirty years. He'll get it. Plus, you two are great agents. There's no way he's going to run you out of the department, especially not after the work you both did on the Arkwell case."

Jumping at the chance to change the subject, Noah said, "Speaking of, Nathan Arkwell's trial is about to start soon, isn't it?"

With a look that landed somewhere between sarcastic and matter-of-fact, Bree shook her head. "It is, but I'd be surprised if it went to trial. The felony murder rule is a stretch for a guy like Nathan Arkwell, especially considering that Cameron is his son. When defense lawyers file a whole heap of motions like Arkwell's lawyer has been, it's because they're trying to drag out the process and make it as expensive for the government as they possibly can."

Noah attacked a knot in his neck with his fingertips. Just thinking of the Arkwells and their fucked-up family caused his muscles to contract. "Right. It's almost like they're showing off or making a point about how obnoxious they can be."

Bree flashed him a thumbs-up. "Bingo. Most charges are resolved with plea deals, anyway. I can't remember the number off the top of my head, but I want to say it was close to ninety percent. That's what I think will happen."

Drumming his fingers on the tabletop, Noah returned his gaze to Bree. "Well, in all fairness, I don't think Nathan Arkwell deserves to be thrown in prison for the rest of his life. He's not a bad guy, just an idiot. There are better ways to get him to give back to society than have him languish in some cushy prison."

The smile that crept to Bree's face was almost prideful, like she was a parent looking over her child's first honor roll letter. "I might not have been around for the investigation, but I think you're right. That's what justice is. It's not about throwing the book at everyone we run into. It's about doing the right thing. Like with Ryan O'Connelly. We gave him the opportunity to do the right thing, and he did."

Noah cast a quick glance around the empty dining room. "Speaking of Ryan, seems like he and Agent Welford have been hitting one brick wall after another looking for the third person in Haldane and Strickland's manifesto."

After the Arkwell case, Bree had arrived back just in time to follow up on a handful of dead end leads in their newest ongoing investigation.

"They have been," Bree said. "It would be really helpful if we could find whoever posted the manifesto in the first place, but I'm not sure how feasible that actually is."

Noah took another sip of water. "I'm not sure, either. I do know that's the first lead they chased down, though. All they could pin down from it was that the document was uploaded from a public wireless network at a restaurant downtown. The wi-fi signal is in range of at least five different places of business, not to mention the apartments above the restaurants and bars."

With a thoughtful look, Bree nodded. "We looked through security camera footage but didn't see anything that looked out of the ordinary. There are tons of people in that area that come to use their laptops for work or school. Even when we narrowed it down to the approximate timeframe of the upload, there wasn't anything that stuck out."

"I guess that's where the old phrase 'needle in a haystack' comes into play, huh? Trying to pick one weirdo out of a whole crowd of people isn't always easy."

It's not easy until they start shooting.

The thought came unbidden, and he took a quick drink to wash away the sudden bitter taste on his tongue.

Even though the past couple months had been mostly low stress, Noah would sleep better at night once they finally found the third person involved in the Riverside Mall Massacre.

5

The harsh white glow of a battery-operated work light cast exaggerated shadows along Jaime Peterson's face as he slid a sheet of paper over to Will. Glancing to the tattered wooden crate they used as a makeshift table, Will slowly reached out to take the paper.

In the two and a half months since Will had helped Jaime bury the body of a man who had threatened to turn them in to the authorities, Will and Jaime had spent more time together than not.

With the potential snitch out of their way, they were free to start their work in earnest. Jaime had taken point, but Will was still in uncharted territory, so he didn't protest his subordinate role.

Soon, however, Will's role would increase. Soon, his involvement in their cause would be unquestionable.

Jaime tapped the top of the paper with a finger. "This is all of them."

Heart in his throat, Will scanned the rows of neat handwriting. "How many are there in total?"

Crossing both arms over his olive drab jacket, Jaime took a step back from the crate. "Twenty-six, but those are just the hostages that survived. There were others in the Riverside Mall who ran away before Tyler and Kent got the crowd under control."

Will turned the page over. "What are we going to do about those people?"

Scratching the side of his face, Jaime shrugged. "The hacker I got in touch with was able to get me the names and information of the people who were there for the whole thing. I've been thinking about it, but I'm not sure there's even a record of everyone who was at the mall when Kent and Tyler got there."

With another quick look to the list of names and addresses, Will tried to think through all the options. He wanted to be helpful. He wanted to make Jaime proud. "I suppose not. It was hard enough to find all the people who were taken hostage, wasn't it? Not all of them let the news media use their names when they ran their articles."

Jaime thrust his hands in his jacket pockets. "No, they didn't."

"What about the hacker? Is he…well, is he part of…" Will gestured to himself and then to Jaime, "this?"

For the second time, Jaime shook his head. "No. I've been trying to get in touch with him, but he dropped off the radar right after he gave me the names."

The first thought to cross Will's mind was that Jaime had killed the hacker to tie up any loose ends, but he mentally scolded himself.

Jaime wasn't here because he was a bloodthirsty psychopath. Jaime was like Will. He was committed to their cause. To the same cause that Tyler Haldane and Kent Strickland had been committed. They were here to rid the world of sin, and as word of their work spread, more would come to join their cause. Of that, he had little doubt.

For the first time in Will's life, he felt like he'd found a cause into which he could throw his full support.

He'd tried other groups in the past, and while a portion of their messages had resonated, Will hadn't been able to envision their goals like he could envision Jaime's.

Will had always been an outcast. In high school, he'd been the kid who sat at the lunch table by himself. Aside from a small group of friends he'd associated with since middle school, Will had been a loner. Sure, he'd *tried* to make friends with the so-called cool kids, he'd *tried* to ask the girl he liked to go to prom. But by the time he finally gathered up the courage to talk to them, they'd looked at him and laughed. Or worse…ignored him completely. Will had been on his own.

Then, for his seventeenth birthday, his parents had scraped together what little money they had to buy Will his first smartphone.

On the internet, Will found friends. Good friends.

Within a month, he was a moderator on a forum dedicated to guys like him—guys who had repeatedly struck out in the real world and who sought to commiserate with other like-minded young men.

Once he found the forum, he no longer cared that his classmates dismissed him. He no longer cared that he didn't have the gall to talk to girls. He knew he wasn't alone anymore, and he knew that he and his online friends would get all the good things that were coming to them.

God blessed those who worked for Him, after all. And Will was his faithful servant. He knew that for sure.

Like so many others on the forum, Will had embraced white supremacy at first. But throughout all the meetings, the posts, and even the rallies, part of the mission had seemed off. Will hadn't been sure what about the neo-Nazi ideology bothered him until he met Jaime.

Jaime had shown him that the problem with their society didn't rest in racial differences. The problem with their society was the amount they'd deviated from the old ways.

Specifically, women overstepping their bounds had led to a decay in moral values. Women were and had always been inferior to men, and until they were reminded of their place, the morals and decency of modern Americans would continue to deteriorate.

There was a measure of cool confidence in the way Jaime spoke that assuaged any lingering doubts in the back of Will's mind. They were doing the right thing. He was certain.

God had called upon Tyler and Kent to rid the world of forty-one sinners at the Riverside Mall that night, but their work had been stopped short by the Federal Bureau of Investigation.

Neither Will nor Jaime could fault the FBI for doing their jobs, but at the same time, they knew that the bureau would never understand. No law enforcement agency saw the problems that were so clear to Will and Jaime. If they did, maybe they wouldn't have fired the shot that almost killed Kent Strickland.

As Jaime reached over to clasp his shoulder, Will almost jumped out of his skin. He barely managed to push aside the shocked reaction as he met Jaime's calm stare.

"Don't worry," Jaime said. "Once we finish our task, God will show me the way. Just like he did for this." He gestured to the paper. "We'll have direction again once we're finished with our task."

Will swallowed as he returned his attention to the list. "Why are there a couple names already crossed out?"

The first hint of a smile tugged at the corner of Jaime's mouth. "Their names were published in the Danville newspapers. When me and Jackson were planning to start our mission, we hadn't worked out how to get the rest of the names yet. These people." He jabbed an index finger at the list. "These were the start. Or, at least, I thought they were the start. I punished them, but then Jackson went soft."

When Jaime's eerie blue eyes met Will's, the chill of fear flitted up his back. He'd never seen Jaime don such an expression before. The look was intense, even piercing—almost like Jaime could see straight through to Will's darkest secrets.

And maybe he could. Jaime Peterson had clearly been chosen by God, after all.

"You won't go soft, right, Will?" Jaime's deadpan expression didn't change as he spoke.

Will straightened his spine, lifted his chin, pulled back his shoulders. "No. I'm like you. I'm a soldier."

Jaime stared at Will for so long that the contents of Will's bowels turned to water. "Good. I knew I could count on you. I know you won't let me down."

The rush of Will's pulse was spurred on not by anxiety, but by pride. For someone like Jaime Peterson—someone who was so charismatic and intelligent—to put his full trust in Will was just short of exhilarating.

"So," Will's voice was strong and confident, "when do we start?"

Jaime's cold smile turned even more dangerous as he dragged the sheet of paper back over to his side of the crate. "Tomorrow. We'll have to take this slow at first since this is new territory for you. Don't take that the wrong way, either." Jaime paused to offer Will a reassuring nod. "Everyone has to start somewhere. I'm going to teach you some tricks of the trade, some things that were passed on to me by my mentor years ago."

Another surge of excitement swept through Will's veins. His smile was just short of an outright grin as he returned his focus to Jaime. "What types of tricks?"

Scratching a scruffy cheek, Jaime shrugged. "Well, we'll start with some of the basics. Our first targets are these two. The top two names."

Will squinted down at the list. Reading upside down was a knack he'd acquired to cheat on exams in high school.

"Sandy and Oliver Ulbrich," he read.

Jaime nodded. "I had a chance to look over them before Jackson turned on us. I've got a good idea of their routine and their interests, but I want to show you how I figured all that out. If we can both work independently, we'll be much more productive."

Will returned Jaime's nod. Even as Will reminded himself that working independently meant that he would be expected to commit a murder, he was ready to do whatever it took for the cause. He believed in Jaime's conviction.

When Will had first asked Jaime how they knew for certain that all the survivors of the Riverside Mall massacre had to be killed, Jaime hadn't balked. The Lord worked in mysterious ways, and the Lord was the one who had herded all those people to that spot.

They'd been put there for a reason.

They were sinners, and they had been put at the mall to be punished for what they'd done. If Tyler and Kent hadn't been interrupted that night, then their mission would have been carried out and completed right then and there. But thanks to the intervention of the Federal Bureau of Investigation, Will and Jaime were left to complete the task themselves.

However, the more time he spent around Jaime, the surer

Will became that the action of law enforcement that night had been part of the plan. Without it, Will never would have met Jaime. He never would have discovered his calling.

His life had purpose. His life had direction.

For the first time in his life, William Hoult had found the place he belonged.

6

A s Autumn approached her and Winter's favored booth, she smiled at the fond memories that came with the homey bar. Her aunt Linda owned the place, and she had decorated the wood paneled walls with memorabilia and pictures reminiscent of a ski lodge—hence the bar's name, The Lift.

Though she hadn't won a medal, Autumn's aunt had competed in Olympic snowboarding in her younger years. The décor was an homage to the sport that had been her life's passion.

Autumn had never been skiing or snowboarding, but maybe now that she'd finally finished graduate school and obtained her Ph.D., she would ask Aunt Linda to accompany her on a vacation to the Rocky Mountains. Then again, after the few months she'd been employed by the prestigious forensic psychological firm Shadley and Latham, she could almost afford to take Linda to the Swiss Alps.

Setting a glass of dark beer down in front of Winter, Autumn took her seat on the opposite side of the booth. When Winter's blue eyes shifted from the drink to Autumn, she looked as though she'd been pulled from a deep contemplation. Wordlessly, Autumn sipped at her beer and arched an eyebrow.

Winter brushed a piece of ebony hair from her face and shrugged in response to the unasked question. "Nothing. I was just thinking."

"Thinking about what you're going to order for dinner since we didn't catch any fish?" Autumn flashed her friend a grin.

With a huff of feigned indignance, Winter took a long drink. "Officially, we caught two fish. They were just tiny, so we put them back. We probably wouldn't have even been able to make a fish stick out of both of them."

Autumn snorted. "Adam Latham is the one who told me about that fishing spot. He said he and his wife caught a, and I quote, 'whole mess of catfish' a few weeks ago."

Winter grinned. "Maybe that's why there weren't any left. They caught all the big ones."

Waving a dismissive hand, Autumn crossed her legs. "No. I mean, I doubt that helped anything, but I think it has something to do with the time of year. Even though it was warm out today, catfish like to huddle down at the bottom of the lake when the weather starts to cool down. At least that's what I've been told. I don't know how accurate it is."

Winter sprinkled salt on her paper coaster, so her beer wouldn't stick to the condensation the icy brew would create. "You should have taken more fish classes when you were in school."

Autumn spread her hands. "You're not wrong. Animal Planet only gets me so far, and I don't even think that counts as a formal fish education."

Winter chuckled. "No, I don't think it does."

As their table lapsed into silence, the first notes of a Led Zeppelin tune rang throughout the sparsely populated space.

Autumn knew from her time working as a bartender that Sundays weren't especially popular nights for bar patrons. However, she also knew that the best bar specials occurred on nights that weren't popular.

Then again, the bartender, Hannah—a sweet, single mother in her early thirties—hadn't charged Autumn for her and Winter's drinks.

While she'd worked at The Lift, Autumn had always looked forward to her shifts with Hannah. Despite the hardships in Hannah's life, or perhaps because of them, she was always in good spirits, and she always had a kind word for her coworkers.

When Winter spoke, her voice jerked Autumn out of the brief contemplation.

"Can I ask you something? Something psychology related?"

As Autumn turned her attention to Winter's curious expression, she nodded. "Of course. Shoot."

Before she continued, Winter took another drink. "I know that the basis for a lot of the information that's used by the Behavioral Analysis Unit at work is stuff that's been picked up from interviews with suspects and convicts over the years. And I know that there are some serial killers like Jeffrey Dahmer who have provided valuable insight about what motivates those types of people."

Autumn nodded again. "That's true. It's still true. It didn't end just with Dahmer. There are still plenty of studies that utilize interviews with convicted killers."

Winter's eyes flicked back and forth, as if searching for the right words before her gaze settled on her beer. "This might be a longshot, because I don't know what happened to Justin after he was kidnapped, but I was wondering what you thought of it. I was wondering if, maybe, to get some perspective on what my brother might be like or even where he might be, it would be helpful to talk to someone who operates kind of like Douglas Kilroy."

Well, that was one of the last questions Autumn had expected.

Based on the work Autumn had done with Aiden Parrish several months earlier, she was confident that Winter's brother had been irreparably damaged by his time with Douglas Kilroy—the serial killer also known as The Preacher.

Of course, that was still a big *if*.

They didn't know for sure that Justin Black had been raised by Kilroy. All they knew was that Justin was alive, and that he didn't want to be found. Whether he was hiding from Winter or from Kilroy, perhaps not knowing the evil man was dead, they still couldn't be certain.

Autumn tapped her fingers against the wooden tabletop. "You want to talk to someone to see if they can think of why Kilroy would have kidnapped Justin, right?"

Winter nodded. "And to ask them what they'd do if they were in Justin's position. I know what Aiden thinks about my brother. I know he thinks Justin's a sociopath, and I guess right now I'm just thinking in terms of worst-case scenarios. I hope he's not like that. I hope whatever's happened to him can be helped, but I'm not naïve."

Their conversation hovered precariously close to a topic that Autumn sought to avoid like the plague—the topic of Justin Black's mental health. She didn't want to give Winter her professional opinion of Justin's fate, but at the same time, she didn't want to lie or give her friend false hope.

"Aiden's always right." There was a distinctive bitterness in Winter's voice that took Autumn by surprise.

"What? What do you mean? I seriously doubt he's *always* right."

Winter let out a sarcastic sounding huff of air. "I've never seen him get a profile wrong. Not in the time I've been working for the FBI, and not during the time when I was friends with him before then. I'm just...I'm trying to be pragmatic. Hope for the best, plan for the worst, you know?"

The phrase was one Autumn knew well. "Yeah, I understand. Just so long as we're clear that, right now, we're operating under the assumption of a worst-case scenario, okay?" She raised her eyebrows and shot Winter an expectant look.

Winter pressed her index and middle fingers together and raised her hand. "Scout's honor. Or, wait, is it three fingers?"

Autumn was grateful for the moment of levity. "I'm not sure. I was never in the Girl Scouts."

Winter lowered her hand, her fingers twisting together. "Neither was I. But, yes. Right now, we're just talking about the worst-case scenario. What do you think about talking to someone who might be in that same type of mental state?"

Autumn pressed a finger to her lips as she mulled over the question. "Do you have anyone specific in mind you were thinking of consulting?"

"Cameron Arkwell." The answer was confident and quick. Clearly, Winter had already put a great deal of thought into the suggestion.

"Cameron Arkwell," Autumn echoed. "Yeah, that would be good. He's roughly the same age, just a couple years older. In a different sort of way, he was alienated from his family, so that's similar as well. Plus, he has a sister who's doing well in life, and he lost someone he cared about when he was young. I think there are several similarities there."

Winter lifted her eyebrows. "Do you think it would be worth talking to him about it? Just to get some insight, all completely off the record."

"My guess is that 'off the record' is the only way he'd talk to anyone, anyway." Combing the fingers of one hand through the ends of her hair, Autumn paused. "I don't know how useful it would be, honestly. That really depends on Cameron. But if he's willing to talk, there's always the potential to learn something that you didn't know before. Personally, I think that's worthwhile, but I don't know that everyone would agree with me."

Though slight, a smile crept onto Winter's face. "I agree with you."

Autumn returned the smile and nodded. "You might have to wait until Nathan Arkwell's trial is over, but yeah, I think it would be worth picking Cameron Arkwell's brain. I can help you figure out some questions to ask him, if you want. Nothing that sounds too much like a psychologist, though. Just a few things to help get a dialogue started. Jeffrey Dahmer and Ed Kemper were chatty, but that doesn't mean that every serial killer is."

Winter's smile was more pronounced. "That would be really helpful, actually."

Maybe with a bit of luck, Cameron Arkwell would be helpful too. Though Winter tended to avoid the topic of her brother, Autumn knew the uncertainty about his fate weighed heavily on her friend. She could only hope that a discussion with Cameron Arkwell would lead Winter to some semblance of peace.

But deep inside, she didn't think so.

She didn't think that anything would.

7

On the same day every week, Sandy and Oliver Ulbrich took an evening hike through a wooded trail about thirty minutes from their house. The couple lived just beyond the outskirts of Danville, and they'd been at the Riverside Mall with their heathen friend, Ellen Santiago. Ellen was long dead—she'd been shot in the back of the head at close range before the FBI had even positioned their snipers that night.

That night.

Sometimes, I had trouble with the fact that the massacre at the Riverside Mall had occurred less than a year ago. To me, the event might as well have transpired in a different lifetime. In the months since that fateful night, I felt as if I'd *lived* another lifetime.

The chatter of birds in the woven canopy of tree branches overhead pulled me back to the present. The rays of sunlight that pierced the relative cover warmed me where they landed on the olive drab jacket I constantly wore. Yesterday had been unseasonably warm, but today was more in line with the normal December weather in Virginia.

I'd almost let myself daydream. Gathering wool, as my granddad would have said. As tempting as it was to give myself over to the sense of nostalgia I felt when I stepped onto the hiking trail, I couldn't afford to lose my focus right now.

Will and I had a task to complete.

As I reached into my pocket for a stick of spearmint gum, I cast a quick glance at Will. His bearded face was stone, his pale blue eyes alight with determination and focus.

I stuffed the gum in my mouth, careful not to let my thoughts show on my face.

If I told Will to jump off a bridge, I was almost certain he'd follow through with the order. He was different than Jackson Fisher or even Shawn Teller before him. Though I told Will that *I'd* killed the three people on our list, they'd actually been killed by Shawn and Jackson. But neither of the two men were here to say otherwise, so I figured I might as well take the credit.

There had always been a certain spark of inquisitiveness in Jackson and Shawn's faces, a spark I hadn't much cared for. I didn't need my lackies to be curious or critical. I needed them to follow orders, to listen to what I asked of them and carry it out without a second thought. I had a job to do on this earth, and I didn't have time to answer some henchman's slew of questions.

Will didn't ask questions. Will just *obeyed*.

Dammit, there I went again. Gathering wool.

Will and I had deviated from the hiking trail to trudge through the brush of the woodland floor. Fortunately, the shrubbery and fallen leaves weren't as much of a hindrance as they'd been in the forest where I'd killed Jackson.

Sure, the plant life was handy for hiding a freshly buried body, but it was unpleasant to navigate. Even with boots and long pants, it never failed that I wound up with a burr or three attached to my ankles. To my relief, it hadn't rained in close to a week. Trudging through mud *and* brush was a nightmare.

No matter how unpleasant it was, the trip through the underbrush was a necessary part of today's plan. The hiking path wound in a wobbly circle through the woods, but Will and I were taking a shortcut. We'd wind up on the trail soon, well before Sandy and Oliver Ulbrich got there.

Reaching out to tap Will's upper arm, I kept the movement slow and measured to avoid startling him. Like me, he'd fixed his attention on the ground in an effort to avoid a hidden pit or a fallen branch.

As Will's blue eyes flicked over to meet mine, he lifted an eyebrow.

I raised a finger to my lips to indicate that we should keep our voices quiet. I wasn't worried that they'd hear or spot us in the middle of the woods—in fact, if they did, it would only lend believability to my cover story about being lost. However, I didn't need them to hear my discussion with Will.

"If we finish cutting through this part of the woods here, we should run into the trail up that way." I gestured past a moss-covered oak. "It's only a little after five right now, but it'll be dark soon."

Will wrinkled his nose. "They hike after dark?"

I was careful to keep my annoyance from my face. "No. They head home before it gets dark. We're going to try to run into them so we can ask them for directions, maybe get a better feel for their routine, you follow?"

Lips pursed, Will nodded. "The more we know about their routine, the better we can plan for things later on."

I clapped him on the shoulder. "That's right. And the better you can plan, the less likely it is that anything will go wrong. You don't have to say anything to them, just follow my lead, okay?"

Will nodded again, eager as a pup for a pat on the head. "Okay."

Maybe I should have felt bad for lying to him. He'd shown me nothing but loyalty, hadn't he? And here I was, lying to him about what I'd planned for Sandy and Oliver Ulbrich.

But I knew better than to feel bad. This was all part of the learning process—the same process I'd gone through more than a decade ago.

I had to see death for myself, had to witness it unexpectedly so I could fully appreciate how fickle life could be. In the same instant I turned my blade on a sinner, they could have pulled out a weapon to turn on me. I had to be faster. Had to be smarter. Had to be more ruthless than the devil worshippers I chased.

After another glance around the tall trees that shrouded the area, I stretched out a hand and beckoned Will to follow me. The bushes thinned, and soon the fallen leaves gave way to a hint of green grass.

I nudged Will with an elbow. "This is it. This is the trail."

Will's eyes darted to the packed earth that cut through the forest. "Now what?"

I shrugged. "We wait. They'll be along soon. This is the part of the trail that leads back to the parking lot. They'll have to come through here to get back to their car. That's another important thing to remember. When you're hoping to intercept someone, you always want to stick to the routes that are necessary for them to get where they're going. That way, you know you aren't wasting your time."

With another nod, Will took a seat at the edge of a large rock. The opposite side of the stone was green with a coat of moss, and a handful of ferns had sprouted from the earth below. "What are we going to say when they get here?"

The kid was obedient *and* sharp. Good.

"That's good, Will. You always want to know what you're

going to say before you run into the person you're tailing. Eventually, you'll be able to wing most of it, but to start with, it's best to be prepared. We'll act like our phones are dead and we're lost."

Will straightened his back and shifted his gaze to me. "If we ask them for directions, then maybe we can get a feel for a little bit more of their routine. Such as how often they come here or where they live."

The smirk that tugged at the corner of my mouth was all but involuntary. "We sure can. That's quick thinking. I'm impressed. I like to crank up the friendly banter when I run into folks like this too. You'd be surprised the type of info people are happy to cough up when you ask them all nice like."

The glint of determination in Will's eyes didn't dissipate. I really had hit the jackpot with him. Will had been a quiet loner for most of his life, but there was another dimension to his seemingly harmless exterior.

There was an animal lurking under that nonchalant façade.

An animal that had been waiting many years to be fed.

Almost fourteen years earlier, I'd learned the same was true about myself. And the hell of it was, I doubted there was any way I would have found out if it hadn't been for my parents' death.

Until that night, I'd been content with trying to cram my thoughts into the mold that society had given me. I'd been certain I'd have to suppress my feelings and urges for the rest of my life.

Then *he* showed up.

In a single night, he changed everything. He opened my eyes. Gave me room to be who I truly was.

Some kids on the internet these days liked to talk about taking a red pill or disconnecting themselves from the

Matrix. I'd done that long ago. I was just glad to know that others were starting to see the same ugly parts of society I'd been taught to see.

Someday, we'd start a revolution. Me and Will were just the start.

As the mournful wail of a distant coyote drifted down to us on the early evening breeze, I smiled to myself. I never did understand why people wanted to live in a place like Richmond—a city infested with car exhaust and police sirens. The woods were beautiful, the air was clean, and the stars shone brightly at night.

Even when I was a kid, I'd loved these woods. We were about fifteen miles outside Danville, on the same hiking trail my parents used to take me and my sister when we were younger.

My mother had lived in Danville for a spell when she was younger, and the woods held a certain sense of sentimentality for her and my father.

We didn't come out here every week like Sandy and Oliver Ulbrich, but we were here often enough that I got familiar with the lay of the land.

I could still remember our last visit to the trail before my parents died. My sister was seven years older than me, and she'd wanted to wander down a slope to the banks of a shallow creek to see if she could catch a frog. At the time, I'd slept with a stuffed frog on my bed, so I was naturally interested.

Our parents told us to stay in their sight, but the banks of the creek were steeper than we'd anticipated. Once we got down to the water, we could no longer see our parents, but we could *hear* them. My sister assured me that was good enough, and our search for frogs began.

Even at six years old, I'd known there was no way our

parents would let us bring a frog back home if we found one, but I'd still held on to a shred of hope.

I still wasn't sure how long we'd trudged along the creek bank, but we'd been so focused on spotting a frog or a salamander that we almost completely forgot about our promise to stay within our parents' line of sight. Eventually, we'd even hopped over a series of rocks to reach the other side of the creek. Maybe all the noise we made had scared away the frogs, and we'd both vowed to be stealthier.

On the opposite bank, our luck had only been slightly better. Though we'd spotted a couple frogs as they hopped from one slick stone to the next, none of them were in range for us to capture. My sister had harrumphed and ordered me to follow her back to the side of the creek from where we'd come. We were prepared to return to our parents with no frogs or salamanders, and we were sure that would be the worst part of our day.

To our surprise, when we'd climbed past the final line of plant life, our parents were nowhere to be seen. Naturally, I blamed my sister, and she blamed me. If we hadn't been searching for her stupid frogs, we wouldn't have gotten lost. But if we hadn't had to throw in my stupid salamanders, then we wouldn't have gotten lost, either.

We bickered back and forth, but when the irritability subsided, my sister was scared. She didn't say it, but I could see it in her eyes.

Though we'd been to the trail a few times in the past, we didn't know it well enough to get our bearings and head back to the family car. I wasn't scared, and as far as I was concerned now that I thought back on the memory, that was just another piece of evidence that I wasn't like them.

I'd thought about what it would be like to live in the woods, to be taken in by a family of wolves or coyotes, to live free of the restraints imposed by mankind.

But my sister, well, she wasn't like me. I hadn't realized back then how different we really were, but we were much, much different.

Sure, we shared the same raven black hair and deep blue eyes, but that was where any resemblance ended. Our similarities were all superficial. I knew that now, but I hadn't known then.

Fourteen years later, I could still picture her as she tugged at the end of her long braid as her eyes darted back and forth, biting her lower lip to keep it from trembling. She'd raised a hand to point and said, "I think it's this way." She'd tried to sound certain, but I hadn't missed the tremor that tinged her voice.

When we found the hiking trail, we'd done exactly what Will and I were doing today. We'd stayed put in one spot and waited. Our parents were frantic when they rounded a bend to spot us, and even though my sister had tried to hide her fright, she was just as shaken as they had been.

We didn't hear the end of their spiel for the entire drive home. They speculated on how we could have been hurt, how we could have fallen into a deep part of the creek and drowned, how we could have been mauled by a wild animal, or even how we could have been carted away by a stranger.

My sister had scoffed at the last scenario, but she shouldn't have. She had no idea how close we'd come to that exact fate.

After all, we weren't the only people in the woods that day. Just like I was now teaching Will, there had been someone following our footsteps...watching, waiting.

Three weeks later, my parents died, and my life started anew.

I took in a deep breath of the crisp woodland air and found myself smiling as I looked up through the bare limbs of the trees. It was fitting that I should begin my mission in this forest. It was a sign from God if ever I'd seen one.

Will's eyes flicked up to me as a questioning look crossed his bearded face.

In response to the unasked query, my smile widened. "They're close."

The younger man's expression was curious. "How can you tell?"

My smile didn't falter as I shrugged. "Just a feeling. Have you ever been to these woods before, Will?"

He was silent for a moment before he shook his head. "No, not that I can recall. Most of my family lives around Fredericksburg. I didn't move to Richmond until about a year ago. Right after I graduated high school."

I nodded my understanding. "I used to come here sometimes with my parents when I was younger. It's been a while, but I still remember the place pretty well."

The lie fell from my lips just as easily as if it had been the truth. I *had* been here recently, within the last year even.

Not far from the part of the creek where my sister and I had emerged all those years ago, I'd buried the first man who had tried to subvert my authority. Shawn Teller's body still hadn't been found by the cops, not that I was trying to keep his death a secret.

Shawn was just some skinhead from rural North Carolina. I knew no one would think much of his passing. Before he met me, he'd been involved with a handful of motorcycle clubs that boasted their black and white Nazi flags like they were a part of their heritage.

They weren't, of course. Those men were nothing more than a bunch of posers, almost as bad as the sinners who'd escaped from the Riverside Mall. Maybe someday God would direct me to punish those heathens too.

However, those types were unforgiving, and no one

would be surprised to learn that Shawn had been killed by an irate biker after he'd threatened to rat them out, or after he'd stolen from them.

One mission at a time, I reminded myself. Even if God directed me to another group of sinners, I had a job to finish first.

"Back when I was a kid, these woods used to be a safe place to be, even at night." I hunched over to carefully pull a string of burs off the bottom of my jeans. I held up the little barbs for Will to see. "It used to be that these were the only things you had to worry about running into if you were out here by yourself."

Will brushed off the front of his plaid shirt. "What happened? Is it not safe anymore?"

I flicked the bur away. "No, it's not. Bunch of those bikers started hanging around here after dark, selling dope and only Lord knows what else. It's the worst during the summer when it's warm outside, but no doubt there's still some of them that creep around here during the winter months."

The look on Will's face soured. "This is supposed to be a place for families."

I nodded. "It's supposed to be. And someday, maybe God will gift us with the task of returning these parts to the way they're supposed to be."

Before Will could make another comment, the light drone of a woman's voice jerked my attention away from my musing. With a quick glance to Will, I tilted my head in the direction of the sound. He squared his jaw and nodded as he pushed himself to stand.

I reached to the interior pocket of my jacket to retrieve my phone. I'd removed the battery earlier in the day, and I'd told Will to leave his smartphone back in the RV we'd been staying in. Living off the grid was easy when you could drive your home anywhere you wanted.

Powering off my phone completely served two purposes. First, it made my dialogue with Mr. and Mrs. Ulbrich more believable when I showed them that I couldn't bring the screen to life. Second, it prevented any likelihood—however small—of a GPS satellite tracing my steps.

Folks these days were so preoccupied with their digital lives that they didn't stop to think of the myriad ways they could potentially incriminate themselves with technology.

Personally, I'd never been a fan of smartphones. The only reason I'd bought one was to avoid standing out too much.

Waving Will forward with one hand, I stepped onto the packed earth trail and started toward the bend in the path. The man and woman were out of sight, but as we grew closer, I could make out snippets of their conversation.

The discussion was inane, something about what the man planned to cook for dinner the following night, since it was his turn to do the chore. *His* turn. My lip curled up in disgust. Cooking was a woman's work. How did they both not understand that? It was clearly written.

And they would both pay for their stupidity. Their eager abandon of life's sacred rules.

As I watched, the color of their clothing was scarcely visible through the barrier of the tree line as I approached the turn in the path. Painting the best bewildered expression on my face I could manage, I shuffled around the bend.

As soon as I spotted the pair, I held up one arm and waved my supposedly dead smartphone. "Hey! Oh, wow." I paused to glance over my shoulder to Will. "Wow, I'm so glad we ran into you guys!"

Orange sunlight glinted off the woman's glasses as she halted in her tracks. A flicker of suspicion flashed over the man's clean-shaven face at the unexpected sight of me and Will. Apparently, they'd heard about the potential for criminal activity in the woods too.

I held out my hands to show that I was unarmed. "I'm sorry. I didn't mean to freak you out. I know how this place can be after it gets dark. That's why we're trying to get out of here. I, um…" I paused to feign a nervous chuckle. "I'm afraid we got a little turned around, though."

As the husband and wife exchanged glances, I took a slight step forward. Just because I didn't have a weapon in my hand didn't mean I was unarmed.

The woman opened and closed her mouth a couple times before she nodded her understanding. "Where are you trying to get to? Back to the parking lot?"

Anger was like a living thing worming under my skin, and I found it difficult not to let it show on my face. This woman should have deferred to her husband. *He* should have answered my question, not her. A wife should not be permitted to speak without her husband's permission, especially to a stranger.

Then again, that's exactly why I was here. They needed to be punished.

With a sheepish smile, I raised my phone. "It died, so I couldn't use it to get us on track. Which way is the parking lot?"

Even when she attempted to return my smile, the woman's face was strained.

The man shrugged, waving a hand in front of him. "If you follow this trail, you'll get there. There's a turn a little ways up ahead. It veers a little to the right. Just keep going straight, and you'll get to the parking lot."

I arched an eyebrow. "Where does the other trail go?"

"Back into the woods," the man said. "It sort of loops around, kind of like a big circle."

With a sudden grin, I snapped my fingers and looked to Will. "That's why we got lost, isn't it? We just kept going in a big circle. I think I know the turn that you're talking about. It's more like a fork in the road than a turn, isn't it?"

They looked to one another again before the man nodded. "I suppose it is, yeah. Just veer to the left and you'll be fine."

I already knew that, of course. But in the moment they looked at one another, I took another step. I was almost within arms' length now.

Though I had a nine-mil holstered beneath one arm, I had no intention of shooting the two of them. The nine-mil was for protection—a safeguard in case the bikers turned up earlier that day. I'd never shot anyone, and I didn't intend to start today.

Guns weren't intimate enough. Too impersonal.

As I returned the phone to my pocket, I inched my hand closer to the sheathed hunting knife at my back. It was the same knife I'd used to kill Jackson Fisher two and a half months earlier. I'd tossed it in a bowl with some water and bleach, but I hadn't been willing to part with the weapon just because it had been used to dispatch one person.

I offered the couple a quick smile as Will made his way to my side. "Thanks for the help, I really appreciate it." With one hand on the hilt of the blade, I extended the other and closed the remaining distance.

The nervousness had started to dissipate from Oliver's expression as he accepted the handshake. Even so, I could already tell that they were glad to be rid of us.

They should have listened to their paranoia. If they were smart, they would have run.

I closed my fingers around the grip of the hunting knife as I clamped down on Oliver Ulbrich's hand. The man's blue eyes went wide in surprise, but before he could make so much as a shocked utterance, I snapped my arm forward and buried the blade in his heart.

Crimson blossomed along the pale blue t-shirt beneath his jacket. As Oliver's mouth gaped open, a trickle of blood ran down his chin. The waning daylight caught his glassy eyes, and I watched his life drain from his face before I released my vice-like grip.

It was beautiful. So perfectly beautiful.

There was a certain sense of catharsis I achieved whenever I witnessed a person's life force fade away. The sensation was one of the few reasons I didn't use firearms when I was carrying out the Lord's work. Unless I was up close, I couldn't watch those last few seconds of their life as it was whisked away into the ether. To God and His judgement.

With a sickening wet tearing sound, I pulled the knife free to let Oliver complete his final slump to the dusty earth.

An ear-piercing shriek jerked my attention away from the sense of consummation that accompanied a close-up kill. Sandy's brown eyes were as wide as a pair of saucers, but to her credit, she recovered from the shock in short order.

With a sharp gasp, she spun around on one heel and started to run in the direction from which she and her husband had come.

She was fast—probably a leftover stress response from the night she'd been at the Riverside Mall and the rush of adrenaline that was certainly flooding her system. I was disgusted by her fear, her sense of self-preservation. The woman hadn't even stopped to assist her husband. She hadn't begged for his life or offered up her own in return.

She was evil, and Earth needed rid of her presence.

I'd been so preoccupied with her husband that I might not have been able to catch up with her if I'd been alone. It didn't matter, though. Even if she made it out of here alive, I knew where she lived, and she didn't know anything about me.

But Will was fast too. In a blur, he launched himself at the woman. Her petite frame was no match for Will's hulking six-foot, broad-shouldered build.

Will's grunt was followed abruptly by another shriek, and then a shout that roughly resembled, "Help."

With a thud, the two collapsed to the ground. Sandy writhed and squirmed beneath Will's body, but she didn't make so much as an inch of progress. She sucked in another deep breath in preparation to scream again, but Will clamped a hand over her mouth.

As I approached, I lamented the fact that Will was here with me. Sure, he'd just done me a solid, but Sandy Ulbrich was a pretty gal for her age. Her chocolate brown hair caught the red glow from the setting sun, and as her chest heaved with each laborious breath, her shirt contoured to the curve of her breasts.

Part of my duty was to punish the women who went against God's will, but those screams she'd managed would soon draw the attention of anyone nearby. Provided there actually *was* anyone nearby. Either way, I wasn't willing to take the chance. I didn't have enough time to baptize her. Punishing women was a lesson Will would have to learn on his own.

The orange sunlight accentuated the red smear of blood as I raised the knife for the woman to see. "I can tell that you need to be punished, Sandy, but I'm afraid we don't have time for that today. I'll let God sort you out."

Her desperate pleas were muffled into an incomprehensible murmur beneath Will's hand, but her eyes told me all I needed to know.

As I dropped down to kneel at Will's side, his stare was fixed on Sandy. Though his jaw was clenched, his countenance was unreadable.

But as far as I was concerned, actions spoke louder than words. Will hadn't hesitated, hadn't balked, hadn't asked for permission. He'd known what our mission was, and he did what was required to make sure we carried it out.

If we had more time, I'd consider handing him the knife to see how he fared when he was given a real job—when he was handed *real* power. For the time being, however, I'd have to take care of Sandy myself.

Raising an index finger to my lips, I locked my eyes onto hers and shushed her frenetic mumbling. The sunlight glittered off the first tear as it inched down from the corner of her eye. I didn't pause to consider the motion, I just acted.

I nudged my hand in beneath Will's to cover her mouth, and the man took his cue to back away. A pebble dug into my knee as I leaned in to brush my nose against her forehead, but I ignored the discomfort.

Without a word of explanation, I gingerly ran my tongue beneath her eye and down to her temple.

My grandfather and mentor had told me long ago that the sweetest sensation in the world was lapping up the tears of a sinner right before they were sent to God. And though the salt tingled against the tip of my tongue, I was in complete agreement with his observation. For good measure, I trailed my tongue back up the other side of her face as she squeezed her eyes closed with a pitiable whimper.

"I'd punish you good right now if you hadn't made all that noise," I murmured. Tightening my grip on the hilt of the hunting knife, I reluctantly pulled away from her flushed cheek.

I didn't bother to acknowledge Will as I snapped my arm back to slam the blade down into the center of Sandy Ulbrich's chest.

As the sinning female's spirit fled her body and sank down into the depths of hell, I knew one thing for certain. God would be pleased.

8

As Winter rapped her knuckles against the metal doorframe of her boss's office, she wondered if she should have been nervous. Noah had relayed Bree's prediction, that neither of them would be removed from the department once they told Max of their relationship.

If anyone knew what to expect, it would be Bree. The woman had worked for the bureau for twenty years. Other than Max, she was the most tenured agent in their part of the building.

Whether due to Bree's reassurance or Winter's own certainty that she and Noah were doing the right thing, she wasn't nervous.

"Come on in, Agent Black. Agent Dalton." Max's gravelly voice filtered out to them through the slight opening in the door.

With a glance over her shoulder to offer Noah a quick smile, she pushed the glass and metal door inward. As the door finished its arc, Max tapped a couple keys on his keyboard and turned to face his newest visitors.

He waved a hand at the two squat chairs situated in front of his desk. "Have a seat, Agents."

The door creaked lightly as Noah eased it closed behind himself. After unbuttoning his black suit jacket, he took a seat at Winter's side.

"I got your email earlier this afternoon. What do you want to talk to me about?" Max's gray eyes shifted from Winter to Noah and then back.

Winter covered her mouth with a fist as she cleared her throat. "I'm not sure what kind of prelude to give here, so I suppose I'll just come out and say it."

As she glanced to Noah, he nodded. "Yeah, not really much of a prelude needed, I don't think."

Folding both hands in her lap, Winter returned her attention to the SAC. "Noah... Agent Dalton and I are..." She cleared her throat again. "Well, we're involved. Romantically."

She might not have been nervous, but she still had a difficult time coming up with a term for their relationship that sounded remotely professional.

Max leaned back in his chair and chuckled. "Involved? Is that what the kids are calling it these days?"

Even as warmth spread over Winter's cheeks, she felt more than saw Noah shift in his chair. Just as she opened her mouth to elaborate, Max waved a dismissive hand.

"You don't need to explain it, Agent Black. I've been an investigator for more than thirty years now, and I've got to say," he paused to let his eyes flick from Winter back to Noah, "it's about time."

Winter's response slipped from her lips before she could rethink it. "Wait, you've known about it? Why didn't you say anything to us, sir?"

Max laced his fingers together and leaned back in his office chair. "I know you and Agent Dalton are both committed to the bureau, and I know you both have plenty of integrity. I figured you'd come to me when you thought the timing was right. Didn't see any need to call you out before then."

"Does this mean that neither of us will be reassigned?" Noah asked.

With another slight smile, Max nodded. "Like I said, situations like this are largely a matter of integrity. As long as I think your relationship with one another doesn't compromise the integrity of this office, I don't see any need to move anyone around. I've got faith in you two. Believe me, I've already noticed the little adjustments you've made so far."

Until Winter felt the flood of relief at the SAC's words, she hadn't realized how the subject had weighed on her in the first place. Somewhere in the back of her mind, she must have been prepared for the worst.

Hope for the best, prepare for the worst.

The old adage stirred up a wave of uncertainty about her little brother, even about Cameron Arkwell. Swallowing, she pushed aside the sudden anxiety and forced the smile back to her face. "Thank you, sir."

In this situation, at least, she had been gifted with the best possible outcome.

She couldn't help but wonder if her luck would hold.

As a form of impromptu celebration, Winter and Noah had stopped by a Chinese restaurant to amass an impressive assortment of food for dinner that night. After a toast, they had settled onto Noah's couch to eat while they watched their newest television obsession. The light from the kitchen at the other end of the living room was the only source of illumination other than the gigantic screen.

With her hunger satiated, Winter stretched onto her side and rested her head on Noah's thigh. The man was methodical about his workout regimen, and she sometimes wondered if there was more than an ounce of fat on his body. Gradually, she shifted her head off the taut muscle of his leg and onto the softer surface of a pillow, giving herself another minute or two of peace.

The conversation with Max hadn't been the only anxiety inducing discussion she intended to have that day.

After twenty-four hours to consider what she and Autumn had discussed, Winter had officially made up her mind. Once Nathan Arkwell's trial came to an end, she would seek out whatever insight Cameron Arkwell had to offer. She would continue to hope for the best possible outcome for Justin, but she had to prepare herself for the worst.

Still, the fact remained that she was planning to voluntarily put herself in a room with the same man who had brutally murdered five women and then held part of his family hostage at the end of the barrel of a semiautomatic rifle.

Winter and Autumn had been all that prevented Cameron Arkwell from sustaining a lethal shot to the head, but Winter wasn't convinced that the little piece of rapport would be enough to assuage Cameron's hostility toward law enforcement.

Then again, she reminded herself what Autumn had told her about Jeffrey Dahmer and Ed Kemper, also known as The Co-Ed Killer. Both men, along with plenty of others, had been more than willing to discuss the disturbing details of their thoughts *and* their crimes. Until she sat down in a room with Cameron, she couldn't be sure he was unwilling to discuss himself and his ilk.

Cameron had been sentenced to life without the possibility of parole, and he was being held in a maximum-security federal prison. The guards were used to a procession of lawyers and law enforcement visitors, and Winter was sure she had no reason to worry for her safety.

But just because *she* wasn't worried didn't mean the same confidence would extend to Noah. Noah Dalton was from Texas, and during their first few months together at the Richmond FBI office, he'd exhibited an obnoxious level of what some might call chivalry.

Winter had never cared for chivalry. To her, it always seemed to be accompanied with a patronizing tinge. She believed in extending kindness to all people regardless of their gender. That was how her grandparents had raised her. They'd raised her to be strong, but they'd also raised her to be kind.

As the credits started to scroll up the television screen, Winter blinked a few times to return herself to the present. Reaching for the remote, she shoved herself to sit before pausing the show.

Noah lifted an eyebrow. His dark hair was still neatly styled, but they'd both changed out of their formal work attire and into t-shirts and comfortable pants.

"What's up, darlin'?"

She swallowed a silly joke about Bugs Bunny and reminded herself that she was about to discuss a convicted murderer.

"I've got something I need to tell you." She regretted the words as soon as she spoke them. That was *not* how she should have started a conversation with her significant other.

He sighed with feigned exasperation. "I told you, if you're a werewolf, it's fine. Really. I mean it. Just don't bite me, and we're good."

She couldn't help a short burst of laughter. With a playful

punch to his upper arm, Winter turned until she faced him more fully.

"No, I'm not a werewolf. That was one time, okay?" She shoved an index finger in his face. "It was a busy week, and I had more important stuff to do than shave my legs."

"Hey." Eyes wide, he spread his hands. "You were the one who called *yourself* a werewolf, okay? I just went with it because I thought it was funny. You know you could go the rest of your life without shaving your legs and I'd still think you were beautiful."

Winter rested a finger over her lips to make a show of considering his suggestion. "Okay, duly noted."

Though she half-expected him to recant the statement, he only grinned at her. "Is that what you wanted to tell me? That you're never going to shave your legs again? Because that's fine. It's your body, sweetheart, not mine. I'm not here to tell you what to do with it."

Her smile widened as she leaned in to gently press her lips to his scruffy cheek. "You're sweet. But no, that's not it."

With an overly exaggerated sigh of relief, he draped an arm around her shoulders. "Okay, shoot, then. What's on your mind?"

She wasn't sure if he'd picked up "shoot" from Autumn, or if Autumn had picked it up from him.

Brushing aside the contemplation, she offered him a reassuring smile. "I had this thought a couple weeks ago, and I talked to Autumn about it last night. I went to her first because it's psychology related."

He stiffened, going on an alert that made her hurry to explain.

"I, well, *we* talked about the similarities between my brother and Cameron Arkwell." Even as she held up a hand to stave off an objection, Noah made no move to speak. "It's preparing for the worst, you know. I mentioned it to her because I've been thinking it might be useful for me to go talk to Cameron. If nothing else, maybe I can get a little more insight into what went on in Kilroy's head when he kidnapped Justin."

Noah gave her a thoughtful look. "That's the sort of thing the BAU does, isn't it?"

Winter nodded. "Yeah. And if Aiden is right about Justin, then..." she let out a quiet curse and shrugged, "it's better to be prepared, don't you think?"

To her continued surprise, a reassuring smile spread over his face. "It is. And if you think it'll help, then I think you should do it."

She'd been prepared for an argument, for an objection, for skepticism. She'd been prepared for him to give a rundown of all the reasons it would be a bad idea for her to visit Cameron Arkwell in his new maximum-security home. But even as she peered into Noah's eyes, she saw only genuine acceptance.

Swallowing, she tucked a piece of hair behind her ears. "You mean that? You're okay with me going to talk to a literal psychopath by myself?"

With a quiet chuckle, he ran the back of his hand down her cheek. "It's a maximum-security prison, darlin'. Guards everywhere, alarms everywhere, cameras everywhere. I know damn well you can take care of yourself. You've knocked me on my ass before, remember?"

As she scooted closer to rest her head on his shoulder, she laughed at the memory. "I did, didn't I? Was that like our first date?"

His laugh sounded closer to a snort. "I don't know if I'd go that far. Jiu Jitsu in a parking lot at Quantico isn't really date-worthy."

Reaching out one hand to touch the side of his face, she tilted her head until their lips met. She hadn't intended for the kiss to become quite so heated, but by the time she pulled away, her entire body was on fire.

"I love you." Her voice was scarcely above a whisper, and if it hadn't been for the wide smile that spread over his face, she wouldn't have even been sure he'd heard her.

"I love you too, sweetheart."

9

As Detective Grace Meyer and her partner neared a halo of white light, she ducked beneath a ribbon of yellow crime scene tape. To either side of the packed earth trail, the shadowy shapes of trees loomed over them. Crime scene technicians and sheriff's deputies milled about beneath the glow of the battery-operated work lights, each of them focused on a different aspect of the scene.

Grace was loath to say she hated to work with the sheriff's department, but she never looked forward to the cases where she had to consult with their deputies.

The sheriff's office exuded even more of a boys' club vibe than the Danville police station. Any time she made her way to one of the rural sheriff's stations, she half-expected to see a sign written in crayon that read "no girls allowed."

Grace's partner insisted that the flippant attitude she received from the deputies had more to do with her status as a newly minted homicide detective than anything, but Grace suspected the treatment would be more professional if she didn't have two X chromosomes.

Whatever the reason for the deputies' demeanors, she'd

vowed not to let the behavior affect her job. Her dream had always been to work as a homicide detective, and she'd worked hard to obtain her position.

That evening, at least, she and her partner—a more tenured homicide detective named Doug Leavens—were able to skip the visit to the sheriff's department.

A handful of battery-operated work lights lit up the isolated hiking area like it was the middle of the day instead of eight in the evening. In the woods to the side of the trail, she caught the occasional shimmer of white light as crime scene techs combed through the trees for evidence.

A flicker of movement drew Grace's attention to an approaching deputy. His brown and gold uniform was neatly pressed, and the white light glinted off his meticulously shaved head.

She extended a hand in a perfunctory greeting. "Evening, Deputy Taylor."

With a nod and a glance to Doug, Deputy Harry Taylor accepted the handshake. "Evening, Detectives. What brings you out here? This isn't the Danville PD's jurisdiction."

Grace offered him a slight smile. "No, but it's a double homicide of two people who *lived* in Danville."

Crossing both arms over his black suit jacket, Doug glanced around the scene. "It's part of the brass's effort to crack down on violent crime. Danville's got one of the highest violent crime rates in the state, and ever since the Riverside Mall, the precinct has been under pressure to cut the violent crime rate down. We're here to help, Deputy. That's all."

At the mention of the mass shooting that had left so many people dead, the deputy's face turned grim. "Yeah, all right, then." He fished a notepad out of his jacket. "You already know who the victims are, then, right? Sandy and Oliver Ulbrich. Sandy was forty-nine, Oliver was fifty-three. They had two kids, both grown, both living in different parts of the state. We've already called them, and they're on their way here."

Grace nodded. "Did they have any idea who might've wanted their parents dead? Any family enemies or anything like that?"

Lips pursed, Deputy Taylor shook his head. "No. They said their parents kept to themselves. Sandy was a librarian, and Oliver was a manager at the post office. From everything we've gathered so far, they were two normal people with normal lives."

Glancing to where a couple crime scene techs photographed the splotch of blood that had seeped into the dirt, Grace racked her brain in an effort to find the incessant buzz that told her she was missing an obvious piece of the puzzle. The name Ulbrich sounded familiar, but try as she might, she couldn't place the source.

She forced her attention back to Deputy Taylor. "What's the CSU been able to find so far?"

He flipped to the next page of his notepad. "Not much, unfortunately. It's been about a week since it rained, so the killer wouldn't have left any footprints. They'll know more at the ME's office, but they didn't see any trace evidence here at the scene."

Doug gestured to the dark crimson that stained the packed earth trail. "You mind walking us through how you think it happened?"

The deputy nodded. "There aren't any witnesses. There was a homeless man clear on the other side of this patch of trees here who thought he heard a scream, but he was so far away that he thought it might've been a wild animal."

Grace lifted an eyebrow. "Where is he now?"

Deputy Taylor's gray eyes flicked from her to Doug. "We brought him in to the station to ask him some questions. Mr.

and Mrs. Ulbrich were stabbed, though, and the witness didn't have any sort of weapon with him. No blood on his hands, nothing like that. He's got a history of a few drunk and disorderly charges, but nothing violent."

"You don't think it's him?" Grace asked.

Scratching the side of his face, Deputy Taylor shook his head. "Detective, I'm not really sure what to think right now. This place has turned into a hotbed of criminal activity over the last few years. It's usually the worst during the summer, but during the wintertime, there are still plenty of shady things that go on in these woods. There's a biker gang that calls itself the Asphalt Devils that started doing business around here a few years back."

Though she still couldn't recall why the name Ulbrich sounded familiar, Grace knew all about the Asphalt Devils. They'd been a thorn in the police department's side ever since they rolled into town.

"So, maybe Sandy and Oliver saw a drug deal go down, or something worse." She looked to Doug. "Maybe they walked in on something the Devils didn't want them to see."

Doug rubbed his chin. "Might be. Deputy, tell us how you think it happened."

With a nod, Deputy Taylor stepped over to stand beside the blood-stained earth. "This was where we found Mr. Ulbrich. He was stabbed right about here." Taylor tapped his two forefingers against his heart.

"Stabbed?" Grace echoed.

Deputy Taylor nodded. "Whoever did it was facing him. They stabbed him, but somehow, they got close enough to inflict the wound without initiating a fight. There weren't any other wounds on his body that we could see, but like I said earlier, we'll know more once the ME gets a look."

Grace waved a hand at the more distant splotch of blood.

The area was labeled with a yellow marker numbered "three."
"Is that where Sandy was killed?"

The deputy nodded again. "Same type of wound as her
husband. There might have been some bruising on her face
or neck, but again, the ME will know more. Bruises tend to
show up a little darker after a while. But based on the position of her body relative to her husband's, we think she
might have been running away. Otherwise," he paused for a
hapless shrug, "we don't have much to go on. Right now, the
best theory we've got is the biker angle."

Doug scribbled down a few notes. "Okay. Thank you,
Deputy. If anything else comes up, give us a call right away.
While you guys chase down the biker angle, we're going to
exhaust any other leads."

Deputy Taylor glanced to Grace and then to Doug. "We'll
let you know. Good luck, Detectives."

FOR THE DURATION of the short trip to the medical examiner's
office, Grace made an effort to rack her brain over the famil-
iarity of Sandy and Oliver Ulbrich's names. However, even
after she posed the question to Doug, she was no closer to
solving the conundrum.

At almost eight-thirty in the evening, the medical examiner's office was just short of desolate. Overhead fixtures had
been turned off, and almost all the staff had left for the day.
Grace and Doug's footsteps echoed off the tiled hallway as
they approached the exam room.

A few years ago, the stuffy old man who used to run the
office had retired. If Grace had met the new medical examiner on the street, she would never have guessed that the
woman did such dark and haunting work.

As Grace and Doug pushed their way through the double

doors, the corners of the medical examiner's dark eyes creased as she smiled. Dr. Mariana Gomez's ebony hair was pinned atop her head in a neat bun, and her olive skin exuded a healthy glow. She looked like a professional athlete, not a person who performed autopsies for a living.

"Good evening, Detectives."

Doug nodded, his nostrils flared against the pungent smell of the disinfectants that was heavy in the air. "Evening, Dr. Gomez."

"I'm assuming you're here about Sandy and Oliver Ulbrich?" With a gloved hand, Dr. Gomez beckoned them over to a silver table.

Though the body was covered with a white sheet, Grace could tell based on the size that it was Sandy.

Glancing to the doctor, Grace gestured at the table. "Have you been able to look for anything yet?"

The harsh lights caught the shine of Dr. Gomez's hair as she shook her head. "Not yet. Sandy's clothes have been cut off and sent to the lab, and I was just about to start the visual inspection and autopsy. I'm not sure what questions I'll be able to answer just yet, but I'll do my best."

"Thank you, Dr. Gomez." Grace reached into the pocket of her leather jacket for a notepad. "Deputy Taylor told us that she was killed with a single stab wound to the heart. Is that right?"

As Dr. Gomez moved the sheet away from Sandy's ashen face, she nodded. "From a cursory examination, yes, that's correct."

"Do you have an idea of the type of weapon that caused the wound?" Doug asked.

Dr. Gomez pulled down the sheet and gestured to the garish mark in the center of Sandy Ulbrich's chest. "I'll know more once I'm able to get a good look at the heart and other tissues, but it looks to be a knife with a smooth blade on one side, and a serrated edge on the other." With a pinky finger, the doctor pointed to the edge of the wound. "See how her skin looks like it's been ripped here, but the other side is a clean cut?"

Grace took a step closer to peer at the body. As she glanced up to Dr. Gomez, she nodded. "A hunting knife, maybe."

Pulling the rest of the sheet down, Dr. Gomez pointed to the other side of the room. "Could one of you hit the lights for me?"

Doug was already moving to the switch by the time Grace looked over to him. When she turned to face Dr. Gomez, the woman had donned a pair of orange-tinted glasses.

As soon as the space went dark, a light click was followed by a violet glow. Gomez shifted the alternate light source down to Sandy's waist, and beneath the light, an angry scar glowed.

"She's been injured before." Dr. Gomez leaned in, her eyes fixed on the healed wound. "It looks like a gunshot wound. Did Sandy or Oliver have any criminal affiliations?"

Doug shook his head. "No, the Ulbrichs were pretty normal people. Nothing out of the ordinary in either of their backgrounds."

When would a librarian have sustained a gunshot wound to the hip?

Grace sucked in a sharp breath as the realization hit her. "She was at the Riverside Mall."

"The Riverside Mall?" Doug echoed, looking as stunned as she felt. "When Tyler Haldane and Kent Strickland took those people hostage? You're saying she was one of the hostages?"

Grace's nod was sharp. "She was. I was there, remember? If I remember right, Sandy was hit by Tyler Haldane just after that FBI agent shot Kent Strickland in the head. Her husband wasn't injured at all."

Scratching his chin, Doug looked back and forth between Sandy's body and Grace. "Don't tell me you're thinking that this is…?" As he trailed off, he held out his hands.

Grace clenched her jaw. "Yes, I am going to tell you. In the past six months, three, now *five* of the survivors of the Riverside Mall Massacre have been killed. None of them had criminal connections, none of them had enemies, but now they're dead."

With a sigh, Doug shook his head. "There were five victims, but there weren't five incidents. Sandy and Oliver were killed together, and so were Kelsey and Adrian Esperson. In both cases, the motive might have been robbery. Honestly, robbery is a lot more realistic than…than…" He waved his hand as he searched for the word. "Whatever this theory you're proposing involves. Plus, Tyler Haldane is dead, and Kent Strickland is in a Supermax prison while he awaits his trial."

As much as Doug had helped Grace during her time as a rookie homicide detective, the man's stubbornness still grated on her nerves. She was certain that his willingness to dismiss her theory about how the murders were connected was due in no small part to the opinions of their colleagues.

When Grace had proposed the idea that a coordinated killer or group of killers could be stalking and killing the survivors of the Riverside Mall shooting, she'd only been a detective for a couple months. The fact that she was a woman under the age of thirty hadn't done her any favors.

If Doug's buddies in the department hadn't been so dead set on dismissing Grace's theory as a conspiracy, she was sure he would have looked at the idea with an open mind. They'd been partnered together since she was promoted, and unless he was posturing for his pals in the department, Doug tended to back her up.

"Haldane and Strickland were radicalized on the internet." Grace narrowed her eyes. "Do you really think they're the only two out there like that? I'm willing to bet they've got a whole fucked-up fan club out there. If someone's taking up their mantle and picking off the survivors from that shooting, then we need to know about it and act sooner rather than later or a *lot* more people are going to die."

Doug opened and closed his mouth a couple times before he managed to speak. "Is there anything else that makes you think these murders are connected? One of the other victims was shot in the back of the head, and the other two had their throats slit. None of them were killed like the Ulbrichs."

As much as Grace wanted to ask him what part of *fucked-up fan club* he didn't understand, she bit back the knee-jerk retort.

"There are five victims now." She held up a hand and wiggled her fingers. "*Five victims.* Three different incidents. I'll grant you that two could have been a coincidence, but *three?* That's not a coincidence. There's no way in hell that's a coincidence."

The dark room lapsed into silence as Doug pursed his lips in thought.

Grace had first proposed the theory months ago after the second two victims had been found dead in their home, their throats cut, and their security system disabled. The deaths had resembled a mafia style hit. Whoever wanted Kelsey and Adrian Esperson dead had known what they were doing.

None of the neighbors could recall witnessing an unfamiliar figure or vehicle, and there were no nearby security cameras to give them a lead in the investigation. Within two weeks, the case went cold, and the rising crime rates in Danville were blamed for the seemingly senseless slaughters.

Though there were other officers who had been present at the mall that night, Grace seemed to be the only one who truly recalled the incident. She'd been a beat cop at the time, and she and her partner were among the first on the scene.

In the days that followed the massacre, the only method Grace found to deal with the heartbreak was to visit with the victims and offer her condolences. She listened to stories about those who had died—everything from summertime pranks to baby showers to tropical honeymoons. Even though Grace hadn't personally known anyone who had been hurt that night, she felt the pain of each victim she'd visited.

Sandy and Oliver had been intensely private people, at least with regards to what they went through at the Riverside Mall. Other than hand the couple's oldest child her card, Grace hadn't interacted with the family at all. There were a few others who had kept to themselves, but for the most part, the survivors of the shooting were grateful for Grace's outreach.

Now, someone was targeting them, as if they hadn't already been through enough.

Doug's voice jerked her from the reverie. "You're right."

The words came with the same ease of two stones ground together. Maybe Grace should have been grateful that Doug had finally set aside his stubbornness, but her jaw was still clenched in exasperation.

If he'd listened to her three months ago, Sandy and Oliver might still be alive.

Coughing into one hand to clear his throat, Doug nodded at her unspoken reprimand. "You're right. Three incidents aren't a coincidence. The department isn't going to like this, though."

Grace barely stopped herself from rolling her eyes. "No one likes a serial killer."

He combed a hand through his dark hair. "No, no one does. But the department's been stretched thin for the past year or longer. We're struggling to keep our heads above water with the way crime's been in this city."

Grace stuffed her hands into the pockets of her leather jacket, suddenly cold. "Well, Doug, considering the nature of these murders, I don't think it really matters what the department thinks. This is Federal jurisdiction now."

Doug didn't have a chance to get a word in edgewise before Dr. Gomez interjected. "Excuse me, Detectives."

In tandem, Grace and Doug turned their heads to the medical examiner. The doctor's eyes were narrowed as she held the ultraviolet light over Sandy Ulbrich's face.

After they exchanged curious glances, Grace and Doug made their way to the exam table.

With a gloved finger, Dr. Gomez gestured to the faint glow smeared to the side of Sandy's eye. "Was there anything at the scene that indicated the crime might have been sexually motivated?"

"No," Doug said, peering closer. "Nothing so far. Why? What is that?"

Dr. Gomez's dark eyes flicked up to them. "I can't be one-hundred-percent sure yet, but my best guess is that it's saliva. I thought at first that it might have just been a mark from a tear, but it's much wider than a tear streak would have been."

Doug looked disgusted. "Wait. You think the killer *licked* the side of her face?"

Dr. Gomez's expression turned grim as she nodded. "Both sides of her face, actually."

Taking in a sharp breath, Grace snapped her gaze back and forth between Doug and Dr. Gomez. "DNA. That means there might be DNA. Do you think you'd be able to do a DNA analysis, Dr. Gomez?"

The medical examiner pursed her lips. "We will surely try."

Doug reached into his black suit jacket for his smartphone. "I've got a contact at the FBI field office in Richmond. Let me give him a call, and then we can get their forensics team to coordinate with ours."

Though part of Grace was reluctant to relinquish control over the investigation, she was tentatively relieved at the idea of turning such a treacherous case over to an entity with the manpower and funding to properly handle it.

She could only hope that the process of transferring the case to the bureau would be quick.

So far, the murders had been spaced out by several months, but Grace had a sinking feeling that the interval was subject to change at a moment's notice.

10

As the glass and metal door swung open with a light creak, Aiden Parrish looked up from staring absent-mindedly at his work laptop. With a quick glance to the computer's clock, he nodded to Ryan O'Connelly.

Aiden had been in the conference room for at least ten minutes, scrolling through the documented evidence that O'Connelly and Agent Ava Welford had collected regarding Kent Strickland and Tyler Haldane's handwritten manifesto.

Although Aiden considered himself fairly tech savvy, he could admit that his eyes had started to glaze over as he'd perused the lists of IP addresses and other digital identifiers. His hope had been to get a better understanding of the information that O'Connelly intended to present in their meeting, but all he'd managed to do was remind himself that online technology was far more complex than he realized.

In the days before the online boom, Ryan O'Connelly had been a proficient thief and conman. Many of Ryan's early exploits had to do with physically breaking into secure areas to steal pieces of priceless art or other valuable trinkets. But as online marketplaces took off, O'Connelly had adapted to the new environment. Gradually, he'd shifted his operation from physical theft to online schemes.

A number of the agents in the FBI's Cyber Crimes Division had advanced degrees in computer engineering and programming, but O'Connelly was self-taught.

In Aiden's opinion, there was something to be said for the former conman's "on the job" experience. After O'Connelly had cut a deal with the US Attorney in order to avoid jail time, he'd become a valuable informant for the bureau.

With O'Connelly's practical knowledge and Ava Welford's vast understanding of modern technology, the two made a formidable team.

But no matter how well their skills complimented one another, the investigation into Tyler and Kent's accomplice had been fruitless so far.

As O'Connelly set his laptop on the circular table, he pulled out a black office chair to sit. "How's your night going so far, SSA Parrish?"

With a slight shrug, Aiden closed his laptop. "Uneventful. Yours?"

It was O'Connelly's turn to shrug. "Uneventful too. Agent Welford was off today so she could go to her sister's birthday party, so I mostly just went over everything again."

Their meeting was a run of the mill update that Aiden had scheduled for twice per week, so he didn't expect any groundbreaking developments. At this point in the investigation, however, almost any update would be groundbreaking.

Aiden lifted an eyebrow. "Have you found anything new?"

As O'Connelly opened the matte silver laptop, he shook his head. "Not really. But I've got a new idea that Agent Welford wanted me to bring up."

An idea was about all Aiden could honestly hope for at this point. "All right. Let's hear it."

After a slight nod, the younger man tapped a few keys.

"It's just a little something I thought of while I was going through the case again. You know how I've been posting in some of these dark web forums pretending to be another extremist over the past couple months, right?"

The pseudo undercover work had been Ava Welford's idea, and they'd all been hopeful at first. But like every other potential breakthrough in the investigation, the plan had deteriorated in short order.

Other than a handful of cringe-worthy responses to O'Connelly's posts, the effort had yielded nothing.

Aiden nodded. "Right. Have you gotten responses that could be useful?"

O'Connelly tapped at the keyboard. "No. Believe me, if I had, I would've led with that."

The start of a smile made its way to Aiden's face. "That's fair. What's this idea, then? Are you thinking of going after those neo-Nazi forums again?"

O'Connelly shrugged. "It's the same concept, I suppose. I'm thinking of expanding the search radius. That's a term that cops use, right?"

Though Aiden might have rolled his eyes if anyone else had made the comment, O'Connelly's perpetually chipper demeanor had grown on him over the past few months. In a line of work that so often dealt with the darkest parts of humanity, an occasional glimpse of happiness was a welcome reminder of why they did the work they did.

Rather than offer up a sarcastic comment, Aiden chuckled. "It is a cop term, yes. How exactly are you planning to expand the search radius in this case?"

O'Connelly turned thoughtful, the lines on his forehead deepening as he clearly considered his explanation. "Well, you know that the dark web is home to all sorts of nastiness, right? There are extremists all over the internet, but only the really serious ones make it to the dark web. We haven't seen the Haldane and Strickland manifesto surface on the regular web, so I think it stands to reason that the fella who posted it in the first place is pretty familiar with the dark web. There's a reason they posted it there instead of on the normal web."

Scooting forward in his chair, Aiden propped both elbows on the table. "So, in this case, 'expanding the search radius' would mean you start sinking deeper into the belly of the dark web?"

O'Connelly's smile widened. "Exactly. There are digital markers associated with every online post, and I'm thinking maybe we can find a match for this fella somewhere else. Maybe the lad who posted the manifesto is a hacker, or maybe he's someone who's been active somewhere else on the dark web before."

Widening the net was a tactic that law enforcement employed when all viable leads had been exhausted, but O'Connelly's combined determination and enthusiasm made the idea seem like it was a new lead in and of itself. Then again, digital searches were vastly different from physical searches.

After a brief moment of quiet, Aiden nodded. "What we've been doing so far hasn't worked, so I think you're right. Like that old saying goes, maybe we've been looking for horses when we should have been looking for zebras."

O'Connelly chuckled quietly. "That's exactly what Agent Welford said when we were talking about it yesterday."

With a slight smile, Aiden folded his hands. "It's the same type of logic we use in the BAU. In a lot of cases, serial killers and other murderers are associated with crimes that seem unrelated at first. Things like animal abuse and domestic violence. When we keep hitting dead ends, expanding the search criteria is a good way to refresh the list of suspects."

O'Connelly nodded his agreement. "That's true. I'm willing to bet the same is true for hackers."

"How about Nathan Arkwell's little circle of friends? Has anything popped up with them?"

The question had become more standard procedure than anything. None of Arkwell's friends or colleagues had made a peep in the last few months.

As O'Connelly scratched the side of his face, he shook his head. "No. They've been quiet ever since Cameron Arkwell was charged. Not even a whiff of insider trading. We're keeping an eye on them, though."

"Then that's that, unless you have anything else you want to run by me. Otherwise, I think your and Agent Welford's plan is a good one. Hopefully, it'll finally turn up something we can use to find this person."

Pushing to his feet, O'Connelly stuck out his hand. "Hopefully. I'll let you know if anything else comes up. Have a good night."

Aiden shook the ex-con's hand. "You do the same."

After the door swung closed and the latch clicked into place, Aiden opened his laptop. The update from Ryan hadn't given much new information about the case, but the new approach was worth documenting.

As Aiden pulled up the file, he groaned when he felt a pronounced buzz against his ribs. With a glance to the clock, he reached to grab the device from an interior pocket.

He didn't stop to puzzle over the reason for the call from a Danville PD detective before he swiped the answer key. "SSA Parrish."

"Evening, Agent Parrish." The caller's voice was tinged with a folksy southern drawl, but the twang was slightly different than Noah Dalton's Texan accent. "This is Detective Leavens of the Danville Police Department."

A hint of recognition flickered to life in Aiden's mind.

Aiden, Winter, Bree, and Noah had first been introduced to Detective Leavens on the night that Douglas Kilroy was shot and killed. Though the majority of the Danville Police Department had been occupied with the shooting at the Riverside Mall, Detective Leavens and his partner at the time had been tasked with documenting the death of an infamous serial killer—The Preacher.

Like Aiden himself, Detective Leavens had worked on The Preacher case. Leavens had become involved back when Kilroy left a handful of victims around the Danville area.

Whether Aiden's sudden clenched jaw was due to memories of The Preacher's case or the grave undertone in the detective's voice, he wasn't sure.

"Detective Leavens," Aiden said. "What can I do for you?"

The detective cleared his throat. "Well, Agent Parrish. I think my partner and I are going to need your help. We've got five people dead, and it's starting to look like we've got a serial killer on our hands."

11

The buzz of anticipation in the air of the briefing room ran through Winter like an electric current. Over the past couple months, life around the field office had been relatively quiet for Winter and her coworkers.

That wasn't to say the work they'd conducted during the so-called downtime had been unimportant—trial preparation, routine training, and paperwork were all essential parts of the FBI's overall operation. Plus, there was never a shortage of cases to work on, but the majority didn't set her heart to pounding like others.

Like this one.

When the team was about to be introduced to a new, exciting case, the atmosphere in the building hovered between foreboding and electrifying.

Winter set her mocha on the polished tabletop before she brushed off the front of her blazer. With a cursory glance around the room, she took her seat beside Noah and crossed her legs.

Bobby Weyrick and Miguel Vasquez sat behind them, and across the row, Bree and Sun had taken up residence at their own table. Sun Ming had a reputation for her take no prisoners attitude and her general standoffishness, but Bree had a knack for getting along with just about everyone. As far as Winter was concerned, if Bree didn't like someone, that meant they were a piece of work.

Sun's glossy black hair had grown out of the angled bob she'd sported for the first year Winter had worked at the FBI office. Today, she'd pinned the strands atop her head in a messy, albeit fashionable bun. With her smart blazer and four-inch heels, Sun could have passed as a runway model or a presidential candidate.

When Winter had first been partnered with Agent Ming, the woman might as well have been carved from marble. After all, her demeanor back then was about as welcoming as a slab of stone.

In the last few months, however, the frigid edge had begun to thaw. Sun still exuded a vibe that told onlookers not to mess with her, but she now came across less like a Terminator and more like a determined, professional woman.

At the front of the room, Max Osbourne sat near the end of a whiteboard, and Aiden Parrish stood behind a podium at the SAC's side.

Once upon a time, Winter had wondered if she'd been falling for the tall, handsome man who headed up the FBI's Behavioral Analysis Unit. Between his neatly styled caramel brown hair, pale blue eyes, and his impeccable style, there was no denying that Aiden was an attractive man. However, if Winter had to guess, she'd say that she had merely mixed up physical attraction with the fondness she felt for him as a friend and mentor.

A friend she hoped she still had. The past few months had been trying for Winter and Aiden's friendship.

Ever since Aiden had pointedly advised Winter and Noah

of his belief that Winter's baby brother was a violent psychopath, she had been dead set on proving Aiden's fallibility.

She had dug through memories of cases he'd worked during her time at the FBI, even during the time she'd known him in high school and college, but she'd come away with nothing. As far as his record with the bureau was concerned, Aiden Parrish was always right.

It was maddening. From a personal level, at least.

Behavioral profiling wasn't an exact science, but whenever Aiden Parrish comprised a profile of a suspect, his analysis was usually spot-on.

The only person Winter knew who was better at understanding motivation, emotion, and mental health was Autumn Trent. To Winter's chagrin, Autumn only ever seemed to confirm Aiden's suspicions.

Like Noah had told Winter when he'd caught her moping around her apartment the week before last, friends had disagreements. Just like romantic couples, friends had to work through rough patches too. In time, Noah said he was sure she and Aiden would find a way to reconcile their differences in opinion.

Winter wasn't so sure.

As Max's voice cut through the quiet chatter, Winter jerked herself out of the contemplation.

"Good morning, everyone. I know this is short notice, and I appreciate you all making it here." Max paused for an appreciative glance around the room. "This is time sensitive. The Danville Police Department has reached out to the bureau for assistance on a handful of cases they think are connected."

When he gestured to Aiden Parrish, Winter sat up straighter. Aiden was never one to smile much, but now, he looked downright grim.

Aiden nodded and cleared his throat. "A contact of mine reached out to me last night. Agents Stafford, Dalton, and Black, you might remember him from the Kilroy case."

At the mention of The Preacher, the taste in Winter's mouth soured. Beside her, Noah leaned an inch closer, and she was comforted by his subtle show of support. She took a sip of her mocha, refusing to let her hands shake, as Aiden continued.

"Detective Leavens and his partner, Detective Meyer, have a total of five unsolved murders starting in June of this year. There were three incidents, two of which were double homicides."

Aiden clicked a button on the remote to bring the projector to life. His blue eyes flitted over the quiet gathering before he reached out to tap an index finger beside the photograph of a smiling, middle-aged couple.

"Oliver and Sandy Ulbrich were killed last night on a hiking trail not too far outside of Danville. They were both stabbed in the heart." He pressed the button to skip to the next image—a photo of a younger couple and their German Shepherd. "This is Adrian and Kelsey Esperson. They were killed in their home about three months ago. Their security alarm was disabled, their dog was tranquilized, and then both their throats were slit."

Winter leaned forward. "Aside from how they were killed, that sounds like a professional hit."

Aiden's expression was still grim as he nodded. "It does. Whoever killed them knew exactly how to get around all their security measures. Nothing was stolen, and according to friends and family, the Espersons didn't have any enemies. Adrian Esperson's ex-wife was questioned, but all accounts indicate that she and Adrian ended their marriage amicably, and they were still friends. Plus, she has a rock-solid alibi.

She works the graveyard shift, and she was at work the night of the murders."

As she blew out a quiet breath, Winter folded her hands. "What about the fifth victim?"

The image projected on the whiteboard flicked over to a graduation photo of a young woman with long braids and a wide smile.

Aiden set the remote on the podium and glanced to the young woman's picture. "Willa Brown, nineteen-year-old African American economics student at Virginia Tech. She was killed while she was in Danville visiting with friends and family over summer break. She was shot in the back of the head with a nine-millimeter. According to the medical examiner, she was sexually assaulted before she was killed. She was watching after her sister's pets while her sister went to a graduate school interview in Boulder. At first, the police thought that her sister might have been the target."

"What happened to her sister?" Bree's voice was as grave as the look on Aiden's face.

The SSA's pale eyes shifted to Bree. "She moved out of the apartment when she was accepted to graduate school in Colorado. Her parents moved with her. None of them wanted to live in the same city where Willa had been murdered."

An image of the dilapidated house where Winter's parents had been killed flashed through her mind.

She knew that feeling. She knew it well. Even almost fourteen years after The Preacher had murdered her parents, Winter could hardly imagine living in Harrisonburg.

To Winter's side, Noah tapped his knuckles on the table. "Willa was sexually assaulted. Were any of the other victims assaulted?"

Aiden shook his head. "No."

"And we're sure these murders are all connected?" There

was no accusatory tinge to Noah's words, only genuine curiosity.

Despite the lack of hostility, Aiden's eyes darkened. "All five of the victims were present at the Riverside Mall when Haldane and Strickland killed fifteen people."

From behind Winter and Noah, Bobby took in a sharp breath. "I thought their names sounded familiar. You think someone's targeting the people who were at the mall that night?"

Aiden's expression didn't change as he nodded. "Yes. And to answer the question of why *all* of you are here for this briefing, this is a high priority case. There are more than twenty other people who were taken hostage by Tyler Haldane and Kent Strickland that night. That's twenty more people this killer or killers may be planning to target."

Sweeping his gaze over the room, Max stepped up beside the podium. "We need to find the person or people who did this, and we need to do it yesterday. We can't keep this from the public for long, and as soon as word gets out, we'll have a circus at our doorstep again. Just like we did with Augusto Lopez."

There was one key difference between Augusto Lopez—the vigilante who had targeted murderers and rapists—and the person after whom they now sought. Lopez hadn't harmed innocent civilians. In fact, if Augusto was still free, there was a distinct possibility he'd take out the newest serial killer before the bureau even got a chance to read them their rights.

Max's gravelly voice cut through her brief contemplation. "Dalton, Stafford, you're going to head down to Danville to meet with Detective Leavens and his partner, Detective Meyer. I want the rest of you to look through the case files for Willa Brown, the Ulbrichs, and the Espersons, as well as get a handle on the other Danville hostages from that night.

Once Stafford and Dalton are back, we'll meet up in here again to figure out where we go from there. Otherwise, as soon as SSA Parrish or I hear anything, you'll hear it too."

Before Max finished, Winter had already scooped up her mocha and pushed to her feet.

Flicking off the projector, Max nodded to the room. "Let's get ahead of this thing. We've got a limited amount of time before we'll have to fight through the media at every turn, so let's make it count. Dismissed."

Just like that, the relative peace of the last two and a half months was shattered.

12

As Noah glanced from one gruesome photograph to the next, the corner of his mouth turned down in a scowl. To Noah's side was Bree Stafford, and across the table were their Danville PD counterparts—Detectives Grace Meyer and Doug Leavens. There were so many crime photographs splayed across the table that the four of them had to stand to get a good view of the entire collection.

A slat of daylight that filtered in through the pane of glass in the door was the only reminder that they weren't in a cave. Though the police station was provided with plentiful natural light, the conference room was a drab, windowless space in the heart of the second floor.

Gesturing to the photos splayed atop the laminate table, Noah flashed a curious look to Detective Grace Meyer. "You've suspected that these murders were linked for a while now, haven't you, Detective?"

Grace brushed a piece of honey-brown hair from her face as she nodded. "Since Adrian and Kelsey Esperson were killed."

Before Noah could open his mouth, Bree's dark eyes

flicked up from the pictures to Detective Leavens. "What about you, Detective? Clearly, your partner was on to something. What exactly was it that made the Danville PD so reluctant to look into Detective Meyer's theory?"

With one hand, Doug reached up to rub his eyes. "It was a mistake. Some of our more tenured homicide detectives dismissed it, called it a conspiracy theory. Those guys have been around for a long time, so I guess the rest of us just followed suit."

Detective Meyer's scowl matched Noah's. "I've been keeping an eye on the cases myself, almost like a side project."

For a split-second, Doug's eyes went wide. "You have? When?"

Grace crossed her arms and shot her partner a dark look. "Off the clock. I was trying to find something else that would tie the murders together so the rest of the department would take it seriously."

As Noah pulled out a chair, he gestured to the chairs on the other side of the table. "Well, have a seat then, Detectives. You two were on the scene of each of these crimes, weren't you?"

Doug Leavens nodded as he dropped to sit. "We were. A couple of detectives in homicide retired at the beginning of the year, and the department hasn't seen fit to replace them, so Grace and I wind up with a lot of extra hours."

Funding was one of the many reasons Noah was grateful for his decision to transition from the Dallas PD to the FBI. Working against the clock to put away violent criminals was a difficult job, and the stress was only compounded in cities like Danville where the police didn't always get the funding they badly needed.

Bree took her seat and tapped the glossy photograph of Willa Brown in her graduation cap and gown. "Willa was the first victim, right? She was killed at the beginning of the summer."

There was a distant look in Grace's eyes as she nodded. "Yeah, she was the first. I double and triple checked to make sure we didn't overlook anyone before her. She was one of Haldane and Strickland's hostages at the mall that night."

Detective Leavens inclined his chin in Grace's direction. "Meyer was still working the beat then. She was at the mall while I was meeting with you guys at that church outside McCook. I was out of town for a concert that night, so I was closer to McCook than Danville when I got the call about Douglas Kilroy. That's why I was at the church. Otherwise, I would've been at the mall as well."

Noah nodded. "A couple of our people were there too. Could you and Detective Meyer walk us through the scene where Willa was killed?"

Scooting her chair closer to the table, Grace looked over the splay of photos before she pulled out a picture of the entrance of an apartment. "Willa was watching over the place while Mary Brown was out of town. The apartment building had controlled entry, and each apartment had the option to pay an extra fee each month for a security system."

Noah and Bree exchanged glances. "Did Mary pay extra for the alarm system?" he asked.

The detective's eyes flicked up to meet his as she nodded. "Yes, she did. The alarm didn't go off, which suggests that the perp knew a way around it. We looked through the security company's logs, and sure enough, it was disarmed." Grace paused to shake her head. "It wasn't disarmed around the time she was killed, though. It was earlier in the night."

The overhead fluorescence caught the face of Doug's watch as he reached for an up-close photo of the doorknob. "No signs of forced entry. Willa was killed a little after one in the morning, but none of the neighbors heard anything. No screams, no loud noises, nothing. We think the killer was waiting for her when she got back from visiting with her parents. We thought it might have been a stalker or an ex, something like that, but…" He left the sentiment unfinished.

Bree tapped a picture of the alarm system. "Your run of the mill ex doesn't know how to disarm one of these things. Plus, it's not like an ex would have known the code. Willa was at her sister's place, and stalkers tend to stick to an area near where they live. If a stalker was going to kill the person they were stalking, they would have done it on their home turf."

A slight flush crept into Detective Leavens's unshaven cheeks. "You're right."

Though Noah thought Doug should feel some level of shame for his department's misstep, he couldn't help a twinge of sympathy at the man's dejected tone.

That same empathy flickered to life in Grace's eyes as she glanced over to her partner. "Well, someone *was* stalking her. It just wasn't your average Peeping Tom."

A hint of determination was back on Doug's face as he met Grace's gaze. "We questioned Willa's ex-boyfriend, but he was out to dinner and drinks with some of his friends that night until about three. Honestly, he seemed pretty broken up about it too. He said they only broke up because she moved away for college, and they were still friends."

Noah pointed to a printout of a mugshot of another man when it caught his eye. The man's blond hair was shaved on both sides of his head, and a handful of black and white tattoos were printed on his forearms. His dark eyes were clouded with anger as he glared at the camera.

Staring at the photograph, Noah tried to place the man before glancing to Detective Meyer. "Who is he? A suspect?"

Her scowl deepened as she picked up the photo. "Yeah. Shawn Teller. Some neo-Nazi punk who'd been seen around

Mary Brown's apartment complex a few times. He claimed he had a friend who lived there, but he wouldn't tell us who it was."

Bree drummed her fingers against the table. "That fits. We haven't made any of the contents public, but we came across Haldane and Strickland's manifesto about two and a half months ago. There were a fair amount of racist musings in it. I can see how their agenda would have appealed to someone like Teller."

"When was this taken?" Noah tapped the picture.

"About a year ago," Doug said. "He was arrested for aggravated assault, but the charges were dropped later on down the road."

"Aggravated assault?" Noah echoed. "What happened?"

"He beat the hell out of a protestor at some political rally. And, well." Doug paused to run a hand through his dark hair. "Teller is, or *was* a white supremacist, and he didn't try to hide it. Willa was an educated, well-liked young black woman. He was suspect number one."

"Was?"

Another nod. "We've been on the lookout for him for the last six months, but we haven't so much as caught a glimpse of him. He just dropped off the face of the planet." With a hapless shrug, Doug spread his hands. "Trust me, we've tried to find him to bring him in. We've gotten ahold of friends and family, and none of them have seen him either. We asked why they haven't filed a missing person report, and they all said they just assumed he'd taken off to live in Alabama to be with some woman he'd started talking to online."

Bree beat Noah to the next question. "Adrian and Kelsey were killed three months after Willa. Do you know where Teller was around that time?"

Shadows moved along Doug's face as he clenched and

unclenched his jaw. "No. He was long gone by then, at least according to the people who knew him."

"Shit," Noah muttered under his breath. "The ME said that Willa was sexually assaulted. Was there any DNA evidence left behind?"

With a quiet sigh, Grace propped her chin in one hand. "There was, but we weren't able to get a sample from Teller before he disappeared. Even though he'd been arrested, his DNA wasn't in the database. There'd been no reason to take it at the time of his arrest, and he lawyered up right away."

"What about his family?" Noah glanced back and forth between the two detectives. "Did you try to get a sample from any of his family? That'd narrow down the suspect pool."

Grace was shaking her head before Noah finished. "No. As far as Teller goes, the apple doesn't fall far from the tree. His family are all just as racist as he is, and to say they don't trust the government would be a grave understatement."

"We didn't have enough for a court order, either," Doug said. "When you get right down to it, all we had was a guy who happened to be around the same area who also happened to have a prejudice that gave him a vague motive. Otherwise, he and Willa had never even met. None of the Brown family recognized him, either."

Crossing both arms over his chest, Noah leaned back in his chair. "Okay. Let's look at the next murder, then. That'd be Kelsey and Adrian Esperson."

Doug nodded and pulled out a familiar photo of the young couple. "We threw out a wide net with them too. Honestly, when we walked through the scene, my first thought was that it looked like a professional hit. We don't see a lot of those here in Danville, but they aren't unheard of."

This time, it was Bree's turn to shake her head. "I've

worked organized crime, and I can tell you that the mob doesn't slit people's throats. That's messy, and it runs the risk of getting blood on your clothes. One bullet to the back of the head. That's how they carry out their hits."

For their lengthy drive to the southern Virginia city, Bree and Noah had discussed the probability that the Espersons had been murdered by a contract killer. The conversation had consisted primarily of Bree laying out a whole host of reasons that contradicted the theory of a hired assassin. At first blush, the precision of the crime *seemed* consistent with a professional hit. However, the theory didn't stand up to scrutiny.

Bree gestured to the photo of Kelsey's ashen face. The gaping wound along her throat was so deep that the white of bone could be seen in the autopsy pictures. "Slitting someone's throat is up close and personal, and when the mob agrees to carry out a hit, it's all business."

Scratching his chin, Doug Leavens nodded. "That's true. But still, Shawn Teller wasn't anywhere to be found when Kelsey and Adrian were killed, and as far as we can tell, he still isn't anywhere to be found. We recovered the bullet that killed Willa, but so far we haven't been able to match it to any of the weapons in the ATF's database."

Noah swallowed a string of four-letter words. Shawn Teller had been a promising lead at first, but the likelihood that he'd killed Kelsey and Adrian dropped lower with each passing minute. The odds that each of the three crimes—all of which were still unsolved—was unrelated were slim. All the coincidence in the world couldn't explain how five victims of the same mass shooting had been brutally murdered in the span of six months.

Most murders were the result of a personal or financial motivator. Crimes of passion, robberies, abusive spouses. More often than not, a violent murder was explained by one of the three elements. Most victims knew their perpetrator, but so far, all signs indicated that none of the five survivors of the Riverside Mall shooting had known their attackers.

As a silence settled in over the small group, the only sound was the drone of the station outside the door.

Noah glanced from photo to photo in a vain effort to connect the three crimes. When a sharp knock sounded out, he barely managed to keep himself from leaping to his feet. It wasn't like him to be jumpy, and he didn't like it.

With a light creak, the wooden door swung inward to reveal a gray-haired man of average height. The man's white dress shirt was neatly pressed, and the gold bars on each shoulder of his jacket distinguished him as the precinct captain.

Nodding to Bree and Noah, he eased the door closed. "Sorry I'm late. I had a meeting with the commissioner that ran over. You must be the agents sent here by the bureau." He stepped forward and stuck out a hand. "I'm Captain Polivick."

Rising to his feet, Noah returned the nod. "Captain, I'm Agent Dalton, and this is my partner, Agent Stafford."

With a slight smile, Bree accepted the captain's handshake. "We've been going over the cases with your two detectives. Our colleagues in Richmond are looking over the digital case files you sent to us, but we came here to get a personal account from the detectives who worked each of the cases."

The captain lifted a bushy eyebrow. "What've you found so far? Do you think these murders are all connected?"

"Yes." Noah answered the man without hesitation. "We don't know who the perpetrator is, or if there's more than one killer, but we are certain they're connected. The FBI will take over the investigation from here, but we'll still need the help of the Danville PD."

"Of course. What do you need from us?"

Noah's mouth tasted bitter as he cast another glance at the slew of graphic pictures. "Right now, we have reason to believe that the survivors of the Riverside Mall shooting are in danger. We don't know how the killer is picking their victims, but we believe they're targeting the survivors from that night."

The captain looked appalled. "That's twenty-one people."

"It's a big ask, but these people are in danger." Noah made sure to keep any hint of impatience out of his voice. It wasn't the captain's fault that his precinct was underfunded.

Captain Polivick shook his head. "I don't have the manpower to spare for that many people, Agents. Danville's crime rates have been on the rise for the past few years, but the city hasn't exactly been throwing money at us. We're short-staffed as it is. If I diverted that much manpower, we'd be leaving other parts of the city at risk."

"I used to work for the Dallas PD, and I get it, Captain. But something needs to be done to protect these people. We've got no way of knowing when they're planning to kill again, and we need to get ahead of them."

Brows furrowed in concentration, the captain nodded. "You're right. How about we split the difference. I'll assign a team of officers to get ahold of the folks here in Danville first, and then we'll reach out to those who live in other places. We'll do wellness checks periodically, and we'll make sure they have safety plans in place. Most of it'll be up to them, but we'll help get it started."

It wasn't nearly enough, but Noah flashed the man a quick smile of gratitude for taking this seriously and doing whatever he could. "That's a good plan. We'll take care of alerting the folks outside of Danville, and we'll make sure the precincts in their areas have an idea of what's going on too.

We're trying to put off the media frenzy for as long as we can, so just ask them to be discrete."

Bree nodded. "If I had to guess, I'd say that we'll have a press conference about the crimes within the next twenty-four to forty-eight hours. That should give you and your people enough time to prepare, right?"

"Right." Captain Polivick nodded again.

Prepare for what, Noah still wasn't sure. The killer was faceless, and they had no idea how this person had gone about selecting his targets.

Right now, their only defense was to fire blindly into the darkness and hope one of the shots hit the mark.

13

Winter slipped back into the routine of an investigation as easily as if the last case had never stopped. She, Miguel Vasquez, and Sun Ming had all taken to their computers to parse through the digital records of each of the three Danville murder cases. After a few hours of working solo, they'd convened in the briefing room to combine their notes.

At one end of the whiteboard, Miguel had written out the names of the twenty-one remaining survivors. To Winter's surprise, the tenured agent's handwriting was neat and precise. Compared to Sun and Winter's chicken scratches, Miguel might as well have been born with a pen in his hand.

Winter, Sun, and Miguel had each taken a different case to look over. As they uncovered details while they continued to review the cases, they had added them to the whiteboard.

When Winter stepped away from her laptop to write the current location of Willa Brown's surviving family, the glass and metal door swung open as Bree and Noah strode into the room.

Glancing to the clock and then back to the newcomers,

Winter lifted her eyebrows. "You guys are early. We didn't expect you to be back for another hour."

Noah cleared his throat overly loudly and shifted his gaze to the shorter woman at his side. "That's because *someone* has a lead foot."

With a sweet smile, Bree offered him a noncommittal shrug. "I don't really like to drive, so when I do get behind the wheel, I prefer to get where I'm going really fast."

The hit of levity was a welcome reprieve after an afternoon of digging through details of the tragic death of a young woman. Willa Brown had survived a veritable massacre only to be brutally murdered in a place where she should have been safe.

They hadn't planned for the afternoon briefing to take place for another hour and a half, but when Aiden appeared in the open doorway, Winter figured their timetables had just been moved up. Aiden's pale eyes flicked around the room before he eased the door closed.

"SAC Osbourne is in a meeting." Aiden nodded at the whiteboard. "We can leave all this up, and I'll give him a rundown of where we are once he's out. Dalton, Stafford, what did you get from the Danville PD?"

Brushing both hands down the front of her leather jacket, Bree looked up to the whiteboard. "They had a suspect for Willa Brown's murder."

Winter nodded. "Shawn Teller. Other than listing him as a suspect and mentioning that he'd been seen around the apartment complex, they didn't have much about him in the case file. What happened to him?"

Bree lifted a shoulder. "They don't know. He just dropped off the face of the planet before they had a chance to find him and bring him in for any real questioning. His friends and family never filed a missing person report because they all just assumed he ran off to live with a girl he'd been talking to online."

Winter snapped the cap onto the dry erase marker in her hand. "That seems convenient. I hadn't gotten to digging into his background yet. All I gathered was that he was a neo-Nazi and was about as cooperative as a stone."

From the corner of her eye, Winter caught a flicker of movement as Sun shook her head. "He wasn't mentioned in the Esperson's case file, or the Ulbrich's."

Bree made her way up to the whiteboard. "He'd already disappeared by then."

Noah shuffled through some papers. "One of the detectives we met with, Detective Meyer, had a theory about why the murders were all so different. She thought that the crimes might have been committed by different people, and that the killers were all part of some deranged fan club devoted to Haldane and Strickland."

"That's a good theory, but there's one thing that still really bothers me about this." Miguel pushed to his feet and stepped around the table where he and Sun had posted up to do their research. "Sandy and Oliver Ulbrich were at the Riverside Mall, and they were part of the group that had been taken hostage by Haldane and Strickland. But…" He held out his hands.

"But their names were never made public," Aiden finished for him.

Winter forced the surprise off her face. Miguel had shared his discovery with her and Sun, but to the best of Winter's knowledge, he hadn't passed the information on to Aiden.

Stuffing his hands in his pockets, Miguel gave the SSA a grim nod. "That's right. Now, if our current theory is that one or two of Haldane and Strickland's fanboys have been tracking down and killing the survivors from the shooting, how'd they figure out that Sandy and Oliver were there?"

"Plus," Winter held up a finger, "Willa and her sister were *both* there, but *neither* of them did interviews with the press afterwards. They didn't necessarily keep their details private like Sandy and Oliver, but their names weren't easy to find, either. The Danville police and the news outlets around the city wanted to protect the victims' privacy."

A chill settled over the room as a spell of silence ensued. There were too many details about the murders that didn't add up to a single, cohesive picture. Even if each crime had been committed by a different person, the question remained how they had gotten ahold of the victims' names and personal information.

Though Winter had learned to live with her sixth sense, she didn't often look forward to the visions. Right now, however, she wished she could coax one of the headaches up from wherever it was they hid in the depths of her mind.

As Winter cleared her throat, the room's collective attention shifted to her. "The first thing we need to do is figure out how the killer, or *killers*, got access to Sandy, Oliver, and Willa's information, and we need to make sure Mary Brown knows she might be in danger."

"Mary and her family have been notified," Noah said, giving her a smile that warmed her toes. "They live in Boulder, Colorado now, and the police department in their area has been notified too. Our drive back from Danville was surprisingly productive."

Aiden scooted his chair back before he stood. "Based on how secretive Sandy and Oliver were, then one of the killers either has to be a proficient hacker, or…"

The implication of Aiden's unfinished observation hung over their heads like a lead weight.

"Or they were there." Sun's voice was as grim as Winter had ever heard.

Slowly, Aiden nodded. "I'll get in touch with Agent Welford and Ryan O'Connelly to let them know that their suspect is now *our* suspect too. Whoever the third person was that Haldane and Strickland mentioned in their manifesto, he's our prime suspect now."

14

The remainder of the night and the first half of the following day flew by. In all honesty, Winter couldn't remember the last time she was so busy at work without the physical presence of a suspect. Max Osbourne had scheduled a press conference for the next day, and Winter and her coworkers were under orders to learn as much about their case as possible.

Ryan O'Connelly and Ava Welford had been briefed on the case so far, and their work had been officially combined into the Violent Crimes Division's investigation. The nature of their search for the third person involved in Haldane and Strickland's manifesto had turned from reactive to proactive quite literally overnight.

For the majority of the morning, Winter had filtered through Shawn Teller's history in order to amass a compelling argument to obtain a court order for his parents' DNA. She even made an effort to look into the supposed girlfriend that Teller had met online.

Just like the Danville detectives had advised, the Teller family was uncooperative. After spouting off a few colorful suggestions about what Winter could do for the rest of her investigation, each friend or family member she contacted had hung up. Without a court issued document to compel them to talk, she suspected she would get more information from a brick wall.

With a quiet sigh, she leaned back in her office chair and glanced to the clock. Noah was out for a much-needed coffee and food run, but Winter and Bree had scheduled a lunch time meeting with Agent Welford and Ryan O'Connelly. The plan was for them to combine notes, but Winter had little to add to the upcoming discussion.

Shawn Teller and virtually his entire family were unpleasant, hateful people. Though their social media accounts were decked with Confederate flags, their Irish ancestors hadn't arrived in the United States until a decade after the Civil War had ended.

It was ironic. During the time when the Teller family arrived in the States, Irish immigrants were treated with the same spite and fear that the Tellers now treated people of color. She couldn't help but wonder if their great-great-great grandparents would be disappointed.

In any case, Winter's research was only more confirmation that Shawn Teller was the prime audience for Kent Strickland and Tyler Haldane's hateful message. There was a great deal of merit to Detective Grace Meyer's theory, and in Winter's opinion, Shawn Teller lent even more viability to the theory.

Winter was so lost in her contemplation that she hardly noticed a figure approach her desk from around the corner of her row of cubicles. Bree's white, button-down blouse was tucked into a dark pair of slim jeans, and her riding boots added at least an inch to her height.

Blinking to pull herself back to the real world, Winter

offered her friend a slight smile. "Hey. How's your morning going so far? Did you find anything new?"

Bree shifted her laptop to the other arm as she shrugged. "Not much, really. Just more and more that makes it seem like the person who killed Adrian and Kelsey Esperson was something of a professional. The tranquilizer they used on the dog was powerful stuff. Usually, it's only kept by veterinarians for surgical procedures on animals. I checked through the records of some vets in Danville, but I didn't see anything out of the ordinary. I'll be finishing up that research today."

As Winter closed her laptop, she rose to stand, stretching out her muscles. "It could have been stolen. If the killer knew how to disarm the security system in the Esperson's house, they might have known how to get past the security at a vet's office too."

With a nod, Bree started off in the direction of the conference room where they were scheduled to meet with Ryan and Agent Welford. "I thought that too, but there weren't any break-ins reported by the vets in Danville, nor were there any reports of missing medication. I checked all the way back through the last two years, and there was nothing. There were a couple attempts, but the burglars took off as soon as the alarms went off. They didn't even manage to steal anything before they ran."

"Maybe they stole it from a different city."

"I was thinking the same thing," Bree said. "Unfortunately, that doesn't give me a lot to go on."

As they approached a glass and metal door, Winter spotted Ryan and Ava seated at a circular table. Ava's dark brown hair was pulled away from her face with a barrette, and her gray blazer matched her slacks.

Even though Ryan wasn't technically employed by the FBI, he dressed as well as any other agent in the building—

maybe even better than most. His black suit was tailored to his lean, muscular frame, and his dark hair was styled in the way of a 1960s businessman.

Bree rapped one hand lightly against the metal frame before pushing the door open. "Good morning, or...wait." Bree rubbed her tired looking eyes as she raised her wrist to check the time. "Oh, well, I suppose it is morning for another five minutes."

The corners of Ava Welford's blue eyes creased as she smiled. "Good morning to you too. I guess this is how we're spending our lunch break today?"

Winter let the door swing closed behind herself. "Noah went out for a coffee and sandwich run. He should be back soon. I'm sure he'll have pastries for us too."

Ryan rubbed his hands together. "Hopefully, he's got some more of those chocolate croissants. So far, they're probably my favorite thing about living in Richmond."

As she pulled out a chair, Winter's stomach growled so loud her cheeks went pink. "Agreed. And I'm betting that's the real reason why your sister is moving out here, isn't it?"

With a hapless smile, Ryan spread his hands. "You might be right. She hasn't ever had one, but she loves chocolate, and she loves croissants, so it seems like a match made in heaven."

Bree held up a hand. "Okay, okay. All I ate before I left this morning was a granola bar, so let's stop talking about pastries until Noah gets back. You guys have been looking into how the victims' information got to the killer, right?"

Agent Welford nodded. "We have. Now, we haven't figured out who exactly was behind it, and we haven't tied the digital activity to any other crimes we're aware of, but..." she waved a hand at the writing scrawled across the white-board, "we've narrowed down the timeframe when each victim's identity was compromised."

A thrum of excitement went through Winter. "Compromised? As in, their identities were stolen?"

"Yes and no." Ava placed both hands on the table and pushed to her feet. "Their identities weren't stolen in the traditional sense of the term. No one went on a spending spree with their bank accounts, and no one tried to open credit cards in their names. That's probably why none of them noticed. If the hacker had done any of that, the folks with credit monitoring would have noticed it right away."

Bree looked as disappointed as Winter felt. "So, what *did* they do then?"

"We're working on figuring that out right now. We're going through each person individually." She raised her arm to tap beside the top-most name. "We started with Sandy and Oliver Ulbrich, since they were quite private about what they went through that night."

Winter squinted to read the text beside Ava's hand. "So, the Ulbrich's information was hacked about a month before they were killed."

Ava waved her hand down the line of names. "Same with all the other victims. All their information was accessed within a period of about two days, or closer to thirty-six hours."

Shaking her head, Winter glanced to Bree. "That doesn't make any sense. Willa Brown was killed almost six months ago, and Kelsey and Adrian were killed three months ago. Are you sure this is when all these people were hacked?"

Ava nodded. "We're certain of it."

Although Winter knew very little about how hackers did their work, she had learned a thing or two since she first stepped inside the bureau's doors. She knew the IT departments could trace where logins came from and were normally alerted when they came from vastly different geographic locations. Even if the geographic locations were the same, the IP address could be different from the usual login, or it might be linked to previous fraud. The person's account activity could change, giving other hints that they had been illegally accessed.

Winter wasn't interested in learning the various ways hackers did their work, she just wanted to know what she could do with the information. She wanted to know the hacker's identification so she could catch his or her insane ass.

As Bree leaned forward, she propped her elbows on the table. "Well, Adrian and Kelsey did an interview with a local news reporter about the shooting. Willa and Mary kept pretty quiet, but their names *were* mentioned in the Danville city newspaper. They were only mentioned once, but if someone picked up a paper or paid attention to the initial news broadcasts about the Riverside Mall or did enough digging, they could have found them that way."

Or they could have been at the mall themselves. Winter kept the grim thought locked inside her brain.

Ava dropped her arms back to her sides. "They could have, yes. Whoever our hacker is, he or she would have had to first access a list of the survivors' names before they went after their addresses, phone numbers, and the like."

Winter wrinkled her nose. "But the only record of that would've been kept with the Danville PD or the FBI."

Glancing up to the names and then back to the table, Ava nodded again. "Exactly. Our hacker broke into the Danville PD's records to obtain the names of all the people who were at the mall when the police arrived. Honestly, that sort of thing happens more often than you'd think. Departments tend to store hard copies of their more sensitive data, but every now and then, hackers will break into digital police records to steal identities. Granted, that's usually just so they can monetize them."

With a sigh, Winter slumped down in her seat. "How about the forums where the manifesto was posted in the first place? Have you seen anything there that might indicate that Haldane and Strickland have a fan club?"

Ava's brown eyes flicked to Ryan.

Raising one hand to cover his mouth, Ryan cleared his throat. "Well, yes and no. Obviously, they've got followers, but that's not unusual. Just about every mass murderer or serial killer winds up with some sort of fanbase. I've been keeping an eye on these forums for the past two and a half months, though, and I haven't seen anything that's really jumped out at me."

"Shit," Winter muttered. "So, none of this." She waved a hand at the whiteboard. "None of these people's names and addresses were dumped somewhere on the dark web?"

Ryan shook his head. "No, they weren't. Not that I've found, anyway." He gave them all a solemn look. "Yet."

A stone had settled in Winter's stomach. She hadn't expected the meeting with Ava and Ryan to break their case wide open, but she'd hoped for a piece of information that would make some sense of the mess they'd inherited from the Danville PD.

Bree drummed her fingers against the table. "What if the hacker is the person who killed Sandy and Oliver? We've already been working on the theory that each of the victims was killed by a different person, so what if the person who murdered Sandy and Oliver is the hacker?"

"I don't think so." Winter shook her head. "If that was true, we'd have seen the list of names somewhere on the dark web. There would be *some* trace of their activity."

Bree flashed Winter a curious glance. "You think that the hacker would have wanted to share the information with the rest of the followers?"

Winter considered the question before answering. "Yeah."

"Followers?" Ava Welford tapped her chin with a slender finger. "You think Haldane and Strickland have a cult, or something like that?"

As Winter's pulse rushed through her ears, she straightened in her seat. She swore she could hear the pieces click together in her head. Manson, something in her head whispered.

"A cult. Yeah. What if the killers and the hacker are all working together? We've been thinking of them as working on their own, but what if they actually know one another?"

The same realization flitted over Bree's face as she glanced to Ava. "Like you said about police departments keeping their most sensitive information in hard copy form, maybe these people are doing the same thing. They haven't posted the list of names and addresses online because they're keeping them written down somewhere."

Ava and Ryan exchanged looks before Ryan nodded. "Radicalizing someone online is one thing, but the pull is a lot more compelling when they're face to face."

Winter barely kept herself from smacking an open palm onto the table. "That's it. The third person in the manifesto, *he's* the one. He's the one who found these other guys and radicalized them. He's the common thread between them."

For the second time, Bree nodded her agreement. "So, we need to double down on our effort to figure out who the third person is. If he's the ringleader, then the first thing we need to do is take him down."

Winter's heart still hammered in her chest from the surge of adrenaline. "This might sound crazy right now, but I think we're dealing with the next Charles Manson."

15

As the quiet buzz of the ringtone filled Aiden's ear, he raised a hand to check the time. Once he'd been briefed on the newest theory in their investigation, he'd worked through his lunch break in an effort to establish a behavioral profile for the ringleader and his followers.

Though he felt the familiar clench of hunger in his stomach, he pushed the pang aside as the other line clicked to life.

"This is Detective Leavens." The detective's voice was thick with sleep, but Aiden didn't pause to contemplate whether or not he'd just roused the man from a midday nap.

"Detective, this is SSA Parrish. I'm calling to follow up on the status of the remaining survivors from the Riverside Mall."

Leavens cleared his throat, and the haze of sleep vanished when he spoke. "Of course. We've gotten ahold of most everyone. Some of them have left town, but there are still thirteen folks who couldn't leave because of work or school, things like that."

"Are your people keeping watch over them?"

"As best as we can. We started reaching out to them all

this morning. There are some we haven't had a chance to talk to yet. We're doing regular wellness checks and having the beat cops drive by their houses during their patrol. We told them to break away from their usual routines, and to be alert for anything unusual in their surroundings."

When the detective paused, Aiden could tell there was more he wanted to add. "And...?" he prodded.

"The bureau is still planning that press conference for tomorrow, right?" Though slight, there was hesitancy in Doug's voice.

"Tomorrow, later in the afternoon, yes. We're doing everything we can to get ahead of it and collect as much information as we can before this goes public. We know it's going to be a media shit storm. Why?"

Doug heaved a quiet sigh. "What if the announcement sends the killer into hiding? As long as they don't know that we're onto the pattern, they don't know that we're onto them too. Is there any way we can keep this under wraps until we've found a suspect?"

Aiden pursed his lips. He'd mulled over the idea himself, but the ethics of withholding such a volatile piece of information from the majority of the public were questionable at best. "We've already told twenty something people about what we think is happening. If one of them doesn't leak something to the press, either accidentally or on purpose, I'd be dumbfounded. If word gets out to the public that way, they'll lose what little faith they've got in the authorities to handle this case."

Another sigh. "You're right. I know you're right, but it just seems like a good opportunity to take this bastard by surprise, you know?"

Aiden nodded to himself. "You're not wrong. But at the same time, once we go to the press about it, we've got the potential for tips to come in from the public. It'll be easier to spread the word across the whole damn country, and we'll be able to look for evidence in some places that might've been off limits to us before."

"Huh, yeah." The trepidation had dissipated from Doug's tone. "You're right. We'll open up a tip line here in Danville, and we'll see what we can do about getting the sheriff's office involved too. I know this is Federal jurisdiction now, but I'll be damned if the city of Danville isn't going to do *something* to help. These are our people who were killed."

"We appreciate it, Detective. The more we look into this, the bigger the whole thing seems to become. I'll keep you posted on any updates we run into, and I'll make sure to let you know before we do that press conference tomorrow. It's scheduled for three, but we might move it up."

"Roger that, Parrish. I appreciate you keeping me in the loop. I'll talk to you soon."

Pulling the phone away from his face, Aiden let it drop into his lap. Damn, he was tired. With a heavy sigh, he tilted his head back to fix his vacant stare on the dimpled drop ceiling of his office.

The theory Winter had proposed made sense, but just because it made sense didn't mean it made the investigation easier.

Charles Manson's case had been intricate and complex, and the trial to convict him was mired in legal speedbumps. Though the law had evolved since the early 1970s, cult leaders were still difficult to track down and prosecute. Their followers were notoriously loyal and closemouthed. Even the mob could take notes on the unyielding devotion of cult leaders and their so-called flocks.

Aiden had kept the sentiment to himself so far, but he couldn't help but wonder if the Charles Manson-type character they sought now had been the motivator behind Kent Strickland and Tyler Haldane's massacre.

Had Strickland and Haldane been coerced and controlled by a charismatic man with a seemingly revolutionary message? Had law enforcement merely put away the tools only to leave the mastermind free to commit more atrocities in the name of his twisted agenda?

If they were looking for someone like Charles Manson, Aiden thought he knew the answer. And if the mastermind was still free, then their investigation had a new, unprecedented level of urgency.

Unless they found him soon, more people would die. In Aiden's mind, there was no doubt. There were no ifs, ands, or buts. The only question was how many.

16

After another fifteen minutes in the cab of the white work van, Will finally managed to calm his racing heartbeat. He and Jaime had gone over his task at least ten times, and by now, Will had a clear mental picture of how his reconnaissance would play out.

A police cruiser had driven through the quiet neighborhood not long after Will parked. At the sight of the black and white vehicle, his heart leapt into his throat, and he'd been convinced that the cops were onto them. He was still paranoid, even though the officer hardly cast a second glance in Will's direction. The front windows of the van were lightly tinted, but they weren't so dark that an outside observer's view of the cab was hindered.

As the cop had driven by, Will made a show of leaning back in his seat to scroll through his smartphone. With the security systems uniform Jaime had stolen, as well as the removable decals they'd plastered to the side of the white van, Will looked like just another repairman. Jaime had even pilfered the technician's ID badge. After pasting Will's picture over the face of the other man, Jaime was certain that no casual onlooker would be able to spot the forgery.

Scratching the side of his bearded cheek, Will glanced back to the house—to the target. The residence was an unassuming two-story family home with a modest driveway and a two-car garage. Beige siding blended in with the other neutral colors that dotted the block, and a chain-link fence surrounded the grassy lawn. A tall oak took up the far corner of the lawn, its branches spread over the roof like a protective hand.

After almost three months under Jaime's wing, Will could hardly believe his time had come. Finally, after all the lessons about security alarms—knowledge that was passed to Jaime by his grandfather—Will was about to embark on his first real mission for their cause.

The modest house across the street wasn't home to just any other family. God had chosen the Young family. The mother, Dana, and her daughter, Sadie, had been at the Riverside Mall for a reason. They had walked away, and there was a balance that had to be restored to the world, and Will was the lucky one who had been chosen to complete the task.

Jaime had warned him not to trust the image portrayed by the Young family. Even if they claimed otherwise, they were sinners, and they needed to be punished in accordance with God's will. Tyler and Kent had tried, but their effort had been unsuccessful.

Now, Will was here to take up their mantle.

With a deep, steadying breath, Will straightened to check his reflection in the rearview mirror. The gray button-down shirt was embroidered with the logo of a well-known security alarm business in Danville. Anderson's Alarms was partnered with a nationally regarded security company—a competitor of the company that provided the Young household with their alarm system.

In the interest of gathering more information about the family's habits, Will would pretend to be keen on selling them a new alarm system. He'd worked in sales during high school, and he assumed the principle of selling alarms was largely the same used as the method to sell televisions.

Readjusting the lanyard around his neck, he nodded slightly to his reflection.

The time had come for him to prove his worth to Jaime, and he intended to pass this test with flying colors.

Clipboard in hand, he pulled on the metal handle and shoved the driver's side door open. Glancing up and down the street, he leapt to the asphalt. As Will approached the house, he went over Jaime's suggestions one last time. If the person to whom he spoke became suspicious, he'd been instructed by Jaime merely to hand them a business card and suggest they verify his identity with their corporate office. Since Will's name today was Jared Gainfort, their call would indeed confirm that Will was an authorized salesperson for Anderson's Alarms.

However, Jaime doubted he would receive much pushback from the homeowners. After all, he wasn't there to interrogate them—he only wanted to get a better feel for the layout of their house and an approximate picture of their nightly routine.

Swallowing any lingering anxiety, Will forced a smile to his lips as he rapped his knuckles against the wooden door. A couple muffled voices sounded out from inside, but he couldn't make out their words.

As the door swung inward, he almost lost his convincing façade. Brown eyes wide, a young girl—Mariah, not Sadie, he realized—regarded him with unabashed curiosity. She was pretty, with a sweet smile that made her face light up. In response, he smiled back.

For a split-second, he'd almost forgotten why he was here. He couldn't forget.

Later tonight, he would be back, and he would be required to carry out the Lord's orders. The Young family, this little girl included, had been sentenced to die by God himself.

They're sinners, he reminded himself.

Swallowing against the sudden tightness in his throat, he forced the smile back to his lips. "Hello. Are your parents home?"

The girl nodded. "Yeah. Just a sec." As she disappeared around the corner, her muffled shout followed. "Mom! There's some repair guy at the door."

"What? I told you not to open…" The woman's voice grew quiet, but he could still hear some mutterings going on. Kid was going to get a lecture after he left, he thought with a smile.

Shifting from one foot to another, Will glanced around the covered porch while he waited. There were a couple potted plants beside a lawn chair, and a planter hung from the banister beside the set of steps that led to the door.

As a tall, willowy woman appeared at the edge of the foyer, Will snapped his attention back to the house.

With a slight smile, he offered a nod of greeting to the woman who stepped into the doorway. Her chestnut brown hair was cut just above her shoulders, and her blouse and khaki slacks indicated she'd only just arrived home from work.

"Hello, ma'am," Will greeted. His voice sounded confident, even chipper.

There's a reason God brought us together, he heard Jaime say. At the thought, his smile only grew wider.

The woman glanced over her shoulder before she returned Will's pleasant expression with a wary smile of her own. "Hello. Um, may I ask who you are? Or why you're here?"

Will flashed her a grin as he held up his ID badge. "Of course. My name's Jared Gainfort, and I'm with Anderson's Alarms. We know that crime rates here in Danville have been on the rise for the past few years, so I'm here to check in with you to see if you and your family have considered looking into an alarm system for your home."

Understanding and relief flashed across the woman's face as she nodded. "Oh, okay, I see. No, um, I mean yes. Yes, we already have a security system. We've only had it for about a year now, but it's working great."

Will spread his hands. "Our systems come with twenty-four-seven support from an on-call team of professionals, many of whom have law enforcement experience. We also give you the option to install motion sensor cameras in or outside of your home."

The woman's smile was a little less strained as she shook her head. "No, that's okay. Thank you, though."

The hairs on the back of Will's neck stood on end as the cadence of his heartbeat picked up. He'd disguised himself as a security salesman to glean more information about the family's home alarm system. So far, he'd collected nothing. Not the location of all the cameras, the manufacturer of the alarm, their chosen method of monitoring the home, nothing.

A real salesman wouldn't give up so easily, though. Will'd had his fair share of run-ins with door to door salespeople, and those men and women were nothing if not persistent. He wouldn't pique Dana Young's suspicion by pressing the issue, but he would pique her interest if he threw in the towel so quickly.

He had to think like a salesman.

Widening his smile, he offered her a nod of understanding. "Well, how about you give me a rundown of what type of system you're using now, and I can see if there is a security gap that we can close up for you. Can't be too careful nowadays."

As Dana Young fixed her dark eyes on him, he wondered for a split-second if he had gone too far. If she grew suspicious, he had to be able to concoct a believable explanation for his curiosity.

The hint of annoyance that passed over her face was more of a relief than a deterrent. If she was annoyed, then Will's act was working.

Smiling politely, she shook her head. "We already have mobile monitoring with our system. We have an app that we can use to set the alarms if we're away, and we have a couple cameras." She stepped forward and gestured to a motion sensor light above the door, and he noted a popular security company logo secured to its side. "That's one of them, actually. We can see the footage on our phones when we aren't home. Helps us keep an eye on the kids too."

He'd already spotted the camera, but he wasn't worried about it showing his face. This footage would all be erased within the hour, Jaime had assured him. Will didn't know how that would happen, but if Jaime said it would, he believed him.

With what he hoped was a good-natured chuckle, Will nodded his understanding, then stopped himself. He was nodding too much. "Of course. I've got a daughter of my own. She's not quite walking yet, but still. I get it."

Every word was a lie, but the tale rolled effortlessly off Will's tongue.

There's a reason I'm here, he reminded himself.

Dana Young's smile looked genuine this time. "Then I'm

sure you understand how expensive children are. My husband and I are still paying off student loan debt from over a decade ago, so I hope you'll understand that we can't exactly afford to install a new security system when our current one is working just fine."

Reaching into the breast pocket of his stolen uniform, Will retrieved a business card. "Of course. I completely understand." Will held out the card he'd taken from the alarm technician's vehicle. "Well, thanks for your time, Dana. I appreciate you answering the door today. If you change your mind or if you have any questions, just give us a ring."

Her smile faltered, her arms coming up to cross over her chest. "How'd you know my name?"

Shit.

A real salesperson would never call a potential client by her first name, which was what had triggered her suspicious question. It was a rookie mistake. Will wouldn't let himself devolve into a bumbling idiot, not when his interaction had gone so smoothly. He now knew to expect security cameras, motion sensor lights, and remote monitoring. If he let the façade slip now, he risked ruining everything he and Jaime had worked toward over the last few months.

Clearing his throat, he offered her a sheepish smile. "From physical phone books and online searches. It's where we get information for sales visits like this. I assure you that our company didn't buy your information or anything like that."

Her lips formed an "o" as her arms dropped to cover her middle, her guard dropping with the movement, but not enough for him to ask about stepping in the house to see the current system. "I see," she said. "Okay, then. Have a good night, Jared. Thanks for stopping by." The smile returned to her face as she accepted the handshake he offered.

Her hand was damp. Nervous. Had some primary self-defense mechanism inside her sensed the werewolf at her door?

I'll huff and I'll puff...

Will smiled as he walked back to the van. Disaster had loomed close by, but Will was proud of how well he'd thought on his feet, exactly like Jaime'd taught him. He'd maintained his cover, got some crucial information. Not all the information he'd wanted, but enough to not feel like a complete failure.

When his mind turned back to the wide-eyed girl who'd answered the door, however, he felt the start of a pit in his stomach.

Clenching his jaw, he shook his head as he pulled open the door to the van. He couldn't think about what he had to do. Not now. He was certain he would pull through when the time came to punish the sinners.

He began to whistle as he turned the key in the ignition. "The End" by Jim Morrison just about sprang from his lips.

The end of what? The question arose unbidden in his mind.

These sinners, of course. Sinners like that little girl, and the sin-filled woman she would never become. The end of their way of life.

This was for the good, he reminded himself. For good. For God.

Peace filled him again, and Will was smiling by the time he pulled to the end of the street. His reconnaissance may not have been as successful as he'd hoped, but one way or another, he would prove to Jaime that he was worthy of their sacred mission.

Later that night, he would make up for his failure.

17

Though Winter didn't work in a field or on a construction site, and even though she'd spent the bulk of her day inside the FBI office, a shower at the end of a long workday still felt divine. And as much as she enjoyed showering with Noah, there was something to be said for not being forced to share the hot water with a six-foot-four man who was built like a linebacker.

Maybe someday, they'd live in a place that had one of the wide showerheads that pointed straight down. Until then, Winter would enjoy her solo showers when she had the opportunity.

Noah had offered to cook them dinner that night, and when he'd left to go to the store, Winter decided to pass the time with a relaxing hot shower. She'd entertained the idea of a bath, but she hadn't indulged herself with a tub soak in years, and she wasn't compelled to put forth the effort.

Humming the tune of a song Autumn had introduced her to during their most recent visit to The Lift, Winter rinsed the conditioner from her long hair as she let her mind go blank.

Well, she *tried* to let her mind go blank. But no matter the effort she used to push the thoughts from her head, her brain kept taking her back to the newest revelation in their case.

Charles Manson had been in and out of prison ever since he was a teenager, and his activities before and after the Tate murders were well documented. How, then, could the FBI *and* the Danville Police Department have missed a figure as menacing and conniving as Manson had once been?

Aiden's got his work cut out for him on this case, she thought. Maybe the time had finally come for them to enlist the help of Autumn and her firm.

Their suspect had to have a history of brushes with the law, or at least a history of associating with those who had criminal records of their own. Who were they? Were they just some unassuming civilian, or were they someone who held a position of power—someone like Cameron Arkwell? Was their lofty social status the reason they preferred to operate behind the scenes?

The infamous cult leader behind the Jonestown Massacre had presented himself as a civil rights leader in the beginning. It wasn't until after over nine hundred people had willingly died at Jim Jones's urgings that the truth of his mania came out.

Both men had been sick, along with those who followed them.

The idea that the sick mind behind the deaths of the many innocent people in the Danville mall was still hiding in plain sight was more unnerving than the prospect of a distant armored compound.

Winter was unnerved. What if the maniac hiding in plain sight now was the brother she once loved?

Still loved?

Would always love?

She shivered under the warmth of the water. She didn't know. God help her, she didn't know.

As she turned off the water, Winter mentally scolded herself. The FBI was doing all it could to uncover the identity of the supposed ringleader, and she wouldn't advance their search by needlessly stressing herself over the details.

Ava Welford was a tenured agent in the Cyber Crimes Division, and her expertise combined with Ryan O'Connelly's experience in the criminal underworld would undoubtedly point them in the right direction.

The world wasn't the same place it had been in the days of Charles Manson and Jim Jones. Advances in technology, coupled with the advances in investigatory techniques made deranged men like Manson and Jones easier to spot than ever.

Jones and Manson had been active in the days before the Behavioral Analysis Unit was formed, before the age of the internet, and before the massive criminal databases that catalogued offenders of all shapes and sizes.

Feeling a bit more relaxed, Winter wrapped her hair in a towel before she dressed in a t-shirt and capri sweatpants. Once she finished combing her hair, she flicked off the bathroom light, padded over to her bed, and flopped down onto the plush mattress. Most of Noah's furniture was of higher quality than hers, but she maintained that her bed was far more comfortable.

With a slight smile at the thought of the time they'd spent together in his bed, she grabbed her phone off the nightstand. Noah's message to tell her he was on his way back from the store had been received only five minutes ago, but her eyes were drawn to the email notification in the corner of the screen.

As if her heart knew something her brain didn't, it started beating harder as she pulled up the email app and squinted at the subject line, or the lack thereof. She didn't recognize the address *or* the domain, and she immediately suspected that the message had been sent from a disposable account.

She'd learned from Ryan and Ava that hackers and other shady characters used disposable email domains to route messages to their primary email, as well as to send messages that couldn't be traced back to them. Once the message was sent, the email account disappeared.

She assumed at first that the email had been sent by a scammer in an effort to trick her into entering her credit card or social security number, but the message made no such request.

"No subject," she murmured to herself. As she tapped on the message, she half-expected her phone to be taken over by an advanced virus that had somehow defied all the safeguards she kept in place.

Hello, Winter. It's been a few months since we've talked. You might not remember me, but I sure remember you. I'll see you soon, sis.

As she took in a sharp breath, she felt like her brain had left her body in those few seconds. At the bottom of the cryptic message, a link had been pasted. She knew better than to follow links from strange emails, but the sender had referred to her as *sis*. There was only one person on the planet who referred to her that way.

Before she could second-guess the wisdom of the decision, she tapped the blue hyperlink.

The webpage was bare bones, and she was reminded briefly of the appearance of the forums that Ryan frequented on the dark web.

As her gaze settled on the photo that took up the body of the post, her jaw went slack and her heart pounded in her ears.

A black cat firework.

The same firework that had been stuffed into a handful of dead rats that Justin had left behind in their childhood home in Harrisonburg. The same firework he'd thrown at her on the Fourth of July before their parents had been killed and he had been kidnapped.

The only people who knew the significance of the firework were those who worked for the Federal Bureau of Investigation. Stella Norcott, one of the bureau's lead ballistics experts, Autumn, Aiden, and Noah. They were the only ones who knew about the summertime prank in which Justin had thrown black cats at Winter's feet.

And, of course, Justin. Her baby brother.

The baby who wasn't a baby anymore.

Maybe wasn't even human. More a monster?

Winter wasn't sure how long she laid at the foot of the bed, her stare fixed unerringly on the screen of her phone. If it hadn't been for the light knock followed by the creak of the front door swinging open, she might have held the position for the remainder of the night.

"It's me." Noah's voice jerked her back to reality.

With a start, Winter sat bolt upright before she all but leapt to her feet, the towel that had been wrapped around her head falling to the floor. Her pulse rushed through her ears as the cold creep of adrenaline nestled in beside her heart.

Noah hadn't scared her. She knew it was him and knew he was coming back.

It was the message, the sudden need to hide it, keep it all to herself that had her so shook.

Six months ago, she would have been inclined to keep the bizarre message to herself for fear that Noah would fret over her mental wellbeing. Back then, she'd been so fixated on a bizarre vision she'd had of Aiden saying *"trust no one"* that she'd been inclined to follow his words to the letter.

Now, after all she and Noah had been through together,

she realized the value of his emotional support. In a way, he and Autumn both kept her tethered to reality when her past reared its ugly head.

Slipping in to a robe and brushing the damp strands of hair over her shoulder, she hurried down the hall to the living room and the front door. She loved him. More than that, she trusted him and could rely on him, both physically and emotionally. She wouldn't hold this message from him for even a second.

Noah's green eyes went wide as he spotted the panic that was undoubtedly etched across her face. "Whoa, are you all right, sweetheart?"

Winter opened her mouth to respond, but she wasn't sure how to answer the simple question. "I…I think so, yeah. But, well, no. Not really. Yes and no?" She blew out a long, frustrated breath. "Is that a real answer?"

He stepped out of his shoes before wrapping an arm around her shoulders, pulling her into his warmth. "Kind of. It's okay, though. It was a stupid question. What happened?"

She allowed him to lead her into the kitchen and settle her into a chair. After he set the reusable grocery bags on the counter, she shoved the phone in his face.

The light from the screen glinted off the whites of his eyes as he scanned the message. "Sis? Is this…?" He left the question unfinished as his gaze met hers.

With a quick nod, she tapped the link to display the photo of the firework. "It says to check back in a few days."

Noah sucked in a breath through his teeth. "Jesus, a black cat? That's…that's really him then, isn't it?"

Winter nodded. "It has to be. Stella, Aiden, and Autumn are the only others who know about the black cats."

Leaning against the counter, he combed a hand through his dark hair. "Shit. You're going to take it to Agent Welford, right?"

Winter closed the email and locked the screen, pushing the phone across the counter. "Yeah. But with this investigation taking off, I doubt she'll have time to look into it anytime soon."

Noah draped an arm around her shoulders to pull her into an embrace. As she let herself meld into the safety of his arms, the rush of adrenaline started to recede, leaving her physically and mentally exhausted. "What do you think he means by 'check back in a few days?'"

"Hard to say, darlin'. Maybe it means that he's finally ready to talk to you."

Winter tightened her grip around him. "Wouldn't it be nice if it was that easy?"

Though Noah's suggestion made logical sense, part of Winter knew that being reunited with her little brother would be anything but easy. In fact, just thinking of him felt like a raging storm coming at her from a distance.

She closed her eyes against the thought that had been coming to her for days. Weeks. Months.

Justin was a storm.

And he was baring down on her.

18

Once the security salesman left, Mariah Young's evening went back to the same school night routine she and her older sister, Sadie, had come to expect. After Mariah and Sadie finished their homework, they each completed their daily chores, and then they sat down to watch television and play video games.

Today had been Mariah's P.E. day at school, and all she wanted to do was curl up in the corner of the couch to watch *Supernatural*. Mariah's mom and dad had told her that the show was for older kids, but they liked it too, so they let her and Sadie watch the episodes on Netflix. Mariah thought they were just glad that she and Sadie had grown out of all their kids' shows, though they still watched *SpongeBob* and *Pokémon*.

Earlier that week, Mariah had learned that Pokémon wasn't even technically a cartoon. Since it was written and drawn in Japan, it was an anime show. The new, unfamiliar term had made her feel very grown up whenever it left her lips.

Mariah had always liked the characters' big eyes and

colorful hair better than American cartoons, anyway. There were other anime shows on Netflix, but she and Sadie hadn't watched any of them yet.

As Mariah pulled a super soft microfiber blanket up to her chin, Sadie flashed her a questioning glance. "What do you want to watch, Ry?"

From beneath the blanket, Mariah shrugged. Other than their mom and dad, Sadie was the only one who called her Ry anymore. "We can watch whatever, just not any more of that stupid show about the guy who's always trying to show off how macho he is."

With a giggle, Sadie nodded and flicked on the television. "That show *is* stupid."

When Mariah was younger, she and Sadie used to fight like cats and dogs. They'd always bicker over whose shows were for babies, or who should get the honor of being player one in Mario.

Their rooms upstairs were right next to one another, and they wouldn't hesitate to bang on the walls when they heard even a murmur of noise. Their parents said that the arguing drove them insane, and a couple times, they'd even made Mariah and Sadie sit down on the couch to hold hands after they'd gotten into a fight.

But ever since Mom and Sadie went to the Riverside Mall that night, things had changed.

Mom, Dad, and Sadie's teachers called it trauma. Even now, close to a year afterwards, Sadie still went to see her counselor every week.

At first, Mariah had been jealous that Sadie got to go hang out with a cool lady and drink a soda each Wednesday, and she'd pestered her mom to let her see a counselor too. Then, one time, Mom had let Mariah go with Sadie to see her counselor.

The lady was just as kind as Sadie had told her, and she'd

explained why Sadie visited her every week. Since then, Mariah hadn't bothered her mom about the visits.

Before the mall, Sadie had been bossy and snotty, but now, she was quiet and sweet. Too quiet and almost too sweet sometimes, letting people walk over her rather than bring attention to herself. Every now and then, Sadie would wake up in the middle of the night from a bad dream, and she'd ask Mariah if she could come sleep with her.

Though Mariah wouldn't admit it to Sadie, it made her feel good to know that she was able to help her older sister.

As the rerun of *Supernatural* flickered onto the wide screen, Mariah's eyelids started to droop. From the kitchen on the other side of a dividing wall, she heard her parents' faint laughter as they prepared dinner.

Even through the haze of sleep, Mariah's stomach grumbled when she caught the first whiff of garlic. Her mom's family was from Italy, so food like lasagna and spaghetti was a regular occurrence.

"Girls." Dana Young's voice drifted over to the sisters.

Mariah reluctantly blinked to clear her vision before she turned to regard her mom.

With a slight smile, Dana beckoned for Mariah and Sadie to follow her to the dining room. "Lasagna's in the oven, but your dad and I need to talk to you about something."

With that single sentence, Mariah's mouth felt like it had been stuffed with cotton balls. She and Sadie exchanged fervent glances before they climbed off the couch. Usually, when their mom and dad wanted to talk to them in the dining room, it was because someone was in trouble, or something bad had happened.

Swallowing to fight the desert that had overtaken her mouth, Mariah followed her older sister to where their mother waited for them at the entrance to the dining area.

The space was just off the kitchen, and a breakfast bar separated it from the cooking area.

As Mariah glanced back and forth between her mom and dad, she pulled out a wooden chair to take a seat. "Are we in trouble?"

Mom's smile widened as she shook her head. "No, honey, neither of you are in trouble. We just need to talk to you about something."

To her side, Dad scooted forward and propped his elbows on top of the table. "You girls remember what a safety plan is, right?"

Sadie nodded, her face as pale as the white shirt she was wearing. "Me and Ms. Stanwell talked about safety plans a few times. Mariah was there for one of the times."

"I remember, yeah," Mariah said, concern settling into her bones. "It's when you and your family come up with a plan in case something bad happens."

Even as Mom smiled, Mariah didn't miss the worry in her eyes. "That's right. That's what we're going to go over right now, okay? We're going to just go over our safety plan and make sure we all know what to do in case something happens."

Mariah glanced to Sadie and then back to her mother. "Are we in danger, Mom?"

She expected her mother to laugh and wave a dismissive hand, to reassure Mariah and Sadie that they were safe, and that the safety plan was just a precaution.

Instead, her mom's smile faded as she looked over to Dad. As she did, Mariah felt her bladder squeeze, and she had the sudden need to pee.

Clearing his throat, Timothy Young nodded. "Yeah, honey, the police think we might be."

Mariah's eyes went wide, but she pushed back the threat of tears and swallowed. She was too old to burst out crying whenever she heard bad news. "How? Why? Who wants to hurt us?"

Dad shook his head, and Mariah could see real concern in his eyes. He was afraid. She never saw her father afraid. Except…

She pushed away the thoughts of the day of the bad men in the mall. Her lower lip began to tremble, and she pulled it between her teeth so nobody would see.

"The police aren't sure, honey," her father said. "They're looking for the person right now, though. They've even got the help of the FBI."

"It'll be okay, you guys." Mom reached across the table to clasp Mariah and Sadie's hands. "The police are keeping an eye on us. There are some other people in danger too, so they're working really hard to catch the person. Right now, this just means that we have to be a little extra careful, okay?"

Mariah swallowed again, but she nodded. "Okay."

"Just so you girls know," Dad's eyes flicked from Mariah to Sadie, "we usually only turn on the alarm at night or when we're all gone, but we're going to be leaving it on all the time now, okay? That means that you'll have to enter the code if you go outside and then come back in. And you can only leave the house with our permission, got it?"

Mom gestured to her smartphone. "You two are practically young women now, so I'm going to trust you with your phones when you go to bed. No games, no internet, none of that, okay? I want you to have your phones in case something happens so you can dial 911."

Sadie opened her mouth to say something, but Dad held up a hand. "Don't hesitate to call, either. That's what the police are there for. If you hear anything weird in the house or you see anyone suspicious, call. Even if it turns out to be nothing, it's better that you call, just in case. Either your mother or I will always be here with you too. I know it's kind of a pain in the butt, but it's not permanent. It's just until the police catch this guy."

Mariah felt queasy, but she nodded, trying to be brave. "Is that why that security guy was here earlier?"

Her mother shook her head. "No, he was just a salesperson out and about."

Mariah scratched at her cheek, wrinkling her nose. "He didn't *look* like a salesperson."

Shrugging, her mom offered her a quick smile. "Not all salespeople look the same, sweetie. Different industries have different dress codes. Apparently, whoever he worked for didn't have any rules about shaving."

Sadie perked up at the change in conversation. "Like that guy at the grocery store with the tattoos on his arms, right?"

With a chuckle, their father pushed up the sleeve of his hooded sweatshirt to reveal a warrior angel tattooed on his forearm. "Ten years ago, no one would have let me wear short sleeves at work with this. But now, most places are okay with tattoos as long as they aren't something offensive."

Mariah finally managed to overcome her unease and a smile came more easily than she thought it would. "When I'm older, I want all *kinds* of tattoos."

WHEN SADIE'S first scream pierced through Mariah's slumber, she thought her sister had suffered another nightmare. But when the second shriek sounded out immediately after, her eyes snapped open.

That wasn't a scream caused by a nightmare. The blood-curdling sound was the result of something worse. Much, much worse.

With a sharp gasp, Mariah sat bolt upright.

Through the faint ring in her ears, she made out the dull

thud of heavy footsteps as someone made their way down the hall.

Even if you're not sure if it's an emergency, don't hesitate to dial 911. As her father's words resonated through her thoughts, Mariah's stomach churned, the taste in her mouth suddenly sour.

Blinking back tears, she cast a desperate glance around the shadows of her bedroom. She couldn't remember closing her door, but one of her parents must have shut it when they went to bed after she and her sister did.

As the footsteps slowed to a halt, Mariah's body might as well have been turned to stone. She felt like one of those knights who had looked at Medusa. She couldn't move, couldn't even pry her stare away from the door, couldn't even *blink*.

The first tear slipped from the corner of her eye, and even though her hands had begun to tremble, she still couldn't break the spell. As her wide-eyed stare remained on the door, she felt like time itself had stopped.

She didn't even know if this was real. Maybe she, and not Sadie, was the one who had suffered the nightmare.

No, that wasn't right. She was *sure* she'd heard Sadie's cry.

A muffled shout came from the end of the hall—from her parents' room. All at once, reality sped back up, and Mariah broke through the spell. Her heart hammered a merciless cadence against her chest, but she grated her teeth against the fear and swung her legs over the edge of the bed.

With one hand, she snatched up her cell phone. Her hands were too shaky to draw the unlock pattern. She tried once, and she was greeted with the angry buzz that told her the pattern was incorrect. Blinking back tears, she made a second attempt, and then a third.

Then, she got the dreaded warning. If she tried too many more times, she'd be locked out.

She couldn't let that happen.

"No," she managed. The word was little more than a squeak. Even though she doubted that the burglar had heard her, she snapped one hand up to cover her mouth.

As Mariah took in a shuddery breath, she squeezed her eyes closed. During Mariah's one time visit with Sadie's counselor, Ms. Stanwell had gone over a technique the girls could use if they felt overwhelmed.

Take a deep breath in and count to three.

Mariah inhaled and counted, careful to be as quiet as possible.

And then exhale and count to five. Do that as many times as you need to until you start to feel better.

Forcing her eyes open, Mariah counted to five as she silently exhaled. Her hands still shook, but the trembling was much less noticeable than it had been at first.

As she focused on the unlock pattern on her phone, Mariah purposefully ignored the handful of shouts in the distance. She had to be brave so she could call the police to come help her family. They were counting on her, she was sure of it. If the burglar had made it to her parents, then she was the only one who could call for help.

Her index finger wavered only slightly as she drew the series of zigzags to unlock her phone. Rather than an angry buzz, she was greeted with the photo of her and Sadie she'd saved as her wallpaper. Though the tremor threatened to return full force, she pressed the phone icon and dialed the numbers 9-1-1.

Swallowing against the tightness in her throat, Mariah pressed the device to her ear. With her other hand, she groped at the darkness between her nightstand and her bed until she felt a familiar wooden handle. Her Louisville Slugger.

"911. What's your emergency?" The man on the other end

of the line sounded calm, like he was ready for anything. Mariah hoped he was.

"H-hello," she whispered, her voice a shaky waver she couldn't control. "Hello, 911? My...my family, they're in danger."

The professional edge in the man's voice softened. "Okay, what's your name, sweetheart?"

"M-m-m-m..." She bit down on her tongue, trying to force it to work. "M-mariah Young."

"That's great, Mariah. What's your address?"

With another paranoid glance to the closed wooden door, she rattled off the same address she'd recited countless times before. They'd lived in this house since Mariah was three and Sadie was five.

"Can you tell me what's happening? Are you safe?"

Mariah's bottom lip trembled. "I'm not sure. I'm in my room and...and the man, I think he's in my parents'—"

Her explanation was cut short as the raucous crack of a gunshot cut through the night air. The sound was so clear, so piercing that Mariah felt as if she'd been physically struck.

"Here's what I want you to do." The man's voice was more urgent now. He must have heard the gunshot too. "Are you with me, Mariah?"

"Uh-huh." She barely heard her own voice over the roaring of blood in her ears. Tears poured down her face, mixing with the snot that began to flow into her mouth.

"Grab a weapon if you have one, and then I want you to *hide*, okay? The police are on their way, but I need you to stay safe until they get there. Do you have a closet you can hide in?"

"Y-yes," she stammered, wiping her face with her sleeve, taking a step backward, then another, desperately afraid to turn around. She didn't stop until her back caused the slats of the bifold door to rattle.

She was just reaching for the knob when the footsteps neared, stopping in front of her door this time. The pace was hurried, and the thud was more pronounced.

"He's here," she whispered, the words barely a puff of air.

"Mariah!" The sound of the dispatcher's voice sounded so very, very far away. "Mariah! Can you hear me? Hide, sweetheart. Hide now!"

To her horror, the bedroom door creaked open in slow motion. Even though she knew she should heed the 911 operator's advice and hide, she had been turned to stone again.

As the door completed its arc, the faint glow of a nightlight near the stairs outlined the hulking silhouette of a man. In one hand, he clutched a gun, and in the other, he held a knife.

The clatter of her phone hitting the hardwood floor was the only indicator that Mariah had lost her grip on the device. She didn't remember reaching down to grasp the Slugger with both hands, nor did she remember her bladder loosening until warm pee soaked her pajama bottoms.

"I c-c-called the p-police!" As much as she wanted her voice to sound menacing, there was an unmistakable hint of fright in the shaky words.

Swallowing the sting of bile in the back of her throat, Mariah raised the bat over her shoulder, the wood causing the slats of the door behind her to rattle. She took a step forward so she could maneuver better, although she was loathed to get even an inch closer to him.

The man was still. Watchful. The waiting was terrible, and her bladder emptied a little more.

"The police are on their way!" Her second shout carried more weight than the first. She had peed on herself, just like she was a baby. The thought made her mad, gave her a little bit of strength. "They'll be here any minute now. Look, they're on the phone right now!" She didn't dare even flick her eyes at the fallen smartphone.

Even as the tears streaked down her cheeks, and the pee ran down her legs, Mariah didn't let her grasp on the Louisville Slugger waver. Her grip was iron, and as soon as the man made a move, she would explode into action. She'd broken through the spell that had turned her to stone, and now she was prepared to fight.

She had no other choice.

When the bad man took a step toward her, she arced the bat behind her head, just like she did in softball practice. She was the best hitter on the team, and today, she knew she needed to make this one count. She fully expected him to raise the gun to take aim, or to charge at her with the knife in his other hand.

Somewhere in the house, something crashed to the floor, making Mariah jump. To her surprise and tremendous relief, the bad man jumped too, his body turning toward the door.

Hit him, Mariah's mind screamed as she gripped the baseball bat tighter. *This is your only chance. Don't wait.*

But she was so afraid. Deathly afraid.

"When life throws you a curve, just drive it." Her softball coach had said that a thousand times.

Forcing her frozen body to move, Mariah raised the bat higher, but before she could take a step closer to him, the bad man ran out into the hallway. She barely heard the thud of his footsteps on the wooden stairs over the pounding of her heart.

Inhale. One, two, three.

Exhale. One, two, three, four, five.

Inhale. One, two…

She burst into tears when the front door slammed shut.

19

For the duration of their drive to Danville, neither Noah nor Levi Brandt uttered more than six words. Detective Doug Leavens had reached out to Noah personally to relay the news of the newest murder. At five in the morning, Noah and Winter had dragged themselves to the FBI office for a short briefing on the situation in Danville.

Due to the nature of the crime, Levi Brandt—an agent from the Victim Services Division—had been tasked with accompanying Noah to meet with the two witnesses who had survived.

Until now, the killer or killers hadn't left any survivors. What had changed? Why had Mariah Young and her father, Timothy Young, been left alive? The father had been shot in the arm, but the young girl hadn't been touched.

Why?

"The next Charles Manson," Noah muttered to himself.

Levi's eyes shifted over to Noah as he pulled the sedan into a familiar parking lot. "Come again?"

Shaking his head, Noah heaved a sigh. "That's what Winter said. She said she thinks we're dealing with the next

Charles Manson. Every one of these cases is different. Different murder weapon, different cause of death. Different time of day. The only thing that's consistent is that all these people were at the Riverside Mall when Haldane and Strickland killed fifteen innocent people."

As he nodded his understanding, Levi's mouth was a hard line. "So, their ringleader is giving them orders to finish what Haldane and Strickland started, killing however they want. The third person in the manifesto."

It was Noah's turn to nod. "It has to be. Nothing else adds up."

After he threw the car into park, Levi turned the key back in the ignition. "Then we need to find one of these fuckers. *Alive*. And then SSA Parrish needs to work whatever magic he used in Baltimore to get the son of a bitch to talk."

A flicker of vehemence passed over Levi's gray eyes that told Noah he never wanted to be on the receiving end of the man's wrath. The Richmond PD had botched their relationship with a potential witness during the Augusto Lopez investigation, and according to Winter, Levi Brandt's scathing reprimand of the precinct's captain had been the stuff of cop ghost stories.

Unfastening his seatbelt, Noah wondered if they would even need Aiden Parrish to interrogate a suspect. Maybe all they had to do was sit the guy in a room with Levi. Between the withering stare and his creative use of four-letter words, Levi would break even the most hardened criminal.

Noah and Levi lapsed back into silence as they made their way up a set of concrete stairs to a pair of heavy double doors. As soon as he shoved the first door open, Levi's badge was in his hand. Noah followed suit in short order, and a uniformed officer behind a wooden desk waved them forward.

"Detective Leavens is waiting for you," the man said.

"What about the witnesses?" Noah posed the question before Levi could interject. Though Noah didn't doubt the man's professionalism, he wasn't ready to test his luck quite yet.

The officer nodded. "Mariah Young is with her father in an interview room."

Noah lifted an eyebrow. "I thought Tim Young was shot?"

"Left the hospital against medical advice. Shot in the shoulder." The officer glanced to the hallway. "Head up to the second floor, then take a right. Go past the desks out in front, and Detective Leavens should be back there before you hit the interview rooms."

Noah gave the man a quick nod of thanks before he and Levi took off toward the elevator.

They followed the officer's instructions, and as promised, Doug Leavens and his partner, Grace Meyer, were seated on a wooden bench beside the entrance to a short hall.

"Detectives." Noah extended a hand as he closed the distance. "I wish I could say it's nice to see you, but I don't think that's the case."

"I'm afraid not." Detective Leavens stood to shake Noah's hand before he turned to Levi. "I'm Detective Leavens, and this is my partner, Detective Meyer."

With a stiff nod, Levi accepted the handshake. "Special Agent Brandt with the Victim Services Division. We've already heard a little about it, but could you two fill us in on what happened?"

Grace's brown and green eyes flitted back and forth between Noah and Levi. "The Young family were the targets. I checked through my notes, and only two of them were at the Riverside Mall. Dana Young and her oldest daughter, Sadie Young."

Noah's mouth was suddenly devoid of moisture. Was *that* why there were two survivors?

Detective Leavens crossed his arms over his black suit jacket. "Sadie Young was stabbed to death three times in her bed, and Dana Young sustained a handful of stab wounds, one of which pierced through her left lung. She died in the ambulance on the way to the hospital."

Scrubbing one hand over his face, Noah clenched his jaw. Timothy and Mariah might have survived, but their lives had been irreparably damaged.

"Timothy Young was the only one who was shot," Grace went on. "He was trying to shield his wife."

Noah shifted in his seat. "Why did the killer leave, then?"

Grace tipped her head to the side, and Noah could hear her neck crack with the movement. "We aren't sure. Tim Young had a sidearm stashed in a nightstand, and he was trying to get to it when he knocked a lamp to the floor."

"Who called 911?" Levi asked.

"The younger daughter, Mariah. The perp barged into her room before he left, but she yelled at him and told him the cops were on their way. Then something crashed inside the house, the lamp we believe, and the man fled."

Levi pursed his lips. "That doesn't explain why he left the husband alive."

Grace shook her head. "No, I know it doesn't. My best guess right now is that he thought he had subdued Tim and he wanted to get out of the house after the noise of the gunshot."

"Either that or he thought his work was finished." Levi's tone was as foreboding as the grim reaper himself.

Grace's expression matched Levi's grave statement. "Detective Leavens and I already went through the usual round of questions with Mr. Young. Between what the daughter witnessed and the physical evidence, we can confidently rule out the possibility that Mr. Young was involved in his wife's murder."

Before they had even left for Danville, Noah was sure that Tim Young was as much a victim as his wife and his daughters, but old investigative habits died hard.

"We were told that Mr. Young was injured," Noah said. "Did he get a look at the killer?"

Shaking her head, Grace crossed both arms over her chest. "No. Well, yes and no. Mr. Young saw the killer, but the perp was wearing a mask that concealed the top half of his face."

Noah gritted his teeth and nodded.

Detective Leavens cleared his throat. "We got Mr. Young's statement when he was at the hospital, so you can feel free to go over it and see if there are any other questions you'd want to ask."

"We appreciate it," Levi said.

Grace gestured to the closed metal door beside the bench where she and Detective Leavens sat. "We told Tim and Mariah that you would be here to ask them some questions. They're in the second interview room, just down this hall."

Leavens buttoned his suit jacket. "We'll be in the next room over, so you can let us know if you need anything."

Levi offered the detective an appreciative nod. "Will do."

The hinges of the old door groaned as Noah and Levi stepped into the dim hall. They passed room one, and Levi paused to straighten his black tie. Levi flashed him a questioning look, and Noah nodded.

When they stepped into the interview room, Noah had to fight to keep the surprise off his face. As soon as Levi's foot touched the tiled floor, he was a different person. He was no longer the methodical, take no prisoners agent who had a reputation for his scathing reprimands and candid observations.

Two sets of honey-brown eyes snapped over to the doorway as Levi and Noah entered the interview room.

Rather than the drab, imposing space Noah had expected, the room felt almost cozy. Against one wall, Timothy Young sat on a leather couch with his one good arm wrapped around the shoulders of his daughter.

The girl was a carbon copy of her father. Their eyes were the same shade of light brown, and their high cheekbones lent them each a regal air.

"Mr. Young, Mariah, I'm Special Agent Levi Brandt. I work with the Victim Services Division of the FBI. This is my partner for this case, Special Agent Noah Dalton."

With a polite smile, Noah extended his hand to Tim Young. Tim nodded slightly as he accepted the handshake before wrapping the arm around his daughter again.

"We're here to ask you a few questions to get a better idea of what happened." Levi pulled a chair closer to the coffee table in front of Tim and Mariah, and he gestured for Noah to do the same.

Tim glanced to his daughter as he straightened in his seat. "We'll do our best. We already answered a few questions for the Danville PD."

Noah dropped down to sit at Levi's side. "We'll skip the usual questions about whether or not you know anyone who would want to do this."

Levi's eyes shifted from Tim to his daughter. "Mariah, do you mind if I ask you a couple questions?"

Shadows moved along her throat as she swallowed. "Okay." The word was hardly above a whisper.

"Let's start with your day. Did you notice anything strange while you were at school?"

The girl shook her head.

Levi spread his hands. "Anything at all? Even if it doesn't seem like a big deal."

She shook her head again. "No, there wasn't anything weird at school."

With a slight smile, Levi nodded. "Okay. What about after you got home?"

Glancing to her father, Mariah frowned with a look of concentration. "No, I-I don't think so. Mom picked me and..." As she trailed off, the overhead light caught the tears that welled up in the corners of her eyes. "Me and Sadie. She picked up me and Sadie, and then we went home."

Tim tightened his grasp on Mariah's shoulders.

Noah had broken bad news to the families of many victims during his tenure in law enforcement, but the sight never got any easier. When Tim blinked against the glassiness in his eyes, Noah felt as if a phantom hand had clamped down around his throat.

Propping both elbows on his knees, Levi hunched forward in his seat. "Okay. What about when you got home? Could you tell me what happened after you guys got home?"

Slowly, Mariah nodded. "Mom made us some French toast because she said the bread was getting stale and she needed to use it. I was reading a book for one of my classes while we ate, but Mom and Sadie were talking about math stuff." Her eyes dropped to the floor as she sniffled.

"It's okay. Take as long as you need." When the girl glanced back up, Levi offered her a reassuring smile.

Dabbing at her nose with a tissue, Mariah nodded. "We did our homework after we ate, and Mom told us that Dad would be getting home a little late. I had to sweep the kitchen, and Sadie had to vacuum the rugs in the living room and the dining room."

Noah wasn't sure how the man did it, but Levi's calm smile never wavered.

"My daughters have to do those same exact chores. My oldest, I don't know what it is, but she *loves* to vacuum." Levi's eyes shifted to Tim as he shrugged. "We have a German shepherd and two cats, so I never argue when she wants to break out the vacuum cleaner. If it wasn't for her, we'd be as furry as the animals."

Through a sniffle, Mariah managed a wistful smile. "I hate vacuuming. That's why Sadie always did it."

"What about after your chores? What happened for the rest of the night?" Levi asked the questions with the same patient smile.

The look in Mariah's eyes turned vacant as she fixed her gaze on the floor. Dabbing at her nose again, she shook her head. "Nothing, really. Before me and Sadie went to watch TV, there was some guy who came to the door, but I didn't talk to him much. My mom did."

As Tim patted Mariah's shoulder, he nodded slightly. "Oh yeah. The salesman, that's right."

Noah leaned forward, every muscle tensing, although he tried not to let his excitement show. "Salesman? What type of salesman?"

Tim shrugged and glanced at his daughter. "I wasn't home yet, but Dana…" His voice strangled on the word, and he cleared his throat with a loud cough. "My wife mentioned it to me while we were cooking dinner. Some security system salesman."

Before the realization fully dawned on him, Noah had already known what Tim was going to say. Anger mixed with excitement at the prospects of a lead made his blood pump faster. "Do you remember the name of the company he worked for?"

As Tim nodded, his eyes met Noah's. "She said he was from Anderson's Alarms."

Maintaining the same pleasant look as before, Noah raised his eyebrows at Levi. "Agent Brandt, could I have a quick word with you in the hallway?"

Curiosity flashed across Levi's face as he nodded.

With a reassuring smile to Tim and Mariah, Noah held up a finger. "We'll just be a second."

By the time Noah and Levi stepped into the dim hall, Noah was ready to kick a wall or scream the rooftop off. Revelations and realizations were always accompanied by a fleeting high, the result of a flood of dopamine and norepinephrine.

The door latched closed with a metallic click. After glancing over his shoulder, Noah returned his attention to Levi.

Though mostly calm and patient, there was a distinct edge in Levi's visage. The man knew that Noah wouldn't have pulled him away from the two victims without a damn good reason.

Noah covered his mouth with one hand as he cleared his throat. "The security salesman. At two of the three previous murder scenes, the victims' home security system was disabled."

Levi took in a deep breath and scratched the side of his face. "You're thinking that the killer might be an alarm technician?"

"If he isn't now, then he might have been at some point in the past. Showing up at the victims' doorstep pretending to be a home security salesman is one way to figure out whether or not the homeowners actually *have* a security system, and even what type it is. If they've got experience as a technician, then they use that knowledge to plan how to disable the system."

With one hand on his hip, Levi rubbed his chin. "You're right. It's pretty unassuming. Most people think of a door to door salesman as more of a nuisance than a threat."

Noah checked the time. "The bureau is holding a press conference about the murders in about four hours. I might want to add something about our home security salesman."

"Tim said he wasn't home yet, so the only people who would've seen the guy would be Mariah and her mother. Any idea how big Anderson's Alarms is? Maybe we can see if Mariah recognizes any of the employees."

Noah tapped at his phone. "They've got locations in Richmond and Norfolk. It's a decent-sized operation, and my guess is that there are enough people who come and go in their business that we might miss our guy if we take that route. Plus, there's no guarantee that the perp actually *works* for Anderson's Alarms. He might have disguised himself as an employee just so he could ask his questions and leave."

Levi nodded his understanding. "A sketch artist."

Noah returned the nod. "Exactly. If we've got that to go on, then we can look through their employees ourselves. And, I'll access the Young's system myself. Maybe we'll get lucky and catch the guy on some hidden camera."

Levi briefly crossed his fingers. "You tackle the alarm system, and I'll get Mariah set up with a sketch artist."

20

Though Autumn made an effort to avoid national news on a regular basis, she still liked to keep up with the goings-on around the city. As long as she was home during the evening broadcast of the local news, she almost always flipped over to the station, at least for a minute or two.

Tonight, however, she and Winter had anxiously awaited the nine o'clock timeslot. The FBI and the Danville Police Department had teamed up for a press briefing that had been aired on Danville's news station earlier that night. Due to a hazardous weather forecast and the fact that the FBI's announcement wasn't local to Richmond, the briefing hadn't made the cut for the earlier broadcast.

With one more sip from her chai latte, Autumn settled back into her corner seat on the sectional couch that took up most of her living room. At the other end of the sofa, Winter scratched the head of the fat, orange cat curled up in her lap. Autumn's little Pomeranian mix had taken up residence in the cat bed beside the entertainment stand—the cat hardly slept in it anyway.

Autumn stretched her legs to prop her feet on top of the

stone surface of the coffee table. "Is Noah still thinking about getting a cat?"

As Winter nodded, she held up two fingers. "Two cats. He doesn't want to get only one because he thinks it'll get lonely since we work so much."

Autumn smiled as Peach turned over onto her back, wanting a belly rub. "He's not wrong. When I adopted Toad, I was at the shelter to find a friend for Peach. I wasn't all that familiar with having a dog as a pet, but little Toad just looked so sad. I figured that since he was about the size of a cat, it should work out."

Winter glanced to the sleeping pup. "They seem to get along pretty well, so I'd say it was a good choice."

The orange cat opened her eyes slightly, almost as if she knew she was the topic of their conversation.

"Sometimes, I'll catch them snuggling together, and then they'll both run out of the room like they're embarrassed that I caught them."

Winter let out a half laugh, half snort. "I'm a little excited for Noah to adopt his cats. It's been a long time since I've owned a pet, and sometimes I forget how comforting it can be. I figure him adopting a couple is the next best thing to me going out to adopt them myself."

Before Autumn could voice her agreement or ask Winter what she and Noah planned for their future living arrangement, the evening news jingle drew their attention back to the television screen.

The newscaster, Rosa Carrero, nodded to the camera. *"Hello, and welcome back to the Richmond nine o'clock news. As we mentioned earlier in our broadcast, we now have a story from our neighbors to the south in Danville. No doubt, we all remember the tragedy that took place earlier this year at the Riverside Mall."*

As Rosa folded her hands atop a stack of papers, Autumn

glanced over to Winter. "So, it's official? You think the killer is targeting the survivors of the shooting?"

Winter's expression grew solemn. "After what happened to the Young family last night, there's no way it's all coincidence."

With a nod, Autumn returned her attention to the broadcast.

The news anchor's dark eyes were fixed on the camera. *"We go now to the footage of a press briefing conducted earlier today by the Danville Police Department and the Federal Bureau of Investigation."*

The scene cut away to a short stage, in front of which sat at least twenty members of the press. A man in a black police dress uniform stood behind a wooden podium. To one side of him was Noah and a federal agent that Autumn vaguely recalled. To his other side was a well-dressed man and woman, each of whom wore silver police badges around their necks.

"Thank you all for coming." As the man at the podium glanced around the room, the glare from the overhead lights caught the two gold bars fastened to the lapel of his suit jacket, causing her to almost squint from the momentary glare. *"As most of you know, I'm Captain Steven Polivick with the Danville Police Department."*

As the captain paused, a quiet murmur ran through the crowd.

Captain Polivick cleared his throat. *"In the past few days, even just the past few hours, we've learned some troubling information about a series of seemingly pointless murders that have occurred in Danville over the past six months."*

Autumn settled her feet on the floor and straightened herself. Winter had given her a high-level overview of the case so far, but Autumn wanted to see how the press would react to the announcement that a serial killer was preying on survivors of a mass shooting. The crime spree was unprecedented—to this day, Autumn couldn't recall a similar situation that had occurred elsewhere in the country.

"However, we now have more than adequate circumstantial evidence to tie these killings together. As of now, we do not have a suspect, but we intend to provide the public with the knowledge necessary to keep themselves and their families safe."

The captain must have been nervous, but to his credit, he hid the sentiment well. However, Autumn was adept at reading people, and she knew anxiety when she saw it.

Captain Polivick rested one hand on each side of the podium. *"As you all no doubt remember, our city was stricken with tragedy when two armed men took up an arsenal of automatic weapons and killed fifteen people at the Riverside Mall. During the shooting, those same men took dozens of hostages, of whom twenty-six survived."*

Another murmur thrummed through the room. Even through the television, the unease was palpable.

"Now, however, we have evidence that indicates a new killer is targeting the surviving victims of the massacre. We've already discussed the threat with the survivors and their families, and we are actively assisting them with maintaining their safety during this troubling ordeal."

Just as the murmur seemed like it would take over the conversation, Captain Polivick held up a hand.

"I'll answer your questions in just a moment. The Danville PD has enlisted the help of the Federal Bureau of Investigation for this case." The captain gestured to Noah and the agent at his side. *"That being said, we'd also like to tap into the resources of our community. If anyone watching has a friend or family member who was at the Riverside Mall on that tragic night, please reach out to them."*

Autumn pointed to the television screen. "Who's the guy

beside Noah? I feel like I've met him before, but I can't remember his name."

"Levi Brandt," Winter said. "He's from the Victim Services Division."

Captain Polivick raised his hand again. *"Now, in addition to checking up on the survivors of the attack, we'd also like to ask our city for its help. So far, the perpetrator or perpetrators of these killings have gained access to victims' houses by disabling their security systems."*

When the captain swept his grim gaze over the gathering this time, he was greeted only with silence.

"The suspect often visits the victims' house under the guise of a security salesman. As I mentioned earlier, we've already discussed this aspect of the crimes with the other survivors, but we'd like to implore our citizens to keep a watchful eye on their friends and neighbors. We'll be providing an anonymous tip line at the end of this briefing. Now, I'll take your questions."

Rather than wait for the first reporter to ask about the case, Autumn turned her attention to Winter. "He didn't mention anything about the third person in Haldane and Strickland's manifesto. Are they trying to keep that part quiet?"

Yanking her hand away when Peach decided she was finished with belly rubs, Winter shook her head at the temperamental feline. "Not necessarily. The press briefing was more to warn the public and ask for their help than anything."

Autumn reached for her mug as she lifted an eyebrow. "What's your take on the investigation so far? Do you think that the third person involved in the shooting is the one who's been killing these poor people?"

Winter's expression turned thoughtful as she scratched the cat's head, getting a loud purr of approval in response. "Yeah, I think they're involved somehow."

"Somehow? What do you mean?"

"You're familiar with the Tate murders and Charles Manson, right?"

Autumn shrugged. "Who isn't? But yeah, Manson was always brought up when we'd discuss conformity in my classes. So many people wondered how he managed to get people to carry out murders for him. It's the same concept as figuring out why all those people followed Jim Jones down in South America."

Winter frowned as the cat hopped off her lap. "Well, so far, each of these murders has been a little bit different than the last. We don't necessarily have anything solid to confirm it yet, but I think that we might be dealing with someone who's a lot like Charles Manson. Someone who's got a cult-like following."

Autumn let out a long breath. "Wow. That's...unsettling."

In the days since Charles Manson, there had been other killers who operated similarly, though none of them had achieved the same notoriety. Then again, if someone like Manson had access to the internet, their reach would extend far beyond the so-called family that Manson had formed in his heyday. If the FBI didn't track down the psychopath behind the series of murders in Danville, there was no telling where their reign of terror would end.

Winter's voice cut in through Autumn's bleak contemplation. "I was actually wondering if I could pick your brain about the whole thing. I think it might be time to officially bring you into the investigation. I'm going to bring it up to Aiden tomorrow, but I didn't want to blindside you with it."

Autumn tucked her legs beneath her, giving herself a few moments to think it all through. "I appreciate that. It'll be good to go into it with some idea of what you're dealing with."

With another nod, Winter rested her feet on the edge of the coffee table. "I thought so too."

Even after the agreement, a glint of contemplation remained behind Winter's eyes. Though Autumn's first inclination was to think that Winter intended to prod her for details about the status of her and Aiden's friendship, she dismissed the idea.

Any time Winter brought up the subject of the Supervisory Special Agent, there was a measure of girlish amusement on her face—almost like she hadn't gotten to tease her friends when she was younger, so she was making up for lost time. Now, however, her eyes darted back and forth as if she was nervous.

Clearing her throat, Autumn turned to face her friend. "Something else on your mind? What's up?"

As she heaved out a long breath, Winter played with the ends of her hair. "I got this message the other night. This weird, creepy message from a disposable email address."

A stone dropped into Autumn's stomach. She suspected she knew the answer to her question, but she asked anyway. "Do you know who sent it?"

"I'm pretty sure it was Justin." Winter's entire body had tightened, as if the thought of her brother had wound her to some breaking point. "All it said was that he'd talk to me soon, and then there was a link to one of those anonymous forums that deletes posts after twenty-four hours. The message said to keep an eye on the link, and then there was a picture of a black cat. The firework, not an actual kitty."

Autumn fought to keep the grim look from her face as she rubbed her chin. "Sounds like it's really him, then, and not a hoax."

Winter shot Autumn a curious glance, the tension releasing a bit after her confession. "What do you think he meant by it?"

A silence descended on them as Autumn tapped an index finger against her mug. "Well, he's been trying to stay hidden for quite a while. It could mean that he wants to reach out to you, but he's not ready to do it in person yet. It's a pretty big step, so there are a lot of reasons he could be anxious about doing that."

Brushing a piece of ebony hair from her face, Winter nodded. "That's what Noah thinks too. I made sure to log the email and the link to the forum as evidence in his kidnapping case, but I'm almost wondering if I should have done that at all. I mean, will it spook him? If he knows that I'm sharing all this with the FBI, what if he turns around and runs off again?"

"He doesn't have to know that you're sharing it with the FBI. Even if he sees that the IP address from the field office accessed the post, he wouldn't have any reason to think it was someone other than you. You did the right thing. We've still got no idea where he is or what kind of state he's in, so it's better to be safe." Autumn lifted a shoulder, tossing her friend a bit of comfort, even if she didn't believe it herself. "What if he needs your help at some point?"

The corner of Winter's mouth turned up for the briefest of moments. "That's what I was thinking too. Thank you. That actually makes me feel a lot better."

Even as Autumn returned the smile, in the back of her mind she wondered about the real reason for Justin's sudden outreach. In all honesty, she *hoped* that Justin was reaching out to her for help, and not for some other nefarious purpose.

That was what her heart hoped.

Her mind and her gut knew better.

21

A s Winter stepped out of the elevator and made her way down the well-lit hall to Aiden Parrish's office, she went over her sales pitch one more time.

When she had proposed that they enlist Autumn's help for the Arkwell case, Aiden's refusal had taken her by surprise. She hadn't prepared a sales pitch then, but she had mentally rehearsed a compelling argument before she and Noah even left for the office that morning.

Winter was certain that there was more to Aiden's affinity for Autumn than just a professional friendship, but she had no idea why he would actively seek to push Autumn out to arms' length. No matter the reason for Aiden's sudden standoffishness, the direction of this case dictated that the bureau consult with a psychological expert.

If Winter's theory was right—and she was confident it was—then there was much more at play than a serial killer.

Who knew how many had fallen under the spell of the mastermind behind the seven deaths so far? Who knew how many were waiting to take up the madman's mantle the second he was captured, imprisoned, or killed?

They needed to know the extent of the killer's influence, and there was no one better suited to unravel the mystery than Autumn Trent. Threat assessment was literally in her job title. And, in the event they came across a suspect, a psychological evaluation would no doubt be required.

If Aiden disagreed with Winter's pitch, she always had the option to make the suggestion to SAC Osbourne. However, part of her was confident that the situation wouldn't devolve that far. Aiden was a professional above all else, and they had a pressing case to solve.

As she neared the end of the hall, Winter popped a mint in her mouth to relieve it of the dryness the thought of this conversation had created. The blinds were closed on the other side of the glass and metal door, but the door was open wide enough to allow a slat of gold light to fall along the carpeted floor.

After rapping her knuckles against the frame, Winter eased the door open until she could see Aiden seated behind his desk.

His pale eyes flicked away from the computer monitor. "Good morning."

Winter took a tentative step into the office, tucking the mint behind her teeth. "Morning. I was wondering if you have a few minutes? There's something I want to run by you."

With a nod, Aiden straightened in his chair. "Sure. Come on in."

Much like a delicate layer of frost on a crisp fall morning, a chill had settled in over top of Aiden's usual cool demeanor. The extra layer of professionalism—if that's what it could even be called—was scarcely noticeable, and Winter doubted that anyone who hadn't known him for over a decade would have noticed.

To be sure, Aiden wasn't an emotionless automaton. Hidden under the sophisticated veneer he portrayed to the world was a man with a strong moral compass and a desire to make the world a better place. However, he wasn't what Winter would call warm. And if she had to guess, the temperature of his demeanor had dropped a few degrees below what was typical.

As Winter closed the door behind herself, Aiden waved to the two chairs in front of his polished mahogany desk. "Have a seat."

Winter managed another nod as she accepted the offer. More than likely, the added chill in his voice was due to their months' old disagreement over his prediction for Justin's current mental state. Aiden might have been professional, but the man had a long memory.

One of these days—a day Winter didn't necessarily look forward to—they would have to bring up the topic if they hoped to hash out their differences. But before Winter had even set off on her way up to Aiden's office, she had decided that this wouldn't be that day.

"What can I help you with?"

With a start, Winter wondered how long she had sat there in silence. She blinked a few times and shook her head to return herself to the present. "Sorry, it's still pretty early. I probably haven't had quite enough caffeine yet."

Aiden chuckled, but she could hear the concern behind the sound. For a split-second, the ice fell away. "It's all right. I can sympathize. I think most of the people in this building are fueled more by caffeine than actual sleep."

Winter forced herself not to fidget. "You're definitely not wrong there."

As Aiden folded his hands over a handful of papers, the familiar chill started to seep back into the air.

Straightening her spine, Winter cleared her throat. "Okay, well, coffee jokes aside. I have a proposition to run by you. Something I think can help with this case."

She knew she didn't have to elaborate on the case in question. Right now, to about half the people in the Richmond field office, *this case* had only one meaning.

"Okay. We could use any help we can get, so I'm all ears."

Winter couldn't have asked for a better lead-in. "This guy, the perpetrator, there's a very real chance that he's been coaxing other people to kill for him, or at least to kill on his behalf, right?"

Aiden nodded, watching her so closely that a bead of sweat popped out on her temple. "With how different all the murders have been so far, I think that's a distinct possibility."

Winter propped her elbows on the wooden arms of the chair. "And with the scope of these killings, with how much of a national, even *international*, impact this has had, I think it's safe to say that we may well be dealing with the next Charles Manson."

When Aiden's expression changed little, she knew he had drawn the same conclusion.

"This is big, and unless we can catch this guy soon, it's only going to get bigger." Winter paused to meet Aiden's intent stare. "Manson didn't have the internet, and this guy does. There's no telling how many people he could reach with his twisted message. There's no telling how many more of the survivors from the Riverside Mall might be in danger."

Lips pressed into a thin line, Aiden nodded. "I agree. I've mentioned as much in the profile I've been working on. What are you thinking, then?"

Winter laced her fingers together. "We need to be fast, and we need to be accurate. And if we want to be accurate in figuring out who exactly we're looking for, then we need to understand the scope of the threat we're facing. We need someone who understands how this type of thinking spreads and what can be done to stop it."

A flicker of understanding passed over Aiden's otherwise stoic face.

Before he could interject, Winter forged ahead. "Look, I know you weren't that thrilled to bring in Autumn's help for the Arkwell case, but look what happened when you did? If it weren't for her, there's no way I could have gotten Cameron Arkwell to surrender without hurting anyone. That case could have ended very, very badly, but it didn't, and Autumn's a big part of that."

Aiden didn't know it, but Winter had only scratched the surface of her lengthy sales pitch.

He offered her an inquisitive look. "Why bring it to me and not Max?"

Winter was genuinely surprised by the question. "Why *wouldn't* I bring it to you? You have the rapport with Shadley and Latham."

His questioning gaze didn't waver. "You seem like you were ready for an argument. Remember, I've known you for quite a while. I've argued with you plenty of times."

Rolling her eyes in feigned exasperation, Winter waved away the remark. To her relief, his quip melted the frost she had noticed earlier. For the first time in months, she felt like she was sitting across from Aiden Parrish, and not the Supervisory Special Agent of the BAU.

As if he could read her thoughts, the corner of his mouth turned up in the start of a smile. "I think it's a good idea. Did you already tell Autumn about it, or will I be blindsiding her when I send the paperwork over to Shadley and Latham?"

"I didn't tell her too much, but I told her we might need her help."

Even though Aiden had just conceded to Winter's point, she had to make an effort to stop herself from launching into the prepared pitch. As much as she wanted to know the reason for his sudden change of heart, she reminded herself that there was more important work to be done.

"I'll get everything sent over to Shadley and Latham within the next half-hour or so," Aiden said.

With a slight smile, Winter nodded, moving the mint to the other side of her mouth. "That sounds good. We have a briefing this afternoon where we're planning to go through the newest updates from the Danville PD's tip line as well as the statements from Tim Young and his daughter."

Aiden scooted closer to his desk. "I'll make sure she's here before the briefing. I'll go over what I've got with her too, and hopefully, we'll bring a more complete profile to the briefing."

Little by little, Winter pushed the curiosity from her thoughts as she returned focus to the investigation.

There would be plenty of time to mend fences with Aiden after they put away the person responsible for orchestrating the murders of at least seven innocent people.

22

By the time their afternoon briefing rolled around, Noah felt like eight o'clock that morning had occurred in a different decade. However, just because the day felt like ten years compressed into the span of six hours didn't mean they had been unproductive.

As Noah closed the blinds on the glass door, he glanced over the room. Whenever the bureau enlisted Autumn's help, she tended to gravitate toward her fellow psychological expert, Aiden Parrish. Though Noah knew he and Aiden would never be friends, he was more than willing to admit that Autumn and Aiden made a good team. It really was too bad that Autumn hadn't accepted Parrish's offer to work for the FBI.

Noah was fresh off a phone call with Detective Grace Meyer from Danville, and Sun and Miguel had spent much of the day parsing through old case files. On the other hand, Bree and Winter had been given the unenviable task of sifting through the phone call notes to determine which tips were valid. Though the Danville PD had manned the phone lines so far, they didn't have the availability to sit down to evaluate each potential lead.

Ever since the press conference the day before, the Danville PD's tip line had been inundated with all types of phone calls. As with just about any outlet for anonymous tips, the majority of the calls had been of little to no consequence. Either the information provided by the callers was already known to law enforcement, or it was irrelevant.

But there was one that stuck out.

Glancing to the front of the room, Noah nodded to SAC Osbourne. "That's everyone."

Max returned the nod before he stepped up to the podium. "It sounds like this has been a productive day. I've been in and out of meetings for most of the day, so this briefing hasn't been ironed out all that well. But essentially, we're all here to combine our notes and see where we end up."

As Noah took a seat behind Ava Welford, Max brought the overhead projector to life.

The SAC gestured to Winter and Bree. "Agent Stafford, Agent Black. Thank you for going through the potential leads that our friends at the Danville PD have collected. Let's hear what you found."

Brushing off the front of her white dress shirt, Bree pushed to her feet. After Winter picked up her matte silver laptop, the two women stepped around the table and made their way to the podium.

Once the laptop was plugged into the projector, Winter's blue eyes flitted around the room. Her gaze settled on Noah's for a moment longer than the others. Of the agents present for the briefing, Noah was the only one who had been informed of Bree and Winter's findings.

As Winter tapped a couple keys to summon up the image of the notes that the Danville police had taken when they received the call, she glanced over her shoulder to the white-board. "As expected, most of the anonymous tips that Danville received weren't viable leads. There were a couple that confirmed information we were already aware of, but we had one that was new."

Bree tilted her chin in Noah's direction. "Agent Dalton, would you mind giving us a rundown of the statement that you and Agent Brandt got from Mariah Young?"

The room's collective attention shifted to Noah.

"Of course. Agent Brandt and I went down to Danville yesterday to talk to Mariah and Tim Young. As you all already know, Sadie and Dana Young were killed the night before last. Sadie was stabbed in the back while she slept, and Dana Young was stabbed a total of four times. Two of the wounds were superficial, and the fatal stab wound pierced her left lung. She was barely alive when the para-medics and the police arrived, but she died in route to the hospital."

From where she sat beside Miguel Vasquez, Sun held up a hand. "I'm still not sure I completely follow what happened. How did it take Tim Young so long to do something? He was shot, sure, but how didn't he wake up before his wife was stabbed four times?"

Noah could admit that the concern was valid. Sun and Miguel had been busy poring through the Danville PD's old case files, and Noah hadn't yet been given a chance to bring them up to speed on the Young case.

"Agent Brandt and I wondered that too. Mariah Young woke up when she heard her sister scream in the next room over, and that's what woke Dana too. But Tim Young suffers from an anxiety disorder that makes it hard for him to sleep. He's had a prescription for Ambien for the past decade. Even if it's not Ambien, he still usually takes something that knocks him out."

Sun nodded. "It would make sense that they had a home security system installed then."

As Noah thought back to the hallowed looks on Tim and Mariah's faces, his expression turned grim. "That's exactly why they had it installed, actually. Dana Young is...or was, a computer programmer. Every third week, she would be on call and she'd work late hours."

A flicker of understanding passed over Sun's face. "Okay. I saw in the case notes that Tim Young wasn't a suspect, I just wanted to make sure I understood what happened. Did either of them get a good look at the perp?"

Noah's nostrils flared. "No. The killer was wearing a partial ski mask that covered the bottom of his face. The house was dark, so neither of them saw him very well, but Mariah remembered seeing something a little out of the ordinary that afternoon."

Miguel tapped his fingers on the desk. "The security salesman."

"Right," Noah said. "Of the three murders that were committed inside the victims' homes, all three security systems were disabled. The guy claimed to be with Anderson's Alarms, but when we sent them a picture of the composite sketch that Mariah helped come up with, they didn't recognize the guy. Plus, one of their technicians had his work van broken into about a week ago."

The irony hadn't eluded Noah when he'd read over the police report filed by the home security tech. The theft had occurred during the man's lunch break. Whoever had broken into the vehicle was brazen enough to commit the crime in broad daylight.

According to the worker, the thief had taken all of his tools along with his spare uniform and ID badge.

"Was there any security footage of the break-in?"

Noah turned in his chair to meet Aiden Parrish's gaze.

"We're working on it right now. The restaurant normally only keeps forty-eight hours of footage at a time, but we got in touch with the company that operates their surveillance system. They're going to see if there's anything they can do to recover it, but it might take a few days."

Aiden nodded. "How about the witness's sketch? Have you been able to turn up anything based on it?"

Noah swallowed a knee-jerk sarcastic rebuttal. "Other than eliminate the employees of Anderson's Alarms, no."

When Bree spoke, Noah and Aiden both shifted their attention to the front of the room. "Maybe it wasn't an easy button to solve this case, but it *has* pointed us in the direction of a solid lead. Now, that being said…" she waved a hand at the whiteboard, "what Agent Black and I found makes every-thing a little…hazier."

At Bree's side, Winter placed both palms on the table. "The Danville PD received this tip earlier this morning, and they sent it over to us along with the notes from hundreds of others. Now, even though the tip line is anonymous, this caller gave her name and address to the officer she spoke with."

Bree tapped a key on the laptop, and the image projected onto the whiteboard changed to a DMV photo of a woman in her late thirties. "The caller identified herself as Beverly Walsh, and she said that she and her husband lived next to Adrian and Kelsey Esperson when they were killed. The Danville PD interviewed them after the couple was killed, but at the time, they didn't have anything unusual to report."

After another key press, the image switched back to the notes from Beverly's phone call.

Glancing to the text, Winter took a step away from the podium. "When the detectives interviewed Mrs. Walsh at the time, they were looking for witness testimony from the time the crime was committed. But after she and her husband saw the press briefing about the murders, she remembered something they had seen earlier in the day. A home security salesman."

Noah swore he could hear everyone in the room narrow their eyes to read over the text.

Max's gravelly voice cut through the short spell of silence. "Do we know yet if it was the same person who was at the Young household?"

Scooting to the edge of his seat, Noah propped his elbows on top of the table. Though Bree and Winter had managed to give him a high-level rundown of the tip they'd discovered, they hadn't gone into detail about the witness's description.

As she shook her head, Winter crossed her arms over her black blazer. "It's not the same person."

"How can we be sure?" Max's question was calm and measured.

Rare were the occasions when the SAC doubted his agents, but the tenured investigator preferred that Noah and his colleagues showed their work. In fact, that might have been the only real-life lesson that Noah had taken away from his various high school math classes. If he wanted to convince a superior that he was right, he had to show his work.

Winter and Bree exchanged glances. "The descriptions are too different," Bree said. "There's no way it's the same person."

Winter nodded. "Mrs. Walsh said that she and her husband were outside working in their garden when the salesman showed up to the house next door. They weren't all that close with the Espersons, but they'd exchange baked goods around the holidays and chat about their houses and their gardens. They were neighborly."

"This happened about three months ago, though." Sun's voice was laden with skepticism. "How can they give an accurate description of someone they saw one time three months ago?"

"Well, like I said, they were neighborly." Winter waved a hand at the text, but her stare was fixed on Sun. "That afternoon, Mr. and Mrs. Walsh were pulling weeds in their garden. Mrs. Walsh wanted to ask the Espersons what type of plant food they'd been using, but she wasn't sure if they were home, so she kept an eye on the door. When the security salesman showed up, she told her husband she was going to go talk to Kelsey now that she knew she was home. She said that the man looked very similar to her nephew, which was why she was able to give a good description. The Espersons were killed that night, so that was the last time Mrs. Walsh ever talked to them."

Though the motion was grudging, Sun nodded. "And that's not consistent with the Youngs' description?"

Winter shook her head. "No. We took into consideration how much time had gone by and how appearances can change, but it still can't explain the differences."

"Mariah Young described a white male, early twenties, with a beard and dark hair." With a couple more taps, Bree pulled up a sketch of a bearded man. "She described him as fairly tall, broad-shouldered, and a little on the husky side. On the other hand, the man that Mrs. Walsh described was tall and lean, with a little stubble and black hair."

As Noah leaned back in his chair, he swallowed a sigh. Though he'd by and large agreed with Winter's cult theory, he had hoped the prediction wouldn't pan out. Dealing with a single suspect could be tricky enough on its own, but dealing with a group of murderous psychopaths came with an entirely different level of chicanery.

"That just about confirms Agent Black's theory, then." Max's gray eyes flicked away from the whiteboard and over to Autumn and Aiden. "Dr. Trent, what are your thoughts?"

If Autumn had been caught off guard, she didn't show it. Then again, with her Jedi mind-reading capabilities, she was almost never caught off guard. When it came to maintaining composure, Noah thought she would be able to give Aiden Parrish a run for his money.

Autumn brushed a piece of dark auburn hair from her shoulder. "I think Agent Black is right. I think we're dealing with a disgruntled group of young men who are following in Tyler Haldane and Kent Strickland's footsteps. They're clearly focused on a singular goal, and that leads me to believe that their leader is charismatic enough to convince them to kill. Based on what I've read in the manifesto from Haldane and Strickland, there's little doubt that we're dealing with a male. Likely Caucasian and in his early to mid-twenties."

Noah laced his fingers together. "Hate is a powerful motivator. And that's what these guys all have in common. They all hate modern society."

Autumn gave him a solemn nod. "That's their goal. They want to start a revolution against modern society. I think our suspect is using the current political landscape as a way to rally them all together, just like Jim Jones and Charles Manson did."

A silence settled in over them like a shroud. Amidst the sudden quiet, Noah could hear the dull taps as Max drummed his fingers against the table.

Though the SAC's gaze wasn't fixed on any of them, he narrowed his eyes as he sat in contemplation. "Agent Dalton, Dr. Trent, you're both right." Max's eyes snapped to Noah and then Autumn. "And now we can safely say that our suspect can no longer be classified as just a serial killer. We are officially dealing with a domestic terrorist."

23

Will couldn't remember the last time he slept. He'd thought that his nervousness about carrying out his and Jaime's plan would abate after he killed his targets.

He'd been wrong.

As he signaled his turn onto a residential side street, he glanced to the rearview mirror. Three intersections ago, he'd noticed the same white truck trailing three to four car lengths behind him. Though he'd initially tried to rationalize the paranoia, his heartbeat pounded in his ears as he caught another glimpse of the vehicle.

Grating his teeth, Will returned his focus to the road. The distance between him and the driver of the truck was lengthy enough that he couldn't make out the driver, but his racing mind was quick to fill in the blanks.

Jaime had been adamant that Will dispatch all the members of the Young family—including the two who hadn't been at the Riverside Mall, Tim and Mariah Young. The reasoning Jaime had provided was straightforward enough. The husband and younger sister were witnesses. They were collateral damage in Jaime and Will's noble crusade. In addition, they were of the same bloodline as the two sinners, and they needed to be treated accordingly.

Will tightened his grip on the steering wheel until the blood drained from his knuckles.

Ever since he'd met Jaime, Will had been sure he was destined for their work. Jaime had reassured him, and he'd believed every word. But when the time came to make good on his commitment, Will hadn't been able to follow through.

Was this how Jaime felt after he killed someone? Did Jaime see the peoples' faces every time he closed his eyes? Especially the girl. Sinner or not, her screams had pierced through his soul even as he was piercing his knife into her body.

The blood. So much blood.

The taste in Will's mouth had turned bitter, and he felt the sting of bile on the back of his throat. He needed to pull himself together. And quick. He needed to think.

By now, the news that Mariah and Tim Young had survived would have reached Jaime. Will had worn a ski mask and had taken precautions to avoid the family's exterior security cameras. Surely that was enough to prevent a witness identification, wasn't it?

He was sure Jaime would see his reasoning. After all, they should *avoid* collateral damage, not actively seek it out. Will had prevented the collateral damage. He'd avoided the deaths of two people who weren't on their list.

Right?

His stomach continued to churn.

If Will was so sure Jaime would see the wisdom in the decision to leave Mariah and Tim alive, then why was he so hesitant to reach out to him? Even the thought of checking for a new text message or a missed call made Will want to toss his phone into the closest body of water.

Before they'd even begun to map out the plans to eliminate the sinners that had eluded Tyler and Kent, Jaime had purchased a pair of prepaid phones so they could maintain contact with one another. Aside from anonymous forum posts or disposable email addresses, prepaid cellphones were among the most difficult methods of communication to monitor or track.

Other than a message to advise Jaime that he intended to maintain a low profile for a few days in order to stave off any potential interest from law enforcement, Will hadn't spoken to his mentor since before he'd left for the Young residence.

But right now, Will wasn't worried about the police tracking his movements. As he managed another glance in the rearview mirror, he knew who he was trying to avoid.

The shame of his failure seemed to trail after him like a shadow, but even more than the failure, he was plagued by another sentiment. A feeling he hadn't expected.

Regret.

Maybe the remorse was normal. Maybe all he needed to do was lay low for a day or two to collect himself. Then, once he'd put his thoughts in order, he could reach out to Jaime. He could explain himself, and he was sure Jaime would understand. Will's dedication to their cause hadn't waned, had it? No, he was certain it hadn't.

Still, whenever he pictured the inevitable conversation with Jaime, Will couldn't shake the image of Jackson Fisher's bloodied corpse. Jackson's grave had taken close to two hours to dig, and throughout the entire time, neither Will nor Jaime had spoken a single word.

Jackson was different. I'm not like him. Jackson was a rat.

Swallowing against the sting of bile, Will looked back to the white truck. The driver was still a respectable distance behind him, but the person hadn't altered their course. Though Will's destination was the Danville city limits, he flicked on his turn signal to veer onto a street with higher traffic than the quiet residential areas he'd driven through so far.

As the hairs on the back of his neck stood on end, he knew he had to lose his stalker. He still hadn't been able to make out the person's appearance, but he was certain they were following him.

He didn't know how Jaime could have found him so quickly. After he'd left the Young household, Will had driven blindly until he reached a dilapidated parking lot. After he'd thrown up the meager contents of his stomach, he'd sat in the shadowy lot until the sun rose. Even now, he still wasn't sure where he'd been. The trip away from the ramshackle neighborhood had all been a blur.

If Will hadn't even known where he was, then there was no way Jaime would know where he was. Besides, Will wasn't *really* trying to avoid Jaime, was he?

No. He just needed to collect his thoughts. He needed to rest. When he talked to Jaime next, he wanted to have a clear mind to articulate himself.

Will wasn't a rat like Jackson. He pounded his fists on the steering wheel. He wasn't!

He and Jaime were still on the same side. Their mission hadn't changed.

A dull ache crept to Will's hands from the abuse he'd given them on the steering wheel. His mind kept wandering, but he needed to focus. If the driver of the white truck was Jaime—or a person sent *by* Jaime—then Will could talk to them. Reason with them. He was on their team, after all.

His tired muscles groaned in protest as he turned his head to look quickly out the rear windshield. Apprehension flooded through his body as he switched over to the right lane.

He spotted a sign for a twenty-four-hour chain restaurant. As the truck changed lanes behind him, he made up his mind. Rather than try to outmaneuver the other driver on his trip out of town, Will would rip off the band-aid and confront the stalker.

Confront Jaime.

No, not confront. Talk to him, share his reasonings, make him understand.

Jackson Fisher's dead eyes flashed through Will's mind, making the hair stand up on the back of his neck.

Yes, he was afraid, but he needed to get this over with. Waiting would only surely make things that much worse.

With one last look at the truck, he eased his foot down on the brake pedal as he turned into a pothole-filled parking lot. As he swung the car into a vacant space, his mouth felt like it had been stuffed with sawdust, and he could hear little over the rapid cadence of his pulse.

He caught a glimpse of white in the corner of his eye as the other driver pulled in three spots away from his. Though he made sure to keep his head turned in the direction of the restaurant, Will watched the truck in his peripheral vision.

Each passing second lasted longer than the one before as he searched desperately for a flicker of movement.

When a middle-aged woman rounded the corner of the brick building, he couldn't keep himself from jerking his head to peer out the driver's side window. A tall man clad in a gray peacoat and dark jeans hopped out of the truck to meet the newcomer at the edge of the sidewalk.

As the man held out his arms to offer the woman a warm embrace, all the bluster and tension dissipated from Will's tired muscles.

He was so relieved that he didn't even bother to question *why* he was relieved.

For what was far from the last time, he reminded himself that he was laying low so he could rest. So he could gather his thoughts.

Jaime would understand.

24

As Aiden made his way down the hall to the Cyber Crimes Division, he fully expected the visit to be a formality. Since he wound up staying at the office late more often than not, he'd made a point to swing by Cyber Crimes every other night to check on Ryan O'Connelly and Agent Welford's progress in their digital investigation. Though Ryan had recently adopted a new tactic to search the dark web for the person who had posted Tyler Haldane and Kent Strickland's manifesto, Aiden purposefully tamped down his expectations.

So far, their two-and-a-half-month-long search had been more akin to searching for a needle in a haystack than a true investigation. Investigations usually had suspects, and right now, they were sorely lacking in that area.

Multi-colored lights twinkled on a four-foot Christmas tree in the corner of the cluster of cubicles. More lights were strung along the top of the partitions that separated each desk from its neighbors. Apparently, the agents in Cyber Crimes were more festive than their counterparts downstairs in Violent Crimes.

Those who knew Aiden might not have guessed, but he was a proponent of festive office décor. Their job was stressful enough to require a mandatory retirement age of fifty-seven, so if they could brighten the atmosphere even a little, everyone benefitted.

Not that he'd be caught dead stringing up garland in his office. He had an image to maintain.

The drone of two familiar voices grew clearer as he approached the door to a small conference room. Though the door was open a crack, Aiden still raised his hand to rap his knuckles against the metal frame.

Ava Welford's clear blue eyes snapped over to the doorway, and Ryan O'Connelly's gaze followed suit.

With a slight smile, Agent Welford straightened in her chair. "SSA Parrish, how are you doing tonight?"

As he eased open the glass and metal door, Aiden lifted a shoulder. "I'm doing fine. I was about to head out for the night, so I thought I'd stop by to see how your day went up here in Cyber Crimes."

When a tall figure emerged from a shadowy corner of the room, Aiden was surprised to recognize Bobby Weyrick. The man's eyes were bright and alert, his dark blond hair fashionably styled, and his black suit and tie as neatly pressed as ever.

Easing the door closed behind himself, Aiden cleared his throat. "Agent Weyrick, I didn't expect to see you here. What brings you up to Cyber Crimes?"

The man shrugged slightly in response. "Same thing as you, I'd imagine. Ryan and Agent Welford think they're onto a new lead."

Admittedly, those were five words Aiden hadn't expected to hear. "A new lead?" He glanced to where Agent Welford and O'Connelly sat at a circular table. "When did you find it?"

Agent Welford gestured to an empty chair across from her. "It's brand-new, actually. We were about to plead with Agent Weyrick to get us some coffee since we'll probably be here pretty late tonight."

Aiden accepted the offered seat as Agent Weyrick returned to the squat chair in the corner. Folding his hands on top of the polished table, he glanced to Agent Welford and then the criminal gone good. "What have you got so far?"

As he scooted forward, O'Connelly rested his elbows on the arms of his chair. "Remember how I was telling you about the dark web the other day? About how someone who posts something on the dark web has to have a good understanding of how all that tech works, especially since they didn't make their post on the surface web at all?"

Excitement caused Aiden's heart to speed up a couple beats, although he strove to maintain a calm demeanor. "And you were going to try to look into some other forums to see what you could find. I remember. Did you get something?"

O'Connelly tapped an index finger against his closed laptop as he nodded. "As a matter of fact, we did. While I was doing that, Agent Welford was looking into figuring out who hacked into the databases to get the identities of the people who were at the Riverside Mall." As O'Connelly turned his attention to Ava Welford, Aiden followed suit.

"I'll spare you all the boring details." Agent Welford brushed a piece of dark hair over her shoulder. "But we noticed some similarities to a ring of credit card thefts that Ryan found while he was looking into the Haldane Strickland manifesto. We're still pinning down everything that links these incidents together, but from where we're standing right now, I think whoever committed those thefts is the same person who broke into the databases that got them all the information about the victims from the Riverside Mall."

If Aiden hadn't been fully alert before, he was now. "And you think that's the same person who uploaded the manifesto?"

The good humor vanished from Ava Welford's face as she nodded. "There are enough similarities that we think so, yes. We're about to do a deep dive of the links between the three incidents. Once we've had a chance to do that, we should know more."

Bobby Weyrick raised a hand. "Didn't you say that there was a suspect for the credit card thefts?"

Agent Welford pursed her lips. "Yes, we had a suspect. But at the time, we didn't have enough to make any charges stick."

Before she finished, Aiden was already shaking his head. "We don't need to worry about making those charges stick. Right now, we just need a solid lead. If we've got enough to point the investigation in this guy's direction, we can *find* the evidence we need."

Aiden half-expected a caveat to the groundbreaking discovery, but instead, Agent Welford merely nodded her agreement. "That's our goal right now. We want to give you a thread to start pulling."

Crossing both arms over his chest, Aiden leaned back in his seat. "Well, I don't have anything to do tonight. While you look through those links, could you send me the file for your stolen credit card case?"

With a nod, Agent Welford pushed open her laptop. "Of course. I'll email you the details for it so you can dig up anything you need before you head out."

Even as Aiden's mind took off with the possible implications of Agent Welford's discovery, he pushed aside any lofty expectations. With so much at stake, he couldn't afford to let himself become entangled in a pipe dream.

As Autumn had said earlier in the day, their suspect fit the criteria for a specific profile. In the entirety of Aiden's FBI career, he could only recall a handful of profiles that were as particular as what they'd created for their current suspect. If the man didn't meet one of their criteria, the likelihood that he was truly their suspect dropped significantly.

So, they'd found a potential suspect, but the real puzzle had only just begun.

25

Noah had to exert a great deal of self-control to haul himself out of bed that morning. The temperature had dropped to nineteen degrees, and he'd let his truck warm up for over ten minutes. All the while, he'd cursed himself for skipping out on the optional heated seats.

To compensate for the lack of warmth, he had made the executive decision to swing by the drive-thru of a coffee shop on their way into the office. If *he* was cold, then he knew for certain that Winter had to be freezing. She sat like a stone beside him, her hands tucked between her thighs for warmth. He vowed to get an automatic started installed in his truck. Couldn't let the woman he loved be uncomfortable.

Which was a funny thought, considering Winter Black was the woman he thought of. Winter Black, who witnessed the aftermath of her parents' violent murders. The Winter Black who lay in a coma and came out with visions and headaches bad enough to make her nose bleed.

Winter had been uncomfortable most of her life, which

made him even more determined to keep her safe and comfortable anytime she was at his side. If he could.

He didn't know if there was a damn thing he would be able to do to keep her emotionally safe once they found her baby brother.

Thoughts still maudlin as they stepped off the elevator, Noah glanced to his side. In light of the cold, Winter had gone through the painstaking task of blowing her hair dry. The blow-dryer wasn't even hers—it was his. An ex-girlfriend from years back had left the device at his apartment, and after they split, he hadn't bothered to toss it. Occasionally, the blow-dryer had come in handy to dry his coat or shoes after an unexpected downpour.

Winter had warned him that, without any product, a blow-drying made her hair staticky and fluffy to the point of comical. Before she'd fashioned the strands into her customary braid, she had tossed her fluffed-up hair back and forth, asking him whether or not he thought the style was suitable for an '80s hair band. Considering her disdain for the glammed-out rock groups from the 1980s, the remark had struck him as particularly funny.

Before they rounded the corner to the Violent Crimes Division, Noah bit down on his tongue to stave off a fit of laughter at the memory. When Winter's blue eyes snapped over to him, he knew he had failed.

She lifted a dark eyebrow. "What? What's funny?"

It took everything inside him not to reach for her, pull her against him. Hold her in this playful moment that would be turning serious soon enough. "Nothing." He went to tuck a piece of loose hair behind her ear and gave them both an electrical shock for his trouble. That made him laugh, as Winter clamped a hand over her ear, her mouth a perfectly surprised "o." Damn how he wanted to kiss her, but this wasn't the time or the place. "I was just thinking of your hair this morning, electric girl."

Winter flipped her braid over her shoulder, her lips parting in a playful grin. At the beginning of the year, such an expression of mirth was rarely seen on her pretty face. As they had tracked down Douglas Kilroy, her demeanor had become standoffish and even hostile. But even though her smiles were more common now, the expressions still gave him a rush of contentment.

Before Winter could reply to his comment, they turned their attention to a flicker of movement. Though Bree Stafford's movements were graceful, her sudden appearance on the other side of the cubicle partition reminded Noah of a groundhog or a prairie dog.

The corners of Bree's eyes creased as she offered them a smile. "Morning, guys. It looks like I'm not the only one who rolled out of bed a little late, huh?"

On any given day during a high-stakes investigation, the air in the FBI field office was tense, even stifling. But whether it was due to the lingering effect of Winter's early morning joke or the upcoming holiday, the atmosphere was different today.

Winter had recently relocated her workspace to sit between Bobby Weyrick and Bree. Her and Noah's desks had been beside one another for months, but in light of their relationship, they had both agreed that the move was the best choice to maintain an air of professionalism.

As Noah approached his desk on the other side of Bree's, he shrugged out of his coat. "I'll be honest. If we didn't have a briefing scheduled for this morning, I would have seriously considered coming in a couple hours late. It's too damn cold out there."

Bree's laugh was light and melodious. "I was thinking the same thing."

After he picked up his coffee, Noah made his way to the end of the row of cubicles and waited for the two women, plastering a smile he didn't feel on his face. As he looked at Winter and thought of the eerie message she'd received, he wanted to pick her up and take her home.

Take her to safety.

For some reason he couldn't completely understand, dread curled and writhed like a living thing in his belly as they walked into the conference room for the briefing.

She wasn't safe.

He knew it. Hell, he thought she knew it too.

He just needed to watch. Wait. Protect her from the evil that had set its eyes on her.

Protect her from her own brother?

Maybe. Probably. Most likely.

And if he was forced to kill Justin Black to save Winter, he would. He just didn't know if she would ever forgive him if he did.

26

Only a few hours before, Winter had been filled with excitement as the team had been briefed on what could be a significant find. Cyber Crimes had been chasing the tail of a hacker they thought might be *the* hacker. Now, they needed to find the real man, not just his digital thumbprint.

"Phil Rossway, where are you," Winter murmured as she backed the car down the gentle slope of a driveway, swallowing the sigh she felt building in her throat. The neighborhood around them wasn't upscale, but the houses were lovingly maintained, and the air was quiet. Though she'd half-expected Phil Rossway's mother to be obstinate—much like Tyler Haldane's mother—Lydia Rossway had been cooperative and accommodating.

But even though she'd been kind enough to offer Winter and Miguel each a homemade cup of espresso, she had been little help.

Winter glanced up and down the road before she pulled onto the street. "What kind of kid lives in the same city as his mom, but doesn't physically visit her for over a year?"

Miguel's dark eyes snapped to her. "I don't know. If I tried to do that, my mom would kick down my door just so she could make sure I was eating enough."

Chuckling quietly, Winter shifted the car into drive. She couldn't imagine going an entire year without seeing Gramma Beth or Grampa Jack. And she felt sure she'd feel the same had her parents been able to live.

Then again, if she'd fallen in with a crowd that worshipped scumbags like Tyler Haldane and Kent Strickland, maybe she would be too ashamed of herself to show her face.

The late morning sun caught the screen of Miguel's phone as he tapped the unlock code, making her squint against the glare going straight into her eyes. "It didn't sound like there was any bad blood between them, either. Lydia and her husband have been divorced for more than a decade, but it doesn't sound like the split was bitter."

Winter eased her foot down on the brake as they approached a stop sign. "She said they kept in touch with one another, just not as much after Phil turned eighteen. Any word on where Kevin Rossway has been?"

Miguel tapped at his phone, scrolling through his messages before tossing it into the cupholder. "Nothing yet."

Although Lydia and her ex-husband, Kevin, kept in contact with one another, Lydia hadn't heard from the man in close to three months. She assured Winter and Miguel that the lack of communication was far from abnormal, but there was something about the radio silence that didn't sit well in Winter's gut.

Kevin Rossway lived just outside the Richmond city limits, but so far today, no one had been able to locate the man. Noah and Bree had visited his house earlier that morning, but no one had been home. Of course, the man was a long-haul truck driver, so extended absences weren't unusual. What was unusual, however, was the fact that his employer had confirmed he wasn't on the road for work.

Had he just taken a side job for a little extra cash during the holiday season, or was there a more sinister reason for his absence? Did Kevin Rossway's sudden absence have to do with his son's inoculation into the cult of Kent Strickland and Tyler Haldane? Had the man discovered a darker part of his son's life only to be killed for the knowledge? Or, was he part of the plan?

As Aiden had told them in the morning briefing, the suspect after whom they sought was far from a normal fanatic. Whoever was involved in the murders of the Riverside Mall victims was charismatic, intelligent, and ruthless. But at the same time, they were a chameleon. Like Dennis Rader or a handful of other infamous serial killers, this murdering bastard blended into his or her surroundings.

His. It was definitely a he, she told herself with little doubt.

As she signaled her turn to an interstate on-ramp, Winter cast a quick glance to Miguel. "What do you think so far? About Phil Rossway being our suspect?"

Scratching his chin, Miguel kept his thoughtful gaze fixed on the windshield. "His mom said he was a pretty good kid. He was quiet and he kept to himself, for the most part. He had a pretty small group of friends, and he was obsessed with electronics."

Winter checked the car's blind spot before merging onto the interstate. "So, he's a nerd?"

Miguel picked his phone back up, tossing it between his hands. "Well, he *does* work at an electronics store where he fixes computers. And he's a hacker. So, yes, I'd say he meets the qualifications."

With a slight smile, Winter nodded. "What about the profile, though? How do you think he stacks up to that?"

In the silence that ensued, Winter looked over to assure herself that Miguel had actually heard her question. His pensive gaze was back on the windshield as he chewed his lip thoughtfully.

When he didn't immediately respond, Winter went on. "Autumn and SSA Parrish seem to think we're dealing with the next Charles Manson. Does Phil Rossway seem like a Charles Manson so far?"

Miguel shrugged. "Hard to say, honestly. We've just gotten his mom's account of what he was like. I'm sure Manson's mom thought he was great too. We'll have to wait and see what his coworkers have to say about him when we get to the store."

"No word on whether or not Noah and Bree ran into him?" Winter veered over to an off-ramp.

Pocketing his smartphone, Miguel shook his head. "Nothing yet. But we've had the city cops posted up around his apartment complex in unmarked cars, and none of them have seen anything, either."

Well, that was peculiar. If Phil was innocent in the recent spree of murders, why would he be so difficult to locate?

Aside from the occasional navigation request, the remainder of the trip to the chain electronics retailer was made in silence. Winter had contemplated reaching out to Phil's employer earlier in the day, but in the unlikely event that he was at work, she didn't want to risk spooking him back into hiding. Besides, she found that she and her colleagues received more honest answers to their questions when they showed up unexpected.

After she pulled into a vacant spot near the back of the parking lot, Winter tightened her jacket around herself in preparation for the late morning chill. Despite her best efforts, her teeth were chattering by the time she and Miguel made it to the automatic doors at the front of the large brick building.

The glass doors slid open with a hiss. As the young man behind the horseshoe shaped front desk glanced to her and Miguel, he set down the paperback he had been reading. A glimmer of sunlight caught a silver nametag that read "Brett, customer service specialist." Brett wore a zip-up hoodie over his company issued blue polo t-shirt. If Winter was in his position so close to the door, she would have seriously considered making use of a cloak or a puffy, down-filled jacket.

The kid's hazel eyes flicked from Winter to Miguel as he nodded a greeting. "Good morning, folks. Do you need help finding anything today?"

Winter reached to the interior pocket of her black coat, mentally cursing the slight shiver in her movements. Decembers in Virginia weren't warm, but they weren't normally this cold, either.

As she and Miguel produced their badges, the young man's eyes went wide.

"I'm Special Agent Black, and this is Special Agent Vasquez. We're looking for Phil Rossway."

Brett's mouth formed an almost perfect "o" shape, the blood draining from his face. "Phil Rossway? I, uh, I've only worked here for the last few weeks. I'm a seasonal hire." Clearing his throat, he pressed the button on the microphone clipped to the collar of his t-shirt. "Hey, this is Brett, could I get a manager to come to the front please. No, it's not a customer service issue." Another slight pause as he looked warily at them. "No. It's the FBI."

Though the expression was slight, a hint of amusement flickered over Brett's face at the response in his earpiece. "No, I'm not kidding, Andi. It's the FBI. Okay." As he let go of the button, Brett offered them a quick smile. "She said she'll be right up."

Winter nodded. "Sounds good. We'll just wait up here."

"So, Brett, you've only worked here for a few weeks, you said?" Miguel followed Winter's lead and stepped out of the entryway. "Did you ever meet Phil Rossway?"

Brett was shaking his head before Miguel finished. Though there was an underlying nervousness in his demeanor, the kid kept his composure. "No, I never met him. I don't ever even think I've heard his name before, honestly. Sorry. I wish I could be more helpful."

Miguel held up a hand. "It's okay. Can't help it if you never met the guy, you know?"

With a slight smile, Brett nodded, looking a fraction more relaxed. "True."

From the corner of Winter's eye, she spotted a woman as she rushed down an otherwise empty aisle. Her pale cheeks were flushed, but she forced a smile to her face as she neared the front desk. Apparently, Brett and Winter weren't the only two who were susceptible to the cold weather. Beneath her blue polo, she wore a long-sleeved thermal shirt.

As she took the last few steps forward, she extended a hand, her wedding and engagement rings flashing in the lights. "Hi, Agents. I'm Andrea Harris. I'm one of the assistant managers for the store. What can I help you with?"

Winter gave the woman a reassuring smile as she accepted the handshake. "Good morning, Mrs. Harris. I'm Special Agent Black and this is Special Agent Vasquez."

The shorter woman gave them a stiff nod. "You can call me Andi. Come on, we can go talk in the back. The general manager is doing an interview in the office right now, but we can find somewhere to chat back there where there aren't any customers."

Miguel shook Andi's hand and nodded. "We're just here

to ask some questions about one of your employees, Phil Rossway."

The woman stiffened. "Phil Rossway? Yeah, I know Phil. What kind of crap did he get into?"

Winter didn't let any of her excitement show on her face. "Why do you think he got into something?"

Andi shrugged and looked over her shoulder. "Well, I'm the one who had to fire him for not showing up to work. Our GM, Chris, he didn't have the heart for it, I guess. I don't know why he liked that kid so much."

They turned to a short hallway, at the end of which was a set of swinging plastic doors marked with a bold-printed "employees only" sign. Just before the entrance to the store's warehouse, a second door was also marked with a smaller version of the same sign.

As they shoved their way through the plastic doors, Winter glanced to the tall shelving. Pallets of shrink-wrapped boxes were stacked on metal and wood shelves that stretched all the way to the ceiling. In the corners to either side of the door were security cameras, and Winter spotted more of the dark bubbles at regular intervals throughout the space. The sheer number of security cameras explained why the merchandise was kept behind an unlocked door. During the busy holiday season, Winter could only imagine the hassle that a locked warehouse door would cause.

The doors swung closed behind them, blocking out the din of the televisions and customers. At one end of the room was a wide shelf used for the storage of warehouse tools such as boxcutters, label printers, and even a shrink wrap machine. A door near the corner had been closed, but through the pane of glass, Winter caught a glimpse of a man seated behind a desk.

Before the office dweller caught her scrutinizing stare, Winter glanced to the shelves that lined the wall. Another row of adjustable metal shelving cut through the middle of the room. Even though the second row of shelves wasn't stocked full of merchandise, it effectively blocked their line of sight to the office. Winter was glad for the relative cover, but at the same time, she lamented the fact that she couldn't keep an eye on the other occupants of the warehouse.

When Andi's voice cut through the sudden silence, Winter snapped her attention back to the shorter woman.

"So, what happened to Phil?" Her green eyes shifted from Winter to Miguel and back.

Straightening, Winter met the woman's curious gaze. "We were hoping you could help us with that, actually. We've been trying to track him down and haven't had any luck. When is the last time you heard from Mr. Rossway?"

The shadows beneath Andi's eyes suddenly seemed more pronounced as she shook her head. "I'm not sure. Like I said out front, I had to fire him."

To Winter's side, Miguel nodded. "How did he take it?"

Andi shrugged, her forehead wrinkling in a tight frown. "I don't know. I had to leave him a voicemail and have the termination papers sent to him. He never answered or got back to me. Is he hurt or something? What's going on with him?"

After Winter and Miguel exchanged glances, Winter returned her attention to Andi. "We aren't sure. But without going into too much detail, we believe he's involved in a case we're currently investigating."

"A case? Like what kind of case?"

Winter brushed past the question. "What's important is that we find him. Why did you fire him?"

Still frowning, Andi tucked a piece of dark brown hair behind her ear. "Well, I fired him because he just stopped showing up to work."

As Andi shifted from one foot to another, Winter knew there was more to the story. "What else?"

Lips pursed, the woman glanced over her shoulder before she took a step closer to Winter and Miguel. When she spoke again, her voice was scarcely above a whisper. "Chris, the general manager for this store, kept making excuses for him. He kept saying that Phil was probably dealing with a family emergency, and he asked me to just cut him off the schedule for a couple weeks to give him a chance to work stuff out in his life."

Winter lifted an eyebrow. "Did he? Work stuff out in his life, that is."

Andi shrugged again. "I don't know. He never came back to work, even after I left him off the schedule for two weeks. Even with Chris basically vouching for him, there was only so much I could do after I left something like seven-hundred voicemails. Corporate audits, that kind of stuff, you know? If we're hanging on to personnel who don't show up to work, it's going to look bad on us. Especially with the holiday season breathing down our neck. We only have so many positions we can fill, and I'd prefer to fill them with people who actually show up and work their shifts."

Miguel made a sound roughly akin to a chuckle. "That's reasonable. What about the general manager, then? Chris. What's his relationship with Mr. Rossway?"

A thoughtful look passed over Andi's face as she absent-mindedly twirled a piece of hair around her finger. "Well, Chris and Phil both used to work at a different store. Chris transferred here around the beginning of the year, and then a few months later, Phil transferred over too. I guess they were buddies before Chris was a manager. Honestly, I'm not really sure. You'd be better off asking Chris about that."

Winter nodded. "We will. Were there any other employees who might have been close to Mr. Rossway?"

Andi tapped her cheek with a finger. "It might not hurt to ask around, but probably not. Most of them couldn't stand Phil. Honestly." Andi cast a quick glance over her shoulder. "I wasn't the biggest fan, either. I guess that's probably why I'm not a lot of help, isn't it?"

As if on cue, the clatter of a door echoed throughout the expansive room. The disturbance was followed by two different voices, one male, the other female.

Brushing off the front of her polo shirt, Andi stepped out from behind the tall row of shelves. Winter and Miguel didn't wait for an invitation to follow her lead.

The same man that Winter had spotted behind the office desk had paused just short of the swinging double doors to shake the hand of the middle-aged woman he had been interviewing. The corners of his light brown eyes creased as he offered her a smile and a wave.

Andi cleared her throat. "Chris. Good timing."

Just as the interviewee pushed her way back into the hall, the manager spun around to face them. "Jesus, Andi." He patted his chest as he took in a sharp breath. "I didn't know anyone else was back here. You scared me."

Ignoring the remark, Andi gestured to Winter and Miguel. "These two would like to talk to you."

Winter reached into her coat and produced her badge. "I'm Special Agent Black."

At Winter's side, Miguel flipped open his own badge. "I'm Special Agent Vasquez. My partner and I are with the Federal Bureau of Investigation. We'd like to ask you a few questions about a former employee of yours. Phil Rossway?"

Before Miguel made it halfway through the sentence, the color had drained from the man's cheeks. His eyes seemed to sink into his skull as he glanced to the door at his back. "Phil Rossway? What...happened to him?"

Winter returned her badge to her coat pocket, but she

didn't let her intent stare waver from the manager. "You think something happened to him? Why is that?"

His Adam's apple bobbed as he swallowed. "Well, the FBI is here asking about him. I doubt you'd be wasting your time if nothing had happened."

Winter would give credit where it was due. The man had a point. "Chris. I'm afraid we didn't catch your last name."

Another swallow. "Erickson. Chris Erickson."

Winter gave him as benign a smile as she could manage. "Mr. Erickson." She waved a hand in the direction of the office. "Would you mind?"

She half-expected Erickson to bolt for the door as soon as she'd finished her suggestion. Instead, he offered a sheepish nod and beckoned for them to follow him. Andi didn't offer a word of farewell as she replaced her earpiece and slunk back out into the store.

Erickson pointed to the two chairs in front of a worn wooden desk. "Have a seat."

Wordlessly, Winter and Miguel accepted the offer and dropped to sit.

As soon as the door latched closed behind them, Winter turned her scrutinizing stare to the manager, who looked close to shitting his pants. Though he'd folded both hands on top of the desk, the blood had already begun to drain from his knuckles where he clasped his fingers. Winter was used to nervousness when she spoke to civilians, but Chris was a few notches above the typical jittery witness.

Chris Erickson was hiding something.

Winter scooted to the edge of her seat. "Mr. Erickson, I don't want to come across as hostile, but we're working on a time sensitive investigation, and Phil Rossway is a key component in it."

Raking an unsteady hand through his dark hair, Erickson sighed. "Well, what do you need to know about Phil, then?"

"That's easy." Winter's voice was flat. "We need to know where he is."

Erickson was already nervous. All she had to do now was turn up the heat. Remind him of what exactly was at stake if he decided to try to cover for his ex-employee.

She didn't wait for a reply. "Have you heard of the murders that have been taking place in Danville lately, Mr. Erickson?"

He furrowed his brows. "Yes. The victims of the Riverside Mall massacre, right? Who hasn't? I mean, it's all over the news and people are freaking out and…" The manager closed his mouth as he apparently realized he was babbling.

Winter leaned closer, taking up his personal space. "That's right. We think that Phil Rossway has information pertinent to figuring out who the killer is. I doubt I need to remind you of what happens when you impede a murder investigation."

Miguel crossed his arms. "This isn't just a murder investigation anymore, though. We're searching for a domestic terrorist."

Erickson's eyes went so wide that Winter worried they might roll right out of his head. "Domestic…terrorist? And you think Phil…my employee, Phil Rossway, had something to do with it?"

As she locked her eyes onto Erickson's, Winter rested her elbows on the arms of the chair. "We do. If you know something about Phil Rossway, you need to tell us, Mr. Erickson. If you aren't completely honest, things can get very messy for you very quickly. Whether we have to use a subpoena to compel you to testify or a court order to search through your work and personal documents, we'll do whatever it takes."

The office chair squeaked as the general manager leaned back and heaved a sigh. "My god, Phil," he muttered under his breath. "What the hell did you get yourself into?"

Winter narrowed her eyes. "What do you mean, Mr. Erickson?"

Raking the fingers of one hand through his hair, the man let his head loll back against the headrest. "I've known Phil for close to three years. Since back before I was even a shift lead. We were even roommates for a little while. I got him his job at my old store. He's not a bad guy, and I don't know what you guys *think* he's been up to, but he'd never hurt anyone."

Famous last words. Winter kept the cynical thought to herself.

Erickson shook his head. "He's a really smart guy too. But he...has a penchant for the finer things in life, you know what I mean? He wants to live like a rock star on the salary of a part-time retail worker. So, he did what smart kids with no real-world experience tend to do." As he shrugged, Erickson finally met Winter's gaze. "He did a bunch of stupid shit to try to make a few bucks."

Miguel tapped his pen on his notepad, not bothering to hide his irritation. "Such as?"

Erickson shrugged. "I'm not sure, honestly. I didn't ask because I didn't want to know. All I knew was that it probably wasn't legal, and he dealt with some pretty shady people online. Look...I..." Sweat popped out on his temple, "I don't know if I should even be telling you guys this stuff. Do I need my lawyer here or something?"

Winter bit back a slew of four-letter words. "Our priority right now is finding Mr. Rossway. We're not looking to haul you away from here in cuffs. We need your help."

Erickson scrubbed a hand over his face as a shroud of silence descended over the room. "Jesus, Phil." The words were muffled. When he finally dropped his hand, his expression had changed from haunted to resigned. "Look, whatever he got into, I didn't have any idea, okay? I still stand by my statement from earlier. He's not a bad guy. But he didn't exactly have the best judgement, especially when it came to people he, um…worked with."

"*Worked* with?" Winter echoed, jumping on the word.

Squeezing his eyes closed, Erickson nodded. "When he told me he needed somewhere to lay low, I just figured it meant he snagged a credit card from some tough guy and wanted to wait it out. I thought he was worried about getting his ass beat. I didn't think he was going to hide from the *FBI*."

Though Winter maintained her calm expression, her heart hammered against her chest. Their case had stagnated for the past two and a half months, but now, they'd finally been pointed in a viable direction. "We're going to need you to tell us everything, Mr. Erickson. Any names you can remember, addresses. All of it."

Erickson shook his head, holding both hands up. "No names. Like I said, I never asked. He was just a friend in trouble, so I thought I'd help him out. I figured he could use the week off to do some self-reflection or something, so I let him use my father-in-law's cabin a little ways north of Richmond."

Winter didn't remember reaching for the pen she held out to Erickson. "We'll need that address." When he hesitated, she lowered her voice and gave him her most penetrating stare. "Now."

27

P eople were so damned disappointing.

As the message blared in my ear, letting me know that the person at that number hadn't yet set up a voicemail account, I dropped the phone onto my bed. It was the seventh time I'd called Will. The seventh time he hadn't answered. I was tempted to text him again. Tempted to scream at him in capital letters or leave a voicemail so scathing my grandfather would rise from hell and wash my mouth out in his own, special way.

But I pushed down the impulse. Pushed down the rage.

Rage wouldn't do.

Rage was an emotion that the Lord did not appreciate. It was an emotion that led to mistakes and miscalculations. It was an emotion of passion.

Passion.

I shuddered at the word.

"Let me in, my son."

I heard the words as if they were being whispered in my ears. Felt the body pressed so hard and tight to mine.

"Let me in. Let me baptize your sins."

The pain. The passion.

I closed my eyes against the memories. Grandfather was my teacher. My protector. My solace in a world gone bad. He had saved me from them. From *her*.

And I was glad. I *was*.

After all, she was now doing men's work. Wearing men's pants. Carrying a weapon as only a man should. And worse, she was looking for me.

Which was just fine. I'd let her find me. Someday soon, I would lead her to my door, just as I'd led her to our old house, the sinning house. She was a rat, and I was her cheese. She would only learn much too late that I was filled with poison.

Another P word I favored.

But I had other things to manage first, other rats to poison before I could give her my full attention.

Picking up my phone, I tapped until I reached the app that monitored Will's phone, accessing the software that let me listen through his device. It was a brilliant little app I'd installed before handing the phone over to him. He was driving, which I already knew because the phone was moving at seventy-six miles per hour.

Naughty boy.

Will was speeding. Running. From me? Or from his sudden cowardness that had taken me by surprise? I wondered if it had taken him by surprise as well.

Rage wanted to swell up, and I pushed it down again.

Will hadn't followed my orders. Worse, he hadn't followed God's will.

He had let the man and the youngest girl live, and now he was avoiding me. He wasn't answering my calls. He was running.

God wasn't pleased.

Neither was I.

The sinners must be punished, Will knew that. I'd thought he understood and agreed. Their sins were a message to others, their blood written on the walls for all to see. To read. To listen.

They couldn't understand the message or heed its call if the message wasn't delivered.

And now my delivery boy was on the run.

So very disappointing.

I'd had such hopes for William Hoult, but as I considered his betrayal I thought of one of the things my grandfather used to say as he bounced me on his knee, his hand making me feel so very good, so special. Baptized in my granddaddy's love. "The only person you can trust is me," he told me over and over and over again.

And now I *was* him, so the only person I could trust was me.

As I watched the dot that represented Will's car pull into the parking lot of some big building, I checked the address to learn it was a cheap motel.

Perfect.

Closing my eyes, I let them rest for a little while. I needed to gather my strength.

Another message must be sent. And soon.

WHEN WINTER and Miguel arrived at the Richmond field office, she had to make a conscious effort not to sprint into the building. She slowed her pace to a brisk walk, Miguel on her heels. Their footsteps echoed through the concrete parking garage, but otherwise, the area was silent. Almost as if it was holding its breath in anticipation of the breakthrough that Winter and Miguel had discovered.

Phil Rossway's former manager, Chris Erickson, had

written down the address of his in-law's cabin. The cabin where their hacker was hiding. Winter knew it. She could feel it in her bones.

Rather than taking the time to visit the courthouse to obtain a warrant to search the cabin and the land surrounding it, Winter had gone directly to Chris's father-in-law. Miguel had expressed his concern that the father-in-law might spread the word to Rossway, but in Winter's opinion, time was of the essence. Seconds later, Miguel had agreed.

They didn't know when the killer planned to strike again. The sooner they had Phil Rossway in custody, the sooner they could fully discern his role in the recent murders in Danville. Besides, the idea that Chris's father-in-law was a part of Phil's circle of confidantes was farfetched at best.

Sure enough, Harry Fallwell had never even heard Rossway's name before today. Though the man was puzzled as to why the FBI would be interested in searching a property he hadn't used in close to two years, he'd been cooperative. He had even agreed to meet them near the property.

If Phil was indeed the third person mentioned in Haldane and Strickland's manifesto, then Winter and her team had to be prepared for the worst.

As Winter pushed through a heavy set of double doors, she felt like a kid who had just returned home from school after receiving all As on her report card. She wanted to hold the piece of paper above her head and wave it around for the entire office to see, but again, she refrained. Just because she was eager to put together the next few pieces of their puzzle didn't mean she could abandon her professionalism.

She was cool, calm, and collected as she and Miguel finished the short trip to the Violent Crimes Division. Rather than wave the paper around like a kid who had aced a test, she had neatly folded the address and tucked it into the safety of her jacket pocket.

Two hours later, she and the team were moving through the woods, closing in on the cabin from every angle. Even under the weight of her ballistics vest, Winter shivered. The unusually cold December wind seemed to be made of ice. Next week, it would probably be seventy degrees for a few days, then a good old blizzard for Christmas.

As she crept to the back of the cabin, she held one hand over her mouth. Not only to warm her frosty fingers with her breath, but to also soften the cloud of foggy condensation that bloomed in the air with each of her exhalations. The steel of her service weapon was like a block of ice in her hand.

But as her heart rate increased, so did her internal temperature, and the cold that had been brutal only moments before faded away as her attention turned to where Aiden and Bree had taken up their stations.

Smoke rolled from the chimney of the tiny cabin, giving the place a homey feel she didn't trust. The place looked too innocent, which was as crazy a thought as she'd ever entertained. Winter knew, almost as much as anyone on the planet, that evil hid behind the mask of innocence.

The mask of good.

The mask of the Bible and the words it held within its pages.

Winter shivered, harder this time.

Forcing those thoughts away, she focused back on the cabin, readying herself for what was to come. From her vantage point, she could see Noah and Sun approach the house from the front. She lost sight of them as they stepped on the porch, but the clap of their boots on the old wood reverberated in the surrounding forest. As did the hard knock that followed.

"FBI," Noah called, his sharp voice disturbing some

animal to her left, causing it to bolt through the dry, fallen leaves. "Phil Rossway. Open up."

They'd come armed with a warrant, so if he didn't answer, they'd breach the door. They were going in, one way or another.

Noah knocked again, then waited before knocking a final time. He must have signaled the tactical team, the men armed with a battering ram and the ability to use it, because they approached the door, then she lost sight of them as they stomped onto the porch.

"Sorry, Mr. Fallwell," Winter murmured just before the door caved in and steel boots thundered into the cabin. In her mind's eye, she imagined the scene, the men sweeping the rooms one by one. Hopefully, they'd find Phil Rossway in one of the corners, his hands up in surrender, willing and eager to spill his guts.

"Clear!"

"Clear!"

"Clear!"

Winter's heart fell as the all clear codes where given, room by room. Had Phil Rossway been there at all? Had he been tipped off about their arrival? Had they missed him by minutes? By seconds? And most importantly, where was he now?

"Dammit." She added a few other choice curse words to the more innocent one, willing her special ability or what-ever the hell it was to do its work. She scanned the back and side of the cabin, praying to whatever god looked over the freaks like her that something incriminating would suddenly begin to glow red.

Her own personal burning bush, she thought with a light snicker. She'd never thought of her ability like that. A beacon. A miracle.

Instead, a different, more real bush moved, the dry

branches hissing together.

Winter peered closer. A rabbit? A different type of animal?

It moved again, and this time, the entire bush lifted. Winter blinked, sure the cold and stress had caused her to hallucinate.

But no, the bush was still rising, and underneath it a cavern was being exposed. And a hand. An arm. A head. It was like a man was being birthed out of the earth.

Adrenaline surged through her system as a man rolled out of the cleverly hidden cellar, mentally cursing Mr. Fallwell for not giving them a heads-up about the underground room. The man crouched, scanning the area, his gaze landing on her. But he didn't freeze. Didn't hesitate for even an instant. He bolted. Quite literally.

Winter screamed the required warning as she gave chase. "FBI. Stop." She didn't have time for anything more. The man didn't even pause, only kicking it up a notch. If he was their hacker, he was the most physically fit computer nerd she'd ever encountered.

Jumping over a log, she yelled at Aiden and Bree, who from their angle wouldn't have been able to see the masked man running into the woods.

Within seconds, the sounds of leaves and broken sticks filled the forest, barely discernable over her labored breathing. Winter cursed herself for not running every day as her lungs began to burn from the cold air. Sex—even the hourslong kind, five times a week—hadn't prepared her for this.

Less than a year with the bureau, and she was getting soft. Complacent.

The thought pissed her off, and she pushed through the pain in her lungs and churned her legs, hopping over more fallen logs to close the gap. Tomorrow, she'd run five miles, she promised herself. She'd do sit-ups and pushups, strengthen her core. No asshole was going to get away from her just because she'd eaten too much cake and chocolate croissants lately.

"FBI. Stop or I'll shoot," she called again as she drew a bit closer. The shooting part was a lie. She'd never shoot anyone in the back, but if it caused the dickhead to hesitate or, please god please, stop, she'd lie until her pants were on fire, not just her lungs.

To her side, limbs and leaves crunched and broke, sounding like a bull barreling through the woods. It was Noah, who shot her a gleaming smile as he pulled ahead, shooting her a thumbs-up sign. She shot him a middle finger in return. His grin gleamed brighter as sweat ran into her eye.

He could see that she was struggling, and that more than anything else, made her kick her speed up a notch. Noah still pulled ahead, taking the runner's right, and Winter curled toward his left, angling in case he turned in that direction.

Phil Rossway stumbled, and Winter almost cheered as Noah closed the distance. Rossway noticed him too, and as agile as any running back, pivoted out of the bigger man's way. Noah sailed past, his arms grabbing nothing but air before he hit the forest floor, leaves and limbs flying as he crashed and rolled.

Internally, Winter laughed, knowing she'd be giving him hell for that one for years.

Externally, she bore down, taking advantage of the angle and telling herself not to fall for Rossway's quick feet.

Rossway hesitated, spotting Aiden and Bree in the distance, and it was just the exact amount of time she needed. Winter launched herself, her hands taking handfuls of his hoodie, turning them as they fell together, until he took the brunt of the impact on the forest floor.

"Phil Rossway..." Her voice was barely more than a pant

as she straddled him, holding his face into the leaves as he tried to buck her off. She maneuvered her knee into the small of his back, jerking his arm up in the awkward angle that pretty much stopped him cold. "You have the right to remain silent…"

As she recited the Miranda rights, she snapped on the handcuffs and turned him over to Aiden and Bree so she could catch her breath. Noah was grinning as he held out his hand to help her up, leaves still stuck in his hair.

"Nice catch," he said, barely out of breath.

She was still panting as she pulled a leaf from his hair. "Nothing but air, huh?"

He grinned. "Man juked me good."

That was one of the things that Winter loved about Noah. He wasn't ashamed to admit when he'd looked like a goober.

Her heart warmed, and she would have leaned in to kiss him if their team hadn't been so close. "You got him to turn, though. He might have gotten away if you hadn't tried."

Noah lifted her braid, and she could tell that he wanted to kiss her too. Instead, he just gave it a tug. "You did good. Finding him. Spotting him. Bagging him after I didn't." He tugged her braid again before tossing it over her shoulder. "Now, let's go find out what he knows so we can put this case to bed."

As Winter watched Noah walk away, the jubilant feeling she'd been experiencing at their catch evaporated on the wind that had picked up all around her.

The case.

And after they'd finished this one, she could focus on her brother.

Would she find him?

She hoped not. She also hoped so.

The waiting. The hoping. The hopelessness was taking bites out of her spirit.

28

A iden could feel eyes on him.

Curious eyes. Surprised eyes. Hostile eyes too.

He'd kept everyone waiting, so he understood how tired his team was. How anxious they were for answers, but still he waited. Watched. Paid close attention to every eye and body movement Phil Rossway made through the two-way mirror.

Aiden watched Rossway's facial expressions as Aiden sent in one agent after another, with instructions to ask a specific question. He watched the alleged hacker blithely disregard the male African American agent, showing neither hostility nor warmth. He watched Rossway sneer in disgust at a different agent with dark skin, this time a female.

Yes...the hacker had definitely reacted to her.

Just as he reacted in a negative way to every female Aiden had sent into the room. Color didn't matter, nor did size or stature. It didn't matter if they went in with a scowl or a smile, he was equally antagonistic.

Rossway hated women. If Aiden learned nothing more

during this interview and the subsequent interrogation that was to come, he knew that.

The question was…why?

And did that hatred have anything to do with why Rossway had used his technical skills to assist in the murder of innocent women?

Men too, of course. Aiden hadn't forgotten that men had also been killed. Nor had he forgotten that little Mariah Young, a female, had been unharmed.

The puzzle pieces didn't fit yet, but they would. He just needed to be patient and not let the eyes of his team make him hurry a process that couldn't be hurried.

That was where many crime television shows got it wrong. In the space of an hour, there was a crime, and investigation, then some badass detective stomped into an interrogation room and elicited a confession in the space of a few minutes.

In truth, the process could take hours. Days, even.

Aiden didn't know Phil Rossway any better than he knew the Queen of England. Aiden didn't know his baseline—what he looked like, sounded like, acted like—anymore more than that of a stranger.

But he was learning.

Over the course of a couple hours, he'd learned that Phil Rossway's natural posture was to sit with his arms crossed over his chest, an ankle hiked on top of his knee. That was how he was most comfortable.

Another untruth that TV got wrong was that crossed arms meant someone was defensive. That could be the case, sure, but it could also be that crossed arms was a comfortable way to sit or stand. For Phil Rossway, Aiden believed that position was the latter. Which meant if he wasn't sitting that way, he was no longer comfortable. That he was alert. Possibly anxious.

Aiden turned to Noah Dalton, one of the sets of eyes that were slowly turning hostile at the lingering delay. "Go inside and offer him a bathroom break. Escort him out and chat about how you missed the tackle."

Aiden only barely suppressed the smile that wanted to creep to his mouth as the tips of Dalton's ears turned pink. The almost-smile died on its own as Winter glared at him, taking up for her man.

He still wasn't sure how he felt about all that. The biggest part of him wanted to be pleased that Winter and Dalton had found each other and appeared to be very well matched. But that little part...the part he refused to examine too closely, felt the knife turn somewhere where in his spirit.

He wanted Winter to look at him like she did Dalton. The way she used to look at him before...before Justin seemingly reappeared in her life, and he'd been forced to share his honest opinion about her beloved baby brother. The brother who was now more likely a savage than anything else.

"What are you after?"

Pulled back from the memories, Aiden eyed Dalton. He had to give the big guy credit. He wasn't exactly pushing back against the request. Instead, he appeared to be genuinely curious as to the purpose of the question.

"Hackers aren't normally physically fit," Aiden replied. "Too many hours in front of the computer make them soft, delay their reactions."

"He could be an Xbox fanatic," Noah countered.

Aiden inclined his head. "True. Which would keep his mind reaction sharp, but not his muscle memory. His agility seems to point in an interesting direction. I want you to uncover what it is."

He didn't want to babysit Dalton, give him a list of questions to ask. In Aiden's opinion, it was still early in the process. They were still in the interview portion of this interrogation. Fact finding. Question after question. Building rapport and establishing a relationship with a perfect stranger. A relationship that would, hopefully, lead to a full confession.

True, Aiden had yet to meet with Rossway face to face yet, but he wasn't treating this as a normal interrogation. There was too much at risk. Too many lives at stake. He needed to see what made this man tick before Aiden made a mistake and caused him to lawyer up.

Right now, Phil Rossway was feeling superior. He was feeling like he was the smartest person in the building. He was feeling confident but also curious.

Rossway wanted to know what the bureau knew. He wanted to discover how good or bad the next few hours could go for him. He wanted to laugh in their faces, tell them to prove him guilty of his crimes.

Hatred was bred from arrogance, and Phil Rossway had arrogance in spades, that much was clear.

Where did it come from? His parents?

From what they'd been able to gather so far, Phil Rossway's parents had divorced amicably. Lydia Rossway was described as a happy homemaker, who paid the bills by sewing in her home. Winter had reported that the woman and her house had reminded her of June Cleaver in the old *Leave it to Beaver* shows.

The father, a long-haul trucker, was nowhere to be found, and they'd secured a warrant to search his house an hour ago. Aiden didn't hold out much hope of finding anything useful, but it needed to be done.

He needed to be thorough.

Lives were at stake. The pressure of that reminder weighed heavily on Aiden's shoulders as he watched Dalton enter the room.

"How're ya doin'?" Dalton said to the hacker, laying on his Texas drawl abnormally thick.

Aiden approved. Dalton would be a skilled interrogator one day since his friendly demeanor seemed to warm just about everyone, men or women.

Except this man. This man, Phil Rossway, only laughed, sitting up straighter, both feet planted on the floor. It was a nasty sounding laugh filled with scorn, but it sounded more like a bully than it did of genuine disgust.

"Better than you, I'm guessing. How many dead leaves did you have to pick out of your teeth?"

Noah just laughed in return, good-natured as ever. "A shit ton. You got me good, for sure. What were you, running back or receiver?"

Rossway snorted and crossed his arms over his chest again. "QB."

They already knew that, of course. Phil Rossway had been a standout quarterback for his local high school team, actively being recruited by a number of D1 colleges. Until one of the cheerleaders accused him of rape. Then another. And another.

Though the charges had been eventually dropped due to lack of evidence and the women's flip-flopping stories, the colleges that had been banging at Phil Rossway's door had turned on their heels.

Rossway had gone to college, but on the Pell Grant instead of a full ride scholarship. He'd gotten his degree in computer science, and...what? Become a hacker? Been groomed into a woman hating cult?

Or had he started the cult?

Had his hatred and missed opportunities bonded him to like-minded men? Men like Kent Strickland and Tyler Haldane? And was his hatred so deep that he wanted to kill innocent people? Men, women, and children alike?

"Where did ya play?" Noah asked, and Aiden watched Phil Rossway turn into a block of stone.

"I didn't." The feet were back on the floor again, the hands on the table, palms spread. "It was stolen from me."

This was interesting, and to his credit, Noah turned in his chair to mirror the man's movements. "You're shittin' me. What happened, man?"

The next hour was spent with Rossway spinning a tale of woe so filled with expletives that it would have made any sailor blush. But it was an important hour, and Aiden learned something important. Noah Dalton was the man for this interrogation.

Not himself.

As former athletes, the two had a natural comradery that no other person in the building could compete with. Within moments, Dalton had gotten more reaction from Rossway than anyone else.

Aiden watched and waited for another three hours. He waited through a bathroom break and a meal compromised of the two men inhaling sandwiches and some chocolate looking croissants. The meal and breaks were important. Also unlike on television, it was important to break bread with the accused, make them feel like the interviewer was on their side.

They couldn't come in like they did on crime stories, slamming doors and tossing chairs. The accused needed to feel listened to, they needed to feel respected before they would let down their guard enough to talk.

"So, how did your parents take the news of the rape allegations?" Dalton asked Rossway after taking another sip of his soda, causing Aiden to straighten in anticipation. He had coached Noah to ask that very question just before it was time to break again.

Rossway snorted. "How do you think?"

Dalton lifted a broad shoulder. "I've seen it go a number of ways. Some families deny, deny, deny, thinking their sweet little boy could never do such a bad thing. Some are too shocked to speak." He lifted another shoulder. "And some pretty much wipe their hands of their kid, sputtering something like 'he was good for nothin' anyway.'"

Rossway leaned back in his chair, tossed his ankle over his knee. Comfortable again. Good.

"Father basically clapped me on the back, congratulating me on getting such fine pieces of asses while my mom twisted her hands in her apron and said nothing." Rossway crossed his arms over his chest. "Just like she was supposed to."

That was interesting.

Dalton smiled, tapping his thumb on the table. "She stayed barefoot in the kitchen, huh?"

"Damned straight. Don't find women like my mama these days. They all talk too much or show their tits then gasp when you reach out to touch them. They spend more time getting manicures than making meals and feeding their families." Rossway leaned forward, a look so earnest on his face it caused the hair to raise on Aiden's neck. "That's the real reason the world has gone to hell. Women don't know their place. Letting the kids do whatever they want to do. Instead of cooking, they're stuffing fast food in everybody's faces."

Beside him, Winter shivered. She'd apparently felt it too.

"But not your mom," Dalton said, giving Rossway a pleased looked that Aiden knew he was faking.

Rossway grinned. "That's right. My mom knew her place. Still does."

"What about your father? What's his place in all this?"

The smile dimmed, then fell away, but only for a second. Recovering quickly, Rossway stretched, planting both feet on the floor. Then he yawned, a sign that he was fighting an adrenaline dump in his system. He covered well, but not well enough. Aiden knew Dalton saw it too, and instead of pushing, the agent looked at his watch. "Need another break?"

Friendly. Caring. *I'm on your side*, the question represented.

Rossway was on his feet in an instant, the adrenaline giving him some spring. "Yeah. That chair sucks ass."

Noah laughed as he turned to open the door. "Thought your ass would be tougher than that from sitting at a computer all day."

Rossway laughed too. "Yeah, but my chair is ergonomically correct, man. Gotta take care of the body, you know."

Then they were gone, chatting like old friends to the restrooms.

"He's doing well," Winter said, standing up to stretch.

Aiden nodded. "Good ole boy works in situations like this."

Winter immediately bristled, coming to her lover's defense. "You might try it one day, SSA Parrish."

Then she was gone.

Well, hell.

For what many people called a smart man, he could also be a bumbling idiot. He was about to go over to her, but another woman who he often became a bumbling idiot in front of swept down the hallway, her black hair swinging side to side with every step.

"Parrish."

He inclined his head. "Sun, what did you find?"

She lifted her chin, and he realized he should have used some bit of greeting pleasantry, but before he could correct yet another bumble, she handed him a file. "Blood spatter. No body, but we've called in the canine cadaver dogs."

Aiden flipped through the file, noticed the pictures of the

blood spatter she spoke of, high on the wall of what he knew was Phil Rossway's father's home. "Thank you. Let me know what you find out."

Without another word, Sun turned on her heel and retreated in the direction in which she came, almost bumping into Phil Rossway as he exited the men's restroom. Aiden watched the man's entire body stiffen when Sun simply marched past him, forcing him to stop on a dime, not even muttering the briefest of apologies.

Rossway opened his mouth to say something, but clearly thought better of it and snapped it closed.

The hatred ran deep for such a slight insult to so enrage the man.

Rossway's jaw was still tight as he passed Aiden and returned to the interrogation room.

Once Dalton had securely closed the door behind the hacker, he shot Aiden a glance. "What now?" Dalton asked.

"Now…" Aiden said, looking him straight in the eye. "You don't fuck it up."

29

*D*on't fuck it up, said the asshole in the three-thousand-dollar suit.

Noah Dalton kept his face carefully blank, refusing to let his thoughts reflect to the man he'd like to punch in the face.

"Thanks," he said, letting sarcasm, not anger, drip from the words. "That's my number one priority." Noah nodded at the folder in Parrish's hands, and in spite of himself, his curiosity was peaked. "What's that?"

Parrish handed him the folder, Kevin Rossway's name written on the tab. Phil Rossway's father, Noah knew. Noah flipped through the contents, stopping at a series of pictures featuring blood spatter.

"Is he dead?"

Parrish lifted a shoulder. "Don't know, but they've called in the dogs, so we'll hopefully know something soon." He held his hand out. "Leave that with me, and don't share any of this information yet."

Noah took his time, skimming the reports just so that he wouldn't be blindsided with anything later. After a few minutes, he handed it over. "What's the plan?"

"When the timing is right, I'll enter the room with any current information. Just wanted to give you the heads-up."

Noah nodded his understanding. "Time to turn up the heat." He rubbed the back of his neck. "You sure you want me to take lead?"

Damn, he was nervous, and he hated like hell to show any hint of it in front of the tenured SSA.

Parrish nodded. "You have the rapport, and you know what to do. I'll break in if I think things need to turn."

Noah blew out a long breath and stretched his arms over his head, giving himself a mental pep talk. Just pre-game jitters, he told himself. It'd always happened before a game, but the second he took the field, the nerves disappeared, and focus took its place.

And he needed to focus. He needed Phil Rossway to vomit out the truth and then sign the confession sheet on the dotted line.

The interview part of the process had been easy. Noah could toss the shit around with just about anyone, prying up bits of information as easily as he brushed his teeth. The interview was just a conversation, just like you'd have on a first date. It had been an important time to give Rossway the illusion of trust.

Tell me about yourself.

What's your favorite food? Least favorite? Most hated subject in school. What are your hobbies?

The questions seemed inane, but the answers could be telling. Useful.

But, unlike most men on a date, Noah's job was to really listen. Deeply listen. Pick up nuggets that could be used later in the interrogation. Understand the man before him and why he made the decisions he did.

That was the interview, but now they were starting the official interrogation where he would control the conversation. Control the narrative. Control Phil Rossway, leading him down a path of giving them the truth.

Charging himself up mentally, Noah clapped his hands together once. "Let's go."

Forcing a friendly smile back on his face, he turned away from Parrish and reentered the interrogation room. Rossway groaned as he sat back into the hard chair, and Noah gave him a sympathetic smile.

"I know you're getting tired, Phil. Frankly, I am too, and since they won't be giving us ergonomic seats anytime soon, let's talk a little more and then we'll be finished for the day."

Rossway perked up at that. "Then I can leave?"

"I hope so," Noah lied, and checked to make sure the cameras were still recording before getting down to business. He also rechecked the folder in front of him, triple checking that the Miranda warning statement had been duly signed.

Once, when he was a newbie detective down in Texas, he'd taken over an interrogation from a fellow detective who hadn't had much luck. Noah had spent five freaking hours with the suspect, grinding him down until he was prepared to lead him to the body of his pregnant girlfriend. It wasn't until the man was signing the confession sheet that Noah realized he hadn't been given a proper Miranda at the beginning.

Even when the man did lead police to the body, they couldn't use that fact in court either because the "fruit of the poisonous tree" doctrine precluded the use of that evidence against the asshole during his trial. The bastard got away with the crime because of a technicality.

He'd never made that mistake again.

Although an officer of the law didn't officially have to Mirandize a person until they were in custody and about to be questioned, Noah always read the familiar lines off to the perp as he was being put in cuffs and before an interview, just in case. Once, he'd read the rights to the same individual six times because he needed to be absolutely certain the asshole's case didn't get tossed out on a technicality. Some of his Texas friends still ribbed him about that.

Closing the file on Phil Rossway's signature, Noah leaned back and propped an ankle over his knee, mirroring the stance of Rossway to continue in this ruse of mutual respect and trust.

"I was just thinking about something," he began. "How did you get to the cabin? We didn't find a car or any other type of vehicle."

Rossway shrugged. "Friend dropped me off."

"Your manager friend? Chris…" Noah made a show of looking at his notes, although the man's name was burned into his brain, "Erickson."

Rossway shrugged again. "Does it matter?"

Noah gave him another friendly smile. "Probably not, but it's important to get the timeline and all the details set in stone. Was it Chris Erickson who dropped you off at his father-in-law's cabin?"

Rossway sat straighter in his seat, his feet planted on the floor again. "No."

The change in position indicated a lie, but it could also have been a protective move to brace for the more specific questioning.

"Then, who was it?"

Another shrug. "Don't know his name?"

Noah arched an eyebrow. "How do you not know your friend's name?"

Rossway sighed. "Friend might be an exaggeration. An acquaintance is a better word."

"How did you convince an acquaintance to drop everything and drive you out to a remote cabin?"

"He owed me a favor?"

"Favor for what?"

Rossway waved his arms, growing agitated. "For doing him a favor. That's how things work. You do something for me, and I do something for you. As the good book says, 'eye for an eye.'"

Noah ignored the biblical reference for now. "What favor?" he repeated.

Rossway rubbed the back of his neck. "Computer stuff."

"What kind of stuff?"

"The personal stuff that any honest businessman wouldn't tell about a client." The words held a bit of bark in them.

Noah leaned his elbows on his knees. "So, the friend that was an acquaintance is now a client?"

Rossway said nothing, just crossed his arms over his chest. This time, the gesture wasn't for comfort. He was agitated. Noah had stepped on a nerve, but which one? And how far could he press before the man lawyered up?

He decided to circle back to that one later. "So, this friend slash acquaintance slash client drops you off at the cabin. What happened after that?"

Rossway relaxed the tiniest of fractions. "I hung out there. Relaxed. Read a book."

"What book?"

Rossway hesitated, and Noah could see him searching for a title. Whatever was about to come out of his mouth was a lie. *"Think and Grow Rich."*

Noah laughed. "That's a good one. Napoleon Hill was ahead of his time. What's your favorite part?"

It was always fun watching a suspect formulate a lie. During the interview process, Noah had fed Rossway baseline questions that he already knew the answers to just so that he could watch his eyes and body language as he answered.

Since they couldn't hook Rossway up to a lie detector machine, it was Noah's job to be that machine. To gauge the microscopic changes in the man's breathing, the way he swallowed, the pores that opened to release little beads of sweat.

Truth had many layers. Someone telling the truth could tell their story forward and backwards, and each layer of that truth would remain the same. Someone telling the truth told a story...this happened first, then this, then this, then this.

A liar didn't do that. Or if he did, he often couldn't remember the story backward or out of order. The layers would be out of line, causing him to stumble in the retelling.

Did Noah care about the book Rossway had been reading? No, he didn't. But he cared about the layer that book represented, and the layers that came before it and after.

"I don't remember," Rossway said with a laugh. "I was tired and was basically just skimming it."

"What had made you so tired?" The question was offered with what sounded like genuine sympathy.

Another shrug. "Stuff?"

"What kind of stuff?"

Killing your father? Slaughtering an innocent woman and little girl?

A bead of sweat appeared above Rossway's left eyebrow. "Just stuff. Work. You know, paying the bills kind of stuff."

"So, computer work?"

"Yeah, computer stuff."

"How did you manage to do so much work and still hold down a job at the electronics store?"

Rossway shifted in his seat. "I didn't manage it worth shit. Got fired." He perked up, like he'd just had an idea. "That was why I was so tired. Holding down two jobs can be exhausting, you know."

Noah gave him an understanding laugh. "Don't I know it.

Too many balls in the air and one of them is going to fall."

"Damned straight."

"I'm curious. Why the job at the electronics store? Hacking not paying the bills?"

Rossway froze, then visibly forced himself to relax. "I'm not a hacker."

Noah held up both hands. "Sure you are, and that's okay. I wish I knew how to hack. That talent would come in handy at times."

Rossway allowed the tiniest of smiles. "Hacking is against the law."

Noah shrugged. "I know, but it would be cool to look into my girlfriend's text messages and see what she's saying to other people." He scowled on purpose. "Other men."

Rossway fell for it. "You need to keep your old lady in line. As the man, you shouldn't even be the least bit worried about shit like that."

Noah made a face as if considering the advice. "True. It would also help me stop her from spending too much money at the mall."

Noah could mentally see Aiden Parrish sitting up straighter on the other side of the two-way mirror.

Rossway sneered. "The mall is the modern-day brothel for whores who don't know their place." The vehemence in his voice nearly took Noah aback, but instead of responding as he wanted to, he laughed.

"No kidding. Just last week, she spent five hundred dollars on a damn coat."

Noah didn't even flinch at the lie.

Law enforcement was prohibited from using physical or psychological coercion like torture, threats, drugging, or inhumane treatment during police interrogations. They could, however, lie, trick, or use other types of noncoercive methods to their heart's content.

Rossway bought the lie hook, line, and sinker. In fact, he looked like he was about to fall out of his seat. "You're shitting me? You let her do that?"

Noah thought of telling Winter that she couldn't do anything, and the ass whooping he'd get in return.

He swallowed a smile. "Her life. Her money. Maybe when we're married..." He shrugged, leaving the statement unfinished.

"You need to put a hammer on that now," Rossway advised, pounding his fist against the table for added emphasis.

"Is that what you do?" Noah asked casually. "Use hammers?"

Rossway laughed and wiggled his fingers, miming like he was typing on a computer. "Nope."

"So, you hack?"

Rossway laughed again. "You're tricky, aren't you? Told you, hacking is against the law."

"Let's pretend that hacking isn't against the law for a moment." Noah took a full two minutes to search through his folder, pretending to search for the printout Ryan O'Connelly and Ava Welford had pulled together. Rossway was squirming in his seat by the time he set the report on the table, turning it slowly so the man could read what it said. "Can you think of any reason why this digital bread trail led to you?"

Rossway swallowed, and Noah caught his fingers tremble before they closed into fists. "I don't know anything about that."

Noah sighed, loud and long. "Phil, do you really think we'd have gone through all the trouble of staking out the cabin, chasing you through the woods, then spend hour after hour in this room if we didn't already know the answer to our questions?"

Rossway swallowed again. "Do I need a lawyer?"

Noah shrugged. "Totally up to you. But between me and you, if you bring a lawyer into the mix, you stop me from being able to help you."

Another swallow. "Help me how?"

Noah mentally smiled. They already knew that Phil Rossway wasn't the third person at the Riverside Mall that terrible night of the massacre. He had an airtight alibi working at the electronic store until closing. Not only did they have his timecard and other employee testimony, but the video file they'd unearthed clearly showed Rossway selling an iPad to a young couple during the moments of the shooting.

"Do you know much about domestic terrorism?" Noah asked.

Rossway's eyes grew wide. "Like 9-11?"

"Not quite. That was terrorism of one country on another." Noah spouted off the FBI's definition, which he knew by heart. "Domestic terrorism is perpetrated by individuals and/or groups inspired by or associated with primarily U.S.-based movements that espouse extremist ideologies of a political, religious, social, racial, or environmental nature."

"So, it's law enforcement's way of locking up the good guys." Rossway clearly intended the statement to be a joke, and then clearly understood how badly it had landed. He opened his mouth, closed it. Opened it again. "Just kidding."

"Were you? It seems to me in the time we've spent together, Phil, that you have some pretty extreme ideologies about some things. Women, for example."

Rossway snorted. "They're not ideologies. They are facts."

Noah leaned back in his chair. "Facts like women belonging in the kitchen, cooking and cleaning for their families?"

"Damned straight."

"And if they don't, and they go to, say a mall, then you think it's your right to show them a lesson." Noah slammed his fist on the table, making Rossway jump. "Bring down the hammer is how you described it, I think."

"I didn't shoot nobody," Rossway practically shouted.

"I didn't say that you did. You were at work, right?" At Rossway's nod, Noah went on, "You were selling an iPad to a man and his wife just as the first shots were being fired." Another nod. Noah tapped the report between them. "But there were so many whores who escaped that night, weren't there?" Rossway's lip turned up into a sneer, but he held his tongue. "Whores who had to pay."

"Yeah." The admission was clearly involuntary. It was barely a breath of sound.

Noah sat back. "Here is what I'm thinking, Phil. I think your friend slash acquaintance slash client has the same thoughts about women as you, and I think you accessed the list of Riverside Mall survivors when he asked you to."

He tapped the report again.

"What I want to know is this…did you know that your friend slash acquaintance slash client intended to kill the people on that list? Did you know that five people from that list you gave your friend slash acquaintance slash client, including a little girl, were already dead?"

Rossway looked like he was about to throw up.

"That is domestic terrorism," Noah went on. "And you're about to be in deep, deep trouble, Phil. You might not have pulled the trigger, but there's this thing called the felony murder rule, and because of that rule, you could be in the kind of trouble that will land you in prison for life." He made his lip curl in disgust. "And in prison, the 'women…'" he air quoted the word, "will be the kind that rape you every night. You'll bleed, Phil. Bad. Then you'll get to the point where you just don't care. And then…" Noah leaned closer, "you'll get to the point of where you crave the connection to another human."

Rossway paled. "I'm not queer."

"Neither are they. Only human beings can be homosexual. These are monsters who watch you during the day and prey on you at night. They'll use your mouth and your body. They'll make you lick their assholes clean. Every. Single. Night. All because you broke into a database and turned over a list of names." Noah's voice was soft now. "That doesn't seem very fair, does it?"

Rossway seemed close to tears, but he didn't say a word.

Noah let the quiet of the room settle all around them. He waited. Watched. Mentally counted to six hundred before Rossway finally answered, "No."

"Who's your friend, Phil?"

More silence, then, "I don't know."

Noah gritted his teeth but kept his voice soft. "Tell me, Phil. Save yourself from a lifetime of abuse."

"I really don't know."

Very slowly, Noah pulled the report back toward himself, then took his time putting it back in the folder and closing the file with a long exhalation of breath.

He stood. "That's too bad, Phil. I really wanted to help you, but I guess you're just on your own now."

His chair scraped over the floor, making a loud shrieking sound that echoed through the room. His hand was on the doorknob when Rossway said, "Wait."

Forcing the smile from his face, Noah turned around. "What?"

Rossway dropped his head. "I don't know his name, but I could describe him. Would that help?"

For the first time in hours, Noah's shoulders relaxed. "Yeah. I think that'd help."

30

Staring at the black screen of the motel room television, Will turned his phone over and over in his hand. He was exhausted, but he couldn't sleep. Every time he closed his eyes, he heard the girl's screams. Felt her blood gush over his hand.

It made him sick, and if there was anything left in his stomach, he'd throw up again. But he was empty. Empty of food, of bile. Empty of tears, of hope.

And beneath it all, he was disgusted with himself.

How had he thought all of this would be so easy? Had he really thought killing someone in person was as simple as punching a button on his Xbox control? Had he really believed he could shoot or stab another human being and then just go on with his life, celebrate his win?

There had been no victory in this, although he'd tried, over and over and over, to convince himself that the sinners had been prophesied to die. The mother and girl were messages to other sinners, and in their sacrifice, many would change their heathen ways, but in the cold aftermath of the murder…

Will shuddered at the word.

Murder.

Jaime could call it what he would. Will could label it anyway he pleased. An eye for eye might have been written by God himself, but the terror in that child's eyes as he plunged that knife into her chest condensed it all down into one thing.

Murder.

Will was a murderer. His hands burned from washing them so much. His eyes burned from trying to not see the blood that now seemed steeped into his own DNA.

He needed to call Jaime. There was no question of that in his mind.

He needed to stop being a damn pussy and just make the call. But even as he brought up his contacts, his thumb hovered over the button.

He was scared.

Because after he spoke to Jaime, he needed to call the police. He needed to turn himself in.

That was his only solution.

No…not his only one.

With trembling fingers, he stroked the cold metal of the gun laying so innocently on the bed next to him. He could make this all go away. Right now. In an instant. All he had to do was pick up the gun, place it in his mouth, pull the trigger and…

And what?

What would come next?

Eternal fire? Flames burning at his feet as he was tormented by demons that breathed an everlasting fire into his mouth, his eyes, his ears? Or was that punishment only for regular sinners? Not for those who murdered little girls?

But she was a sinner. She was a message. It had to be done. God demanded it.

He knew that would be what Jaime would say. Heck, it was what he had said just before the blade of a knife transformed into a point of no return. He tried saying it again now.

"But she was a sinner." His voice cracked with the words, so he cleared his throat and said them again. "She was a sinner. She was a message. It had to be done." He was weeping by the time he shouted the last. "God demanded it!"

Even though his voice was stronger, he felt no better.

Weeping in earnest now, he fell back onto the bed.

He should call Jaime.

No, he should just call the police, confess everything, and put the gun to his head.

Yes, that was what he would do.

Wiping at tears and snot running down his face with his sleeve, he picked up his phone and thumbed to the call app. He tapped 9, then 1, then the phone rang in his hand.

He jumped so hard that the device fell onto the bed. It landed face up, and Will saw the name of the caller. Those five letters turned his bowels to water.

Jaime.

Was this a sign? He didn't know, but he'd take it as one.

Closing his eyes, Will tapped the button that accepted the call. "Hello?"

"There you are," Jaime said, his tone almost sounding amused. "Thought you'd lost your phone or ran away or something."

Will swallowed hard. "Just lying low, you know. Letting things blow over for a couple days."

"That wasn't the plan." A barking laugh followed, but it ended as abruptly as it had started. "Of course, there were a few things…two things to be exact, that didn't go to plan, wasn't there?"

"Yeah…" Will tried to force bravado into his voice. He'd

been thinking about his argument, his defense for many hours now. It was a good defense, if not the correct one, but it was all that he had, and he needed to sell it. "That's exactly right. We didn't plan on the motherfucking father having a gun, did we? Almost got my ass shot." He forced out a laugh, but it sounded on the edge of hysterical.

"So, that's why the man and girl are still alive?" Jaime asked, his tone conversational now.

Will sputtered, wiping his sleeve over his forehead to mop up the sweat. "Of course. What other reason would there be?"

Please believe me. Please. Please. Please.

It was so strange. A minute ago, he was ready to put a gun to his head, and now, he wanted to live more than anything. Wanted to correct his wrong.

As if Jaime was able to read his mind, he said, "It's time to correct that."

Will stood up from the bed, started pacing the small room. "Why? I mean, don't you think that'll be a big risk? I got the ones on the list and—"

"But that wasn't your orders, was it, Will?"

Will turned to pace back across the room, caught sight of himself in the bathroom mirror, and nearly pissed his pants. He blew out a shaky breath before saying, "The cops will be watching them."

"It doesn't matter. They need to die."

"Why?"

One moment of silence stretched into the next, then the next. It stretched out so long that Will checked his phone to see if they'd been disconnected.

"Are you still there?"

"Yes, Will. I'm still here. I'm just trying to think of what I should say to someone who has so blatantly broken my trust."

"The man had a gun, Jaime," Will cried. "What was I supposed to do? I...I...I..." He snapped his mouth shut, hating how weak his voice sounded. How desperate.

"I...I...I..." Jaime mimicked, "I know that the man had a gun, and I...I...I...know you had one too. Why didn't you use it?" Jaime's voice was growing louder. "Must I do everything? Is there no one on this god-forbidden planet that I can trust to help me do God's work?"

"Me," Will said in a rush. "Just not the kids, okay? I don't want to do the kids."

Another long pause was followed with a snorting sort of laugh. "I thought you were different, Will."

"I am, and I'm still a warrior for the cause."

"No, you're not. You're weak, Will. You can't pick and choose. Only God can do that."

What should he do?

Will had never been more scared or confused.

"I'm sorry. I'll do better." Will laid back on the bed, covering his eyes with his arm. "Just not the kids," he repeated. "Not the kids."

"Did you know that, if spiders all worked together, they could eat all humans in a year?"

Will blinked at the change of subject. "What?"

"It's true."

"If scientists gathered up every spider on Earth and weighed them, it is estimated that they'd have a combined weight of around twenty-five million tons. The Twin Towers had a total weight of about one and a half million tons, so the mass of all those spiders is equivalent to about sixteen Twin Towers."

Will wasn't sure what to think or say, so he settled on, "Oh."

"Fascinating, isn't it?"

Will was still bewildered. "Sure."

"In fact, spiders are all around you all the time. Some studies show that you're never more than four feet away from a spider. Just think, one is probably staring at you right now, its black, glistening eyes sizing you up, wishing his friends would come so they could gang up and devour you, tiny bite by tiny bite. They could, you know. It would only take about two thousand of them to consume you in a day's time."

"Why are you telling me this?"

Jaime sighed, a drawn-out exhalation of breath. "Because there's a moral to this story, Will. Don't you get it? The moral is that the weak can outnumber the strong. The few overtake the many. The improbable can become possible when the devoted join forces and work together. You get it now?"

Will nodded, even though he knew Jaime couldn't see him. "Yeah. You know, you missed your calling. You really should have become a preacher."

Jaime laughed, the sound going on and on. "That's funny you should say that because I *am* becoming a preacher."

Will sat up in surprise. "You are?"

"Oh yes," Jaime said, his voice more a whispering hush. "I'll baptize the unholy, inspire warriors to kneel at my alter and worship with me, to me."

The hair on the back of Will's neck raised in alarm. "Worship *to* you? You're not God."

"Yes, I am, Will. Don't you see? I was born from the blood of a preacher man, baptized on his knee. I was raised for a single mission, and only death will stop me from achieving it. There are those who wish to stop me, punish me, nail me to the cross of man's law. Not God's law. *My* law. Sound familiar?"

Will pulled the phone away from his ear as the roar of the last two words pierced his sensitive eardrum.

Jaime was insane. He was either joking or insane. And the hell of it was, Will couldn't tell the difference.

Did that make him insane too?

"Um, Jaime, I need to go."

He did. For so many reasons he couldn't even articulate.

But before he tapped the button to end the call, Jaime said, "Yes, you do, William Hoult. You very much need to go."

The lights went out, creating a darkness so complete that Will froze where he sat. He fumbled with his phone, but it slipped out of his suddenly damp fingers.

Creeeeak.

Every single cell in Will's body responded to the sound that was little more than a hiss. He scrambled backward, falling off the bed in his haste.

Spiders.

All he could think of was the tons and tons of spiders that had to be scurrying all around him. In the old carpet. Under the bed. In the cracks of the wall and the ceiling. In the—

Something whispered across his skin.

Will screamed, and he tried to run, tried to hide, but the darkness was so disorienting that he only turned in circles. His gun. Where was his gun?

"In the name of the Father…"

Will whirled, trying to find the source of the voice.

"…and the Son…"

He began to cry, deep, chest-rending sobs that shook his entire body. Where was his gun?

"…and the Holy Spirit…"

He lunged in the direction he thought the bed was in, but only landed on the floor. He began to crawl, his fingers clawing at the carpet. Try as he might, he didn't make it very far.

The hand that gripped his hair yanked his head back so

far that his neck cracked and popped, the roots ripping out of their protective follicles.

"...for dust thou art..."

The blade of the knife was cold against his throat, then hot as it took its first bite.

Will screamed, but no sound escaped. Only a gurgle as he swallowed a mouth full of blood.

"...and unto dust shalt thou return..."

He thought about the girl, wondered if he looked as terrified as she did. Had she pissed her pants as he was doing now? Had she mentally begged him for her life, even as that life leaked out of her?

I'm sorry, his mind screamed. *Please forgive me.*

Was he asking for forgiveness from the girl? From God? Or the man who was taking his life?

Lips pressed to his ear as the knife moved to his chest, the very tip breaching his skin. As it drove deeper, Jaime whispered one last word.

"Amen."

31

I blinked as my eyes adjusted from the green of the night vision goggles, then I blinked some more when I tapped the app to turn the lights back on.

The place was a mess. That didn't matter. It would be even messier soon.

I took off the bloody rubber gloves that had grown damp on my hands. Dropping them into a plastic bag, I wiped my sweaty palms on the disposable white jumpsuit I wore before slipping into a new pair, snapping them in place.

I needed to be careful. Much more careful than I'd previously been.

But I couldn't think about the past and the mistake I'd made. I couldn't regret the momentary joy of licking the tears from Sandy Ulbrich's face, although Grandfather wouldn't be pleased at my lack of willpower.

"Devil's in the details," he'd often told me.

The mistake could be fixed, though. It was always a good idea to have a hacker on the payroll. After I spoke to Phil, I didn't think he'd have any trouble deleting my DNA results from the appropriate databases.

If I could ever get ahold of the man, that was.

I closed my eyes, feeling the anger build. People were so trying, and I cursed myself again for not focusing more time on honing my own hacking skills. I was a fair hacker and could break through many firewalls, but not the ones I most wanted to break through.

That was Phil's job, and until then, I'd just have to be extra careful about sharing my DNA with the world.

It was passion that had made me do it, taste her tears. Passion and the joy of doing God's work that had precipitated that poor decision. A man couldn't be faulted for his good work, could he?

But I knew there were few who would see it that way. Few who could take off their blinders long enough to view the world as men like Kent Strickland and Tyler Haldane, like my grandfather, had been able to. Like I did.

There were many others, I knew, who also shared my view but were too afraid of modern law to do more than type 160 characters at a time on places like Twitter and in forums, spouting their truths behind the cloak of anonymity.

I wished to change that. I wished to reach out to those who felt muzzled by society, bring them into the light of day to stand together as one so that the vile disbelievers would cower...would learn...would see the truth and kneel down in gratitude to me as I showed them the way to salvation.

Couldn't they see that?

Couldn't they see the overpopulation that was draining Mother Earth? Couldn't they see the liberal thinking that had turned the people from the church? See the way modern women were destroying their children one day at a time? Feel the heat of climate change and do more than toss a plastic bottle into a recycling bin, thinking they were making a difference?

No. Not yet, I knew. That was why I needed to be careful,

leave no more traces of my DNA until the day I too could step into the light and preach the word of God to the masses.

The world needed a good shaking. An earthquake that was beyond all measure.

It needed a storm strong enough to wash away the sin.

It needed me.

I was the storm. The storm brewing on the horizon, gathering strength as I gathered latent heat and energy from those who believed. Those who were willing to do. Those who didn't cower in the face of the tasks set before them.

In disgust, I kicked Will in the face, then kicked him again just because it felt good to do so.

He had failed me, but it wasn't fury at his betrayal that brought my foot back to kick him a final time. It was fury at myself.

How had I not seen this coming? How had God failed to put the right men in my path? How had he not opened my eyes to the treachery that was bearing down on me?

It was those questions that boiled and churned in my gut.

It was...fear. Yes, I could say that word now.

"I was afraid," I said aloud to the man on the floor, bending low so that I could look into his vacant eyes as I said the words that had been burning in my soul.

I would never say them again.

Didn't Jesus Himself lose His faith as He hung on the cross, turn His eyes from His Father, ask, "Why have you forsaken me?"

Yes, he did, and I stood in this depressing motel room and raised my face to the heavens to ask the same question. "Why have you forsaken me?"

My phone rang, and I wasn't even all that surprised to see Phil's name come up on the screen.

I smiled, raised my face to the heavens in gratitude for this blessed sign before accepting the call and lifting the phone to my ear. "Perfect timing, Phil. Tell me that you have what I asked for."

There was a stuttering silence, followed by, "Yes, I have it. Where, um, can we meet?"

Meet?

I looked at Will's body. "Sorry, I seem to be indisposed at the moment. Load it onto the secure server as I requested."

"I...I...I..."

What was with all the stuttering nonsense today?

"Speak!"

And why was he so nervous?

"I need to meet with you, point out some, um, things that you'll find interesting."

I pulled the phone away from my ear and looked at the screen. I'd been on the call for twenty-four seconds. Not that time mattered in this digital age.

I knew immediately what had happened. Phil was betraying me, betraying the cause. After our last meeting, our only meeting, when I deposited him in that remote location, I knew he hoped to never see me again.

The coward.

Hollywood still tried to make their flock believe that it took sixty seconds to trace a call. I called bullshit on that. Ma Bell had gotten savvy and traces happened near instantaneously. Grandfather told me that, and I believed him. I believed everything he told me. He loved me.

"He's dead," I told Phil as I started moving. "You just killed him, you know that? You just killed your father." I ended the call, then texted the damn hacker a picture of his father handcuffed to a radiator that had seen better days, adding, *If you don't follow orders within the next 60 mins, he's dead.*

Kevin Rossway was a mess too. But alive. For now.

He had refused to be taken the easy way, and I'd been forced to shoot him in the shoulder and haul him to a secure location to use as leverage. From what I could ascertain, Phil's father was the only person in the world the hacker cared about.

Not waiting for a response, I powered off the device and popped the SIM card out for good measure. I had work to do and very little time in which to do it. I couldn't get caught. Not now. Not before the message was sent.

Dipping a finger in Will's blood, I wrote a single word on the wall before stripping off those gloves and pulling on a new pair. It wasn't how I'd envisioned it, but it would do.

More quickly now, I searched the body, taking Will's identification and the phone I'd purchased. I also took the cash, dropping the empty wallet onto the floor.

Moving to the door that adjoined this room to the next, I stepped from Will's room to mine, keeping my feet carefully planted on the plastic I'd laid down on the dingy carpet before placing a final call to the bastard.

Had he felt me on the other side of the door, so close? Had he shivered as I told him the story of the spiders, not knowing I was the one spinning the web?

I hoped so. I hoped his skin had crawled and shivers had raced up his back in the final moments before my knife ripped his head nearly off his neck.

Stripping out of the disposable suit, gloves, paper cap and shoe covers, I changed into a pair of tennis shoes that actually fit instead of being two sizes too big.

No DNA.

No shoeprint.

Devil's in the details, boy.

As I pulled a hat down low onto my forehead, then yanked up the hood of the jacket I wore, I added an ugly pair of horn-rimmed glasses to my face. Tugging on the leather gloves was as necessary to combat the cold weather as they were for fingerprint coverage.

I'd already checked the surrounding area for cameras and blocked all that I could see. Grabbing my laptop, I stuffed it in my backpack. Killing the lights of the entire hotel had been brilliant. I added the night vision goggles to the pack, then shoved all the dirty plastic on top of it all.

I had to go.

Checking my watch, I was pleased with my efforts. One minute and twenty-seven seconds was probably my new record. I was out the door, my ears alert for any hint of a siren.

But all was quiet as I jogged across the parking lot and into the forest beyond.

Something howled in the distance, and I was tempted to howl back.

A small laugh escaped me instead, then another, then more.

Devil's in the details, boy.

Oh, how I missed him.

Oh, how glad I was that he was gone.

Oh, how happy I was to take his place. Expand his mission. Preach to the world.

I jogged the entire two miles, not stopping until I tossed my pack into the passenger seat of the car I'd stolen just that morning. I changed out the plates again, just in case, before pulling out onto the empty street.

From there, I'd find a place to destroy any evidence, then I'd pay Phil's daddy a visit, take some of my frustration out on him.

It was all good. I had more faith than a mustard seed, so I knew everything was working out as it should.

That was the problem with this human form I inhabited. This form had fear, doubts, moments of uncertainty.

But if I believed in the good book, then I had to believe every single word of it.

If God so loved the world, so did I.

Oh, how I envied Noah and his ark. How I wished I could lift my hands and cause the rains to fall for forty days and forty nights, leaving only my people to safely join the animals to repopulate our earth.

One day, when this human form no longer served me and I was raised to the heavens, to my throne, I would do just that. Or maybe it would be fire this time. Or famine. I hadn't quite decided the most fitting punishment.

Maybe I would cast down a spell that forced women to clean toilets for all eternity. I snickered, clearly seeing those females in their business suits kneeling in front of a different type of throne.

Those thoughts kept me entertained while I went about my business. I fed the bloody evidence containing Will's and my DNA to a barrel of fire. His phone followed it inside, but my phone had one more chore to do before it met a similar fate.

Another hour, and I was at my last stop. I opened the cooler in the passenger floorboard and grabbed an ice-cold energy drink, popping the top. It burned my throat as it went down, but soon my heart was pounding with the additional strength I needed after an especially tiring night.

The house was but a shack, really. There was no heat, no power, no water. No anything.

The radiator was rusty. The man shackled to it was rustier still.

His lips were blue, the pile of blankets I'd tossed on him clearly not warm enough.

He was alive, for now, but he was at the end of his use. His message needed to be delivered first.

Powering on a different disposable phone, I checked the secure server one last time. It was empty. So disappointing.

Pointing the phone at him, I tapped the video app. "Hi, Daddy," I said to the man. "Your little boy failed you."

Kevin Rossway began to cry. For such a big, burly guy, the tears were especially funny to witness.

"You d-don't h-have to do this?"

I closed my eyes, irritation clouding my reasoning.

"I d-d-d-don't? T-t-tell me why n-n-n-not?"

I moved closer, watched him try to shrink away.

"I d-don't want to die."

"But you're the message. You were born for this moment. Rejoice in the knowledge that your name, Kevin Rossway, will be written in the history books."

"No…please."

He was still pleading, but behind the horror in his eyes was resignation. Deep in his very being, he knew I was right.

Sheep were slaughtered to serve the needs of man. Cows. Chickens. Animals of all kind.

How arrogant was the human race to believe that we two legged mammals were no different? Pure arrogance. Just one of the many negative traits I needed to correct.

After changing into a fresh set of disposable clothes, I took my time carving my message in his meat, letting his screams increase my energy as no caffeine-infused drink could ever do.

There was no rush this time. I could play as long as I wanted. And play I did.

When I was finished, I burned the clothes and all possible evidence. After leaving the shack's doors open so that the forest creatures could more easily access their next meal, I drove three hours before uploading the video onto my favorite forum.

Only ten bitcoin to watch the snuff film. A man had to finance his mission, after all.

As the money rolled in, I sent a message to Phil Rossway, letting him see what his betrayal had caused.

After that, I reset the phone, took out the SIM card, and tossed it all into the lake. As it sank, I yawned. I needed some sleep.

But not yet. I had more to do before I could close my eyes.

Devil's in the details, indeed.

32

Winter gave Noah a dirty look as he opened the pastry box filled with a mix of donuts, bagels, and yes, chocolate croissants.

"No," she told him in a stern voice. "Take that away from me this instant." She was still pissed at how out of shape she'd been while chasing Phil Rossway through the woods.

Noah wiggled his eyebrows. "I'll work the calories off you later tonight."

She forced her scowl to deepen, although she found it hard not to laugh. He was just so goofily adorable. And the croissants did smell awfully good.

Summoning all of her willpower, she pointed a finger at him. "Get thee behind me, Satan."

He wiggled his eyebrows again. "Mmm, doggy style. One of my favorite positions."

She couldn't help it. She laughed this time, then caved and broke off a small corner of a croissant. But the moment it hit her tongue, she already knew she wanted more and took the whole thing, practically inhaling it in one bite.

"You're so bad for me," she groused as he held out the

box for her to take another. "I'm done." And miracle upon miracles, her willpower locked back into place and she turned her back on the pastries. She didn't even turn around when Noah pulled on her braid, giving three gentle tugs.

I. Love. You.

She smiled at their own personal code.

One tug meant, "I want sex." She got that single tug a lot.

Two tugs was a question. "You okay?"

They'd recently added the three tugs, and this was the first time he'd done it in their office.

"Gag," someone muttered, and Winter whirled around to see Sun Ming standing at the opening of her cubicle, glaring at them both. "You two need to get a room."

Was it that obvious?

"What did we do?" Noah asked while Winter just stared.

Sun waved her hand between the two of them, her nose wrinkled in distaste. "You two just reek of sex."

Unable to help herself, Winter rubbed her chin on her shoulder, giving her armpit a delicate sniff. Just deodorant and the scented lotion Noah particularly liked.

The big man laughed and thrust the pastry box out to Sun. "Here. Maybe a couple of these will sweeten your sour attitude." When the surly agent didn't take one, he did, popping it between his lips before closing the lid. "See you later," he said around the donut that was half in and half out of his mouth.

Winter was actually a little surprised by Sun's attitude that morning. Although naturally hostile and bristly as a porcupine, the agent had softened a little over the past year.

Emphasis on...a *little*.

"Can I help you, Agent Ming?" Winter asked, using her own icy tone.

"Thought you'd want to hear that Arkwell cut a deal."

Winter shouldn't have been surprised, but her eyes widened just the same. "Nathan?" she asked, just to be sure.

Sun rolled her eyes. "No, the sadistic son." She threw up her hands. "Of course the senior Arkwell. He got a sweet deal too."

It was Winter's turn to roll her eyes. "Did you really expect anything else?"

Sun crossed her arms over her chest. "A girl can hope that white privilege and money doesn't always win the day, but…" She shrugged.

Winter wanted to argue about that, but Sun wasn't wrong, unfortunately.

"What was the deal?" she asked instead.

A snort so loud that people turned their heads came out of the petite woman. "Pled down to a misdemeanor, so he got time served, a big fat fine, and three years of probation." Another snort. "Oh, and community service."

As much as she hated the thought of anyone getting off so easily, Winter was happy for Nathanial Arkwell's daughter, Maddie. The young woman had already experienced so much loss in her life. Her mother's death, and her brother's… whatever disorder his newest psychiatrist was calling it now. And though the former judge had made some terrible mistakes, he loved his daughter. It would be good for Maddie to have his solid presence in her life.

At least, Winter hoped that would be the case.

Who knew? After all, Nathan was also the father of a murderer, so perhaps nurture could trump nature where the brain was involved.

She needed to talk to Autumn about that more. Just thinking of her friend sent a flurry of excitement through her. With the plea deal, that meant Cameron Arkwell wouldn't be called to testify in his father's trial. It meant Winter could now schedule a visit.

"What?"

Winter blinked, realized she was already reaching for her phone, having completely forgotten that Sun was still standing there.

She gave her head a little shake. "Sorry, you just reminded me to do something."

"Do what?"

Dammit. Sun could be so infuriatingly abrupt.

"Something personal."

Sun narrowed her eyes. "My telling you about Nathan Arkwell's plea deal reminded you of something personal?"

What was this? An interrogation?

"Actually, you did." Winter pressed her lips together, wondering what would happen if she shared her desire to see the Arkwell son.

Would Sun laugh? Think she was crazy?

And why exactly did Winter care what the tiny scrap of an agent thought anyway?

She decided to toss it out, see where it landed. Test the waters and any other clichés that applied. She leaned back in her seat, crossing her arms over her chest. "I'm actually planning to interview Cameron Arkwell for a project I'm working on."

Sun's eyes were tiny slits. "What project?"

Winter was about to say "personal," but she was already in for a penny so she might as well make it a pound. "To discover what makes him tick."

"Why do you care about that?"

Gritting her teeth, Winter regretted bringing this up, but plowed on. "Because he is a young man with serious mental health issues, and I can't help but wonder if he'll be able to—"

"Give you some insights into your brother," Sun finished for her.

Was she really that obvious?

"Yes, that's right."

Sun took a step into her cubicle, leaned down, and lowered her voice. "Let me save you some time, Winter," she said, not unkindly. "If your little brother spent more than one day with Kilroy, he won't ever be the same again. And no matter how much research or wishful thinking, nothing will make it otherwise."

"But—"

"But nothing. This can't be sugarcoated, Winter. The brother you knew is dead. He died thirteen years ago and whatever thing inhabits his body now will only hurt you in the end. Whether he is mean or simply pathetic, emotionally or physically, it will hurt you, and you'll end up blaming yourself, thinking you should have had some superpower to make it different."

Winter wanted to punch the woman, but she was glued to her seat. Because, somewhere deep inside herself, she knew what Sun was telling her was true. Justin would be different. There was little doubt about that. But did that mean she shouldn't reach out to him? Try to help him? Do…something?

She lifted her chin. "I appreciate your honesty, Sun, but I can't just turn my back so easily, and I'll do anything I can to help or at the very least understand Justin better. And if spending a half-hour or so with a convicted felon helps me do that, then I don't see the harm."

Sun took another step closer. "You can't see the harm because you refuse to see the truth. Douglas Kilroy was a murdering bastard who used religion to make himself feel better about killing innocent people, including your parents. You know how easy it is for a predator to groom a child. They do it online, in person. It can take minutes or days."

Winter wanted to cover her ears. Sun was right, she didn't want to see this, to hear.

Sun went on. "Kilroy had him for a long time, Winter. We don't know how long, and we don't know where he was or who he was with when Kilroy wasn't around. He could have handed him over to someone even worse. Why wouldn't he? Don't you think someone with a sadistic nature would find it amusing to watch his victim suffer even more?"

"Stop." Winter held up both hands, like she was warding off a physical blow. "Just stop. You aren't telling me anything I don't already know."

Sun just shook her head. "And yet you're going to meet with Cameron Arkwell and soak up all of his bullshit like a thirsty little sponge? He's a liar, and you think he'll just spill the truth and give you real-life advice on how to deal with your psychopath brother? I never thought you were that dumb."

Without another word, Sun turned on her heel and walked away.

Winter could do nothing but listen to her heels as the sound of their clicking faded down the hall.

Sun was right. God, she hated to admit that, and she'd never say the words out loud. But the woman had hit every nail in its very center, driving each and every syllable straight into her heart.

And if Sun was right, then Aiden was right as well.

Her jaw hurt from where she gritted her teeth. She didn't want them to be right. None of them.

She wanted a miracle.

She wanted Justin to be happy and sane. She wanted him to have escaped Kilroy's hold intact.

Some people did.

Human beings were highly resilient and could persevere in spite of tragedy. She did. Many other people did too.

Was her brother one of them like she desperately hoped?

Turning to face her computer, Winter dropped her head into her hands.

Would a sane and happy brother leave her cryptic emails and reminders of a time when he had wanted to hurt her? Would he decapitate rats and leave bloody messages on the wall of their childhood home?

She knew the answer, but she just didn't have it in her to brush him off without at least trying to get through to him. And the only thing she could do right now was to prepare for their eventual meeting. Because she felt sure that day was coming. Soon.

Picking up the phone, she dialed the number of the prison where Cameron Arkwell was being kept and requested a meeting with the convict for the next morning.

Of course, Arkwell didn't have to see her. He could simply deny the request and that would be that.

She didn't think he would. He would be curious, probably desperate for some company, longing for someone to torture yet again, even if it was only emotionally this time.

After being told that someone would be in touch to confirm the time, if Arkwell approved, Winter hung up the phone. There really wasn't much else she could do.

It wasn't much, but it was something. And sometimes, the little things meant everything.

She just didn't know if that would be good or bad.

33

The past twenty-four hours had been shit, and Aiden Parrish had only left the FBI building long enough to sleep for a bit, shower, and change. He'd been guzzling coffee since, but it wasn't the caffeine that forced him to stuff his trembling fingers into his pockets. It was the sudden adrenaline rush he was trying to hide.

Ryan O'Connelly's face looked as grim as his own as he pulled up the video he'd found posted on some deep web forum only a few minutes ago. There would be no need to try to identify the victim. That much had been spelled out quite clearly.

This man's son, Phil Rossway, is a traitor to the cause. He sentenced his own father to death, and the execution was carried out by God himself. Burn in hell, Kevin Rossway, for spawning a traitor. Ten bitcoin to witness justice being served. #snuff #justiceprevails #execution #iamthestorm

Even as Aiden's eyes widened in surprise at how many bitcoin had been earned in the past hours—sixty damn thousand—Aiden concentrated on the last hashtag. *I am the storm.* And even as O'Connelly looked up at him, waiting for his nod to go on, Aiden hesitated. Did he really want to see this? Have one more horrible thing burned into his brain?

He was sleeping less and less, drinking more and more. Guilt and anxiety were poor bedfellows best left to drown in a cup. Not that he couldn't handle it. He was handling everything just fine. He just needed to solve this damn case so he could take a day or two off.

He gave O'Connelly the nod, then braced himself as the video began to play, forcing his face to remain carefully neutral while he watched Phil Rossway's father being killed.

This wasn't an execution.

This was a slaughter.

And the man wielding the knife was enjoying his work.

Once it was over, Aiden said, "Play it again." This time, he didn't take his eyes away from the killer.

The man wore a white disposable jumpsuit that grew redder and redder as the minutes passed. The hood covered his hair and was tied so tight around his face that only a small circle for his eyes remained open. Dark glasses covered those eyes, gloves covered the hands.

There wasn't even a millimeter of the killer left open to examine. No hair color. And he hadn't spoken a word, so there were no verbal clues left either.

He looked to be about six feet tall, and his body shape was difficult to distinguish under the heft of the billowing suit.

"We need to find out the brand of that suit, see if we can locate the point of purchase." But even as Aiden gave the order, he knew the possibility of finding the suspect that way was slim to none. They had to try, though.

"Screenshot the knife, blow it up for better examination."

The room itself left no clues. Paneled walls. Dirty wood floors. Rusty radiator. The killer had been careful to zoom in on only what needed to be shown.

"He's comfortable, and isn't afraid of being caught," Aiden

murmured. "He's arrogant, and his ego may end up being his downfall."

Aiden looked down at the official transcript from the call the killer had made to Phil Rossway's phone earlier.

Subject A: Perfect timing, Phil. Tell me that you have what I asked for.

Phil Rossway: Yes, I have it. Where, um, can we meet?

Even as Aiden read the response, he could feel the hacker's nerves. Was that what had tipped the suspect off?

Subject A: Sorry, I seem to be indisposed at the moment. Load it onto the secure server as I requested.

Phil Rossway: I...I...I...

Yes. The stuttering, the hesitation had been the tipoff. They should have coached Rossway better before they'd instructed him to call. They should have gone over every possible scenario over and over.

Kevin Rossway's death was Aiden's fault, he knew. It was his fault because he'd rushed something that had no business being rushed.

Guilt tore at him, much like the knife that had torn at Kevin Rossway's body. God, he needed a drink.

Subject A: Speak!

Phil Rossway: I need to meet with you, point out some, um, things that you'll find interesting.

Subject A: He's dead. You just killed him, you know that? You just killed your father.

Phil Rossway had been nearly incoherent when they received the text message shortly after. He'd identified the man in the text picture as his father. The man had a wound high on his shoulder, and Aiden already knew it was the source of the blood splatter in Kevin Rossway's home.

The message had read: *If you don't follow orders within the next 60 mins, he's dead.*

Rossway had tried, screaming over and over that he needed a computer and that White Ghost, as the man had instructed him to call him, had wanted contact information on every police officer and detective in Virginia. He also wanted contact information on every FBI agent.

Rossway had been in the process of hacking the FBI system when they'd come pounding at his door. Ava Welford had come in to assist, generating a false report with false information to upload to the remote server White Ghost had indicated.

The ruse clearly hadn't worked.

Aiden knew that for a fact because the father had been killed anyway. Or, had White Ghost killed the man for spite?

He'd already been in contact with the local police departments, asking them to help cover all the fake address locations. If White Ghost showed up at one of the addresses, they'd have him.

Maybe.

"What do we do next?" O'Connelly asked, and Aiden just stared at the man, trying to sort through all of his options.

"We don't tell Phil Rossway about his father. Not yet. We need the sketch artist drawing of White Ghost nailed down first."

That had to be the priority.

They also needed to find the more accurate location of where the suspect's cellular device had been. Aiden picked up the phone and called Ava Welford's extension.

"Welford," she said, her voice sounding tired.

"Update."

The woman didn't need to ask who was speaking or what kind of update was needed. She and her team had been working to pinpoint White Ghost's exact location. The man had enough technological savvy to have bounced his cell around from tower to tower. It wouldn't save him from being pinpointed, but it would slow them down.

"We have three possible locations left, pinpointed down to just under a mile."

Christ. That didn't help much. And did it really matter?

White Ghost would have been long gone by then, and the only advantage would be to comb the space he'd evacuated with a fine-tooth comb, hopefully find a nice juicy thumbprint that would lead them straight to the bastard.

"Okay. Let me know what you find."

He tossed the phone onto the cradle, then picked it back up and called the extension of the bureau's lead sketch artist.

"Where are you with the Rossway case?"

"Hello, Agent Parrish," came the overly cheerful response. "I hope you're having a wonderful day too."

Aiden always thought artists were temperamental, but Jana White—not to be confused with Vanna White, she always added to her introductions—was irritatingly cheerful.

"Fabulous," he deadpanned. "What's the status?"

"Well…" he heard typing in the background, "if you'll look at your email in three…two…" Aiden gritted his teeth, "one, you'll see for yourself."

"Thanks, Jana. You're a peach." He actually managed to make the words sound like he gave a shit and was rewarded with a cheerful laugh. He hung up on the sound, then pressed his palms into his eyes.

Allowing himself only five seconds of this very unpersonal personal time, he dropped his hands and moved to his laptop, opening the lid. He felt O'Connelly's eyes on him as he accessed his email and clicked on his newest message.

Heart beating faster, he waited for the large file to load.

Then he simply stared at it.

A young man, clean shaven, with black hair and vivid blue eyes stared back.

Aiden heard O'Connelly's chair scrape against the floor, he felt the man move to stand behind him. Heard him ask a question he couldn't comprehend.

He couldn't breathe. His chest hurt from a surge of anxiety so intense, he thought for a moment he might be having a heart attack.

"Know 'em?" O'Connelly asked.

The question broke the spell, and O'Connelly jumped out of the way as Aiden pushed his chair back from the table, nearly overturning it in his haste.

Without a word, he headed to his office, his mind screaming, *No, no, no.*

He found the file, pulled out the picture, laid it on his desk.

Stared and stared.

It couldn't be. It shouldn't be.

But it was.

Pulling out another folder filled with random pictures, Aiden placed the one on his desk in with the rest. Then he was out the door, his mind still screaming, *No, no, no.*

Jabbing his thumb at the down button of the elevator, he stared at the seam of the doors until they opened.

"Oh...hi," Winter Black said, looking startled as he barged in before waiting to see if anyone needed to get off.

Christ.

Looking into her vivid blue eyes, he was filled with too many emotions to name. "Hi," he managed only because he was able, just barely, to lock every single one of those emotions away as he jabbed the button for the basement floor.

"Are you okay?" she asked.

Okay, maybe he hadn't managed to lock them away completely successfully. "I'm good. You?"

She smiled, although the movement of her lips seemed hesitant. "Yes. I…" she blew out a breath, "I scheduled an appointment to speak with Cameron Arkwell, and he approved my request for the meeting."

Aiden narrowed his eyes, trying to process her statement. "Why would you do that?"

Winter's hands went to her braid of black hair, and Aiden's own hand clamped down on the folder he held.

"With the messages from my brother," she licked her lips, "I was thinking it might help me to help him when we finally meet to better understand how his mind works. By interviewing Cameron Ark—"

"No!"

The word was closer to a roar, and Winter took a step back, her hands coming up as if to shield herself from his rage. Anger quickly replaced the surprise on her pretty face. "You don't get to tell me what to do!" she shouted back, this time with a finger poking at his chest.

The door opened, and someone was about to step in, but Aiden pointed at the man. "Not now." Hands up, the man stepped back, and the door slowly closed. Aiden held his thumb on the "stop" button, ignoring the warning sound that rang out.

Winter pulled at his arm, trying to force him to release it.

He wanted to shake her. "Winter, listen to me." He didn't know how to finish. He couldn't do this now. Not in his state of mind and certainly not in an elevator. This wasn't the time or place. For him, or for her.

Using both hands, she pulled his arm away, and the irritating loud sound stopped, and the cart began to move again. "I'm done listening to you. I'm not a child." She jabbed at the button for the next floor.

"Winter, I've got something to—"

The door dinged, slid open, and she slipped out. He watched her stalk off and didn't even try to follow. Just as the door slid closed, she turned and lifted both hands to flip him off, blue eyes flashing.

Could he blame her? In the elevator mirror, he flipped himself off too.

He was sweating by the time he reached the basement floor. His head was pounding, his chest aching. He needed to gather himself.

Heading straight into the men's restroom, Aiden locked himself inside. He tossed the folder onto the back of the toilet and promptly threw up, heaving and heaving until nothing but bile hung in a long strand from his mouth.

It took a long time before he could straighten, and when he did, he staggered to the sink to splash cold water onto his face. He soaked a few paper towels and pressed them to the back of his neck.

Minutes later, he was breathing normally again. His face wasn't as pale. But he gave himself another few minutes to pull his shit together.

Straightening his tie, he smoothed down his suit jacket, and finger-combed his hair back into place. Taking a mint from his pocket, he tossed it into his mouth before picking up the folder and opening the door.

He was ready.

He hoped.

The cell in which Phil Rossway was being held would be considered a luxury suite by normal prison standards, but Aiden didn't want Rossway to be reminded in any way that he was being held as a prisoner. Instead of going inside the cell, he instructed the guard to bring the hacker to the small conference room, then went on in and poured them both a cup of water.

Phil Rossway looked as exhausted as Aiden felt when he walked into the room and took a chair.

"Any word on my father?" he asked.

"Not yet," Aiden lied without blinking.

Breaking the news would come later. Now, important matters needed to be settled.

"We appreciate your cooperation with the sketch artist," Aiden began. "I'd like you to now examine each of the pictures I lay out, see if you recognize any of them."

One by one, Aiden placed the random photos of random men on the table, placing the one he'd pulled from the other file somewhere in the middle.

"Him. That's White Ghost."

It hadn't taken more than a cursory glance for Rossway to tap the picture Aiden had already known he'd choose.

It had come from a folder inside a folder, really. A folder marked "Jaime Peterson," and the picture had been taken from the yearbook of Bowling Green High School.

The kid had offered the camera a small smile, but there was something in his blue eyes that caused the hair on the back of Aiden's neck to stand up.

His stomach churned some more.

He wasn't looking at the picture of White Ghost. He wasn't even looking at the picture of Jaime Peterson.

He was looking into the face of Justin Black.

34

Chelsey Jones hated her damned job. She didn't mind cleaning, and she didn't mind hard work, but people and their slobby ways just pissed her off.

But what pissed her off more was the memory of her deadbeat husband still snoring in bed while she'd fed the kids, gotten them off to school, taken the baby to the daycare that cost too much, then trudged into the job that paid too little.

"Disgusting bastard," she muttered as she picked up a used condom from the floor with a wad of toilet paper. The double layer of rubber gloves she wore didn't feel like enough protection from the pot smelling room and the nastiness left behind by the previous guest.

She snorted. Management made her call the asswipes "guests," like the no-tell motel she worked at was the freaking Hyatt instead of the flea-ridden place most *guests* used for only a couple of hours.

Well, except for the last room she'd cleaned. It had actually been spotless. The bed hadn't been slept in, the sinks and showers hadn't been used. If it hadn't been for the chair that had been pulled away from the table, she wouldn't have thought another soul had entered it since she'd cleaned it the day before.

"But that's not the typical guest at this fine establishment," she said, chuckling at her humor. Then she got excited when "Good as Hell" came up next on her playlist. Lizzo always made doing any chore much easier. So, for the next few minutes she tossed her hair and checked her nails while she got the room ready for the next guest.

She jumped when her radio squawked on her cart. "Chelsey, this is base. Report in. Over."

Chelsey snorted again, adding an eye roll for extra measure. Management of this fine establishment had lost their freaking minds. They weren't soldiers on a battlefield. She thought about the condom and the other landmines she sometimes encountered and decided that maybe they were.

Playing along, she used her best military voice. "Base, this is Chelsey, reporting in. Over."

"Chelsey, add 316 to your list. Over."

Chelsey frowned and backed out of the door to look down the concrete walkway. Room 316 still had the "do not disturb" sign on its door. She reported this newsflash back to base, almost forgetting to add, "Over," at the end.

"They haven't paid, and it's hours past checkout. Knock and go in. If it's still occupied, call for backup. Over."

Sigh. If she hadn't still been wearing nasty gloves, she'd bonk herself on the forehead.

"Sure thing, base. Chelsey signing out."

"Base, over and out."

She almost corrected the manager. She'd learned while watching a documentary on the History channel that real military didn't use both "over" and "out," since the words were basically redundant. But she needed her job and the lead manager didn't think he could ever do no wrong, so she kept her knowledge to herself.

Finishing the current room, she applied a liberal dose of air freshener around the space, holding her breath until she could escape onto the landing. If she didn't die from HIV or hepatitis, her lungs would surely one day explode from all the chemicals she used on a daily basis.

Pushing her cart down to 316, Chelsey pulled on a fresh pair of gloves and knocked on the door. She waited for ten seconds before knocking again. After another wait and another knock, she used her master key to access the room.

"Housekeeping," she called as she slowly opened the door. "Anyone here?"

Once, she'd done this very thing, only to find a man masturbating on the bed. The even more dumbfounding thing was that he wasn't as equally mortified to have been found in such a position. Instead, he bobbed his eyebrows and asked if she'd be willing to "finish him off."

She really hated people.

As she opened the door, it took her mind a few seconds to process exactly what she was seeing.

Blood.

So. Much. Blood.

The air was thick with it too, and she gagged as she inhaled, practically tasting the copper scent on her tongue.

"Aaaaaa…" She tried to scream, but the sound got stuck in her throat.

She once watched a documentary on a medical channel, and she learned why we make the stereotypical scared expression when something frightens us. It was interesting. Our eyes grow wide so we can see the danger coming, our mouths and noses flare so we can bring in the needed oxygen we need to run and escape.

Chelsey could only imagine the face she was making now,

even after the initial shock of seeing the nearly decapitated body on the floor. What allowed her to finally scream, finally turn and run, was the cross drawn on the wall in what could only be the man's blood.

And the word. The single word written below it.

Judas.

MARIAH YOUNG CHECKED both locks on the hotel room she and her father were staying in, then lifted up on tiptoes to make sure the swinging bar latchy thing was closed all the way too. For good measure, she pushed the chair in front of the door then looked around for something else.

"Honey," her father said, "we're safe here. I promise."

Tears welled in Mariah's eyes, and she wanted to shout that she'd heard that lie before, that they were supposed to have been safe in their home with their new security system and look what happened!

But she didn't.

Her daddy looked too tired and sick to fight back. The doctor said the hole in his shoulder had gotten infected, so they'd had to get some medicine to make it better again.

On the way to the hotel from the hospital, they'd picked up take-out for dinner. Chinese was one of her favorites. Her father's too. But while she had gotten her normal orange chicken with noodles, her dad had only ordered a bowl of sweet and sour soup.

She watched him closely. Watched him labor to lift the spoon to his mouth, the lines on his face growing deeper.

"Let me help." Mariah sat on the side of the bed and took the hot plastic bowl from his hands, then carefully fed him one bite at a time.

She had to make him stronger. Make him better. She had

to do everything in her power to make him not die too.

What if he did die? What would happen to her?

Would she have to go to an orphanage, like Orphan Annie? Or go into the dreaded foster care system?

No.

She had grandparents who loved her. Aunts and uncles too. But as much as she loved them back, she didn't want to live with any of them. She wanted her family back. She wanted her mom. She wanted Sadie. She wanted her house and she wanted her bed.

"You okay, champ?" her father asked, and Mariah realized she was holding a spoon full of soup about six inches from his mouth. Making herself stop being stupid, she finished raising it, giving him his bite. With a wince, Timothy Young reached out and touched her hand. "Honey…talk to me. You know you can."

It was true. She knew she could talk to him. The problem was that the words refused to come into her brain. She was just too sad. Too afraid. Too lonely for her sister and mom, but she couldn't tell him that because it would make him sad too.

So, instead of talking about what was hurting her heart, she talked about school and how she didn't want to go back because she hadn't been able to study for the math test coming up before school broke for Christmas.

"I've already talked to your principal, honey. We agreed that, under the circumstances, you wouldn't have to go back until school starts back again in January."

The news was both good and bad. She really had been worried about the math test because she had to study extra hard in math. But that wasn't the real reason. The truth was that she was even more afraid of all the kids staring at her. Pointing. *That's the girl whose mom and sister were murdered.* She could almost hear the words being whispered.

At the same time, she was sad to miss all the Christmas fun. There was ugly sweater day, and pajama day, then her choir concert she was supposed to have a solo in. And the parties and presents. Mariah and her mom had already shopped for her teachers' gifts. What did she do now? Just throw them away?

But even while she was thinking such things, she felt terrible. Here she was all upset over some parties and presents when her mom and sister were dead and not even buried yet. The funeral was tomorrow, and she didn't want to go. But her Aunt Lisa had already brought her a new dress and new shoes and everything, so she guessed she'd have to.

She was a terrible person. Maybe she should have been the one who died. Sadie would never be worried about presents or people looking at her or going to a funeral if something terrible had happened to her.

It was all so confusing. Overwhelming. Mariah had never felt so much grief. And guilt.

She wished that she had just died too.

"Honey...?"

Mariah blinked, realizing she had tears on her cheeks. She rubbed her face with her arm, wiping them away before sniffing hard, trying to keep the rest at bay.

"Do you remember the therapist you saw that one time?"

She nodded slowly. The therapist she'd been so jealous of after Sadie had just about almost died. She really was a terrible person. "Yeah."

"What do you think about me making you an appointment to see her?"

Mariah just stared into her daddy's soup, then remembered she was supposed to be feeding him and gave him a bite.

When she didn't answer, he went on, "I think it's a good idea, and I think I'll see a therapist too."

That surprised Mariah. "You will? The same one?"

Tim Young smiled. "No. A grown-up one."

Mariah studied her father's face, trying to see if he was being serious. She could remember overhearing him and her mother fight about the therapy bills for Sadie, so learning that he'd be willing to pay for therapy now came as a surprise.

Maybe he really was serious. Or maybe he just thought there was something really wrong with her.

That didn't make her feel any better.

He swallowed the next spoonful of soup she gave him, then he closed his hand over hers. "That's enough for now, sweetheart."

She looked worriedly into the plastic bowl. He hadn't eaten very much, but he did look really tired and pale. She was tired too.

"Would it be okay if I took a bath?"

He actually looked relieved. "You need to eat first, sweetheart, then you can soak for as long as you want."

Mariah made herself smile and put the lid back on the bowl before climbing onto the other bed with her chicken and noodles. But like her father, she wasn't very hungry either and just kept pushing the food around, only taking a little bite when he looked over at her.

When she couldn't stand the thought of eating another bite, she closed the lid and set it on the table between them. Her dad was sleeping now, so she tried to be very quiet as she dug through the bags Aunt Lisa had brought them from the mall.

They'd needed everything new since they weren't allowed to go back to their house. It was a crime scene, her father had told her, so Aunt Lisa had bought them new shampoo and pajamas and clothes.

Mariah wrinkled her nose as she pulled out a bottle of

Johnson & Johnson shampoo and conditioner. She wasn't a baby, but when she opened the top and took a deep smell, she had to admit that the scent was comforting. Pulling the tags from the new pajamas, she took everything into the bathroom and started the water, making it extra hot.

It wasn't until she sat down, lowering herself under the water until her hair swirled all around her like a mermaid's that she allowed herself to really cry. Breaking back to the surface, she covered her mouth so her father wouldn't hear and just cried until all the tears disappeared. Then she washed her hair, left the conditioner on for a full two minutes like her mom taught her to do.

"You don't want a rat's nest in your hair, do you?"

That got her to start crying again. What other things had her mom taught her? What other things would her mother not be around to teach her in the future?

She knew about periods, but would she now have to ask her dad to buy her the stuff she'd need to deal with them? How embarrassing!

Mariah forced herself to stop thinking about that and think about something else. The problem was that nothing else in her life didn't involve her mom or her sister. It was kind of like that song that talked about wherever you go or do, I'll be there waiting for you. Or something like that.

She rinsed her hair and washed quickly, using the rough hotel towel to dry off before changing into the new pajamas. Unwrapping the second towel from her head, she squeezed the water out of the long strands. *"Don't rub or you'll get split ends."*

She couldn't even brush her teeth without hearing her mother's voice. *"Sing the birthday song three times to make sure they get all nice and clean."*

She couldn't escape it. Escape them.

They were like ghosts, but instead of saying "boo," they whispered things in her ear.

Fleeing the bathroom, she was glad to see that her dad was awake. He smiled at her as he flipped through the channels on the TV, stopping on the news. She groaned. Terrific.

"The body of a man found slain in a hotel room yesterday has been identified as William Hoult," the TV woman said with a wide smile on her face.

Mariah didn't want to even think about dead bodies, but her eyes were drawn to the screen. A picture of a man flashed up, and Mariah gasped.

"What's wrong, honey?" her father said, but his voice sounded very, very far away.

She just stared. She knew that man. It was him. The smiling salesman who'd been standing at the door, the door she hadn't been supposed to open. But she had forgotten. And she hadn't really realized that her mom had been serious about opening doors until they'd had that talk later that night.

Did that mean that everything that happened was her fault? Mariah had opened the door. Didn't they say that a vampire couldn't enter your house unless he was invited? Is that what Mariah had done, invited the evil in?

"Mariah!"

Her dad was getting up from the bed, calling her name, sounding very concerned. Mariah tried to look at him, tried to tell him that the man on the television was the same man who'd come knocking on their door that terrible day. And now, as she looked at him again, she realized he had the same dimple in his chin that the man in the ski mask had.

It was really him. The man who'd killed her mother and sister.

For the second time in only a few days, Mariah Young peed her pants.

35

Winter was still shaking with rage...and fear...and a sadness so deep she felt like her insides were being squeezed by a giant's hand. First Sun...then Aiden. What had that been all about?

Forcing her mind to release the emotions rattling around her brain following her run-in with the SSA, she blew out a deep breath and practiced an enhanced breathing technique she'd learned long ago. Five minutes later, it hadn't helped much, but she did feel more in control.

At least a little.

And now she was regretting having scheduled this meeting with Cameron Arkwell at all. What was she doing? Did she really think some rich judge's spoiled brat could give her insight into her little brother's mind?

Somewhere deep inside her, she'd known that the Arkwell kid and her brother would be nothing alike, but when Noah and Autumn hadn't tried to dissuade her from the meeting, she'd decided it wouldn't hurt and might even be interesting to see inside a sociopath's mind.

But one thing Winter had learned long ago was that

knowing what another was thinking wasn't always a good thing. Words could be as vicious as a knife.

In fact, studies suggested that the same part of the brain that lit up when a person was stabbed was the same part of the brain that lit up when someone was verbally abused. And it was well known that, in children, those who experienced verbal abuse and bullying at a young age had a different type of brain than did children raised in a loving home. Their left and right brains didn't connect and communicate in the same way, leaving them open to being abused later in life. Or becoming the abuser.

Even though Winter was no longer a child, words still hurt, and she was still aching from them, especially from the ones from Aiden. True, he didn't actually say much, but his tone and temper, his facial expression and body language had filled in the blanks.

Did he really think he could treat her like a child? Like the thirteen-year-old girl she'd once been?

As Winter paced in the stark reception area of the prison, her phone buzzed in her pocket. It was Noah: *Did you see the news? Will Hoult killed Dana and Sadie Young.*

Heart beginning to gallop in her chest, Winter paged to a search engine and pulled up the latest story. As she read, her knees weakened, and she sank into a nearby seat.

For a terrible moment, Winter had imagined how she'd felt if her brother had been the one to kill the mother and daughter. The thought hadn't really even surprised her that much because some part of her mind knew that any man raised by Douglas Kilroy would be capable of such a thing.

She continued to read about the body found in a hotel room and how little Mariah Young had recognized the man's driver's license photo on the news. Such a brave girl.

And so young. Younger than even Winter had been when she had faced a similar tragedy, although Winter had been lucky in one important sense. Back when she was thirteen years old, social media was only a baby beast. Today, it was a giant monster that could swallow a person whole, and Winter couldn't imagine surviving any type of tragedy during a time when news outlets were spouting the news before the blood even dried.

"Agent Black?"

Winter turned to the voice, pocketing her phone as she headed to where the guard was standing. "Yes."

"We've got Arkwell ready. Just need to do the security check, and we'll get you through."

Winter signed in, went through the appropriate checks, and didn't hesitate to walk into the room where Cameron Arkwell sat, his hands chained to a heavy table.

He licked his lips as she walked toward him, a slow drag of muscle over skin that left his lower lip unpleasantly damp. She kept her face carefully blank, refusing to let him affect her.

But his eyes. She'd forgotten how pale they were, and how they seemed to penetrate everything around him. Forgot the smirk that made his pretty face turn into a sneer.

"Hello, Cameron..." she purposely used his first name to remove the respect he'd glean if she'd used his last. "I'm Agent—"

"Winter Black." He ran his tongue over his lip again, even slower this time. "I know who you are. I know you."

Son of a bitch.

She played along, lifting her elbows to the table and planting her chin on her hand, feigning an expression of fascination. "You do? I'm flattered, but I'm really not here to talk about me. I—"

"You were made an orphan by The Preacher, and even as an agent of the big bad Federal Bureau of Investigation, you've still not been able to find your brother. Not very detective-y of you, is it, Agent Black?"

She didn't take the bait. "Where did it go wrong for you, Cameron?"

"For me?" He laughed. "It—"

"I'd imagine that when you were a little boy, killing frogs and kittens and small helpless creatures, that you had imagined a long life filled with multiple murders and records for most bodies buried on your thousand-acre estate." She waved a hand at him. "But here you are, in prison without a possibility for parole at the ripe old age of twenty-two, so I ask again, where did it go wrong?"

She'd hit a nerve. Good. Because at that moment, she didn't care.

Sure, she'd come into this room with the best of intentions, wanting to see inside of the mind of someone who was similar to her brother. Screw that. This bastard would only play with her if she used kindness and consideration to tap into his world. If she wanted to see the real Cameron Arkwell, understand how he ticked, she needed to piss him off. She could do that.

"It's funny. I had an ulterior agenda of meeting with you today, Cameron, but I honestly don't know what I was thinking." He licked his lower lip again, in that same suggestive manner, and she exploded, "Is that all you have?" She licked her own lip, giving it a quick swipe. "Is that the only play you have in your playbook? Look like a dick and watch all the girls go weak in the knees? Does that actually work?"

She was making him angry now. No, not angry. Embarrassed. Little Cameron Arkwell wasn't used to anyone standing up to him. He was used to his daddy judge and a shit ton of money having his back.

"Actually, I can get all the pussy I want."

She laughed, long and loud. "Not anymore. You better be

careful how you lick those lips now, because the only pussy you'll get in here comes with a set of balls."

He actually looked sick, which made her feel more than a little guilty for the jab, but she was in the position to use any means necessary. "Nobody's going to touch me."

She immediately backed down and took a deep breath. "I hope so, Cameron." She looked at him sincerely now. "I deeply hope so. Nobody deserves to be raped."

Something flashed across his features. Was that guilt? If it had been, it was probably one of the few times this sociopath had felt it. People like Cameron could experience the emotion of guilt, but it was weak, and it didn't deter them from doing whatever they had set out to do.

Still, something in her heart cracked open just a little. "I'm so sorry, Cameron, that your brain works this way."

His nostrils flared. "I don't need or want your pity."

"Then, don't take it, but I'm sorry all the same. You see, I'm worried about my brother. As you already know, he was taken from my family at a very young age. We don't know how he was raised, or by whom exactly, but I'm afraid, very afraid, that his mind is..." she looked deeply into Cameron's pale eyes, "like yours."

Cameron said nothing.

"And yes, I worry about him hurting people. I worry about what he has done and what he might do next, but what I worry about the most is what makes me so sad for you. With the type of brain you have, and the type of brain I fear my brother has, he and you will never be able to feel true joy. True happiness."

"I'm happy," he argued, pulling at his chains.

She gave him a sad smile. "But the feeling is so fleeting, isn't it, Cameron? Because in your mind, all emotions are fleeting. Guilt and empathy are fleeting, which means that happiness and hope are fleeting too."

He was quiet for a long time, and she watched an array of emotions flicker over his expression. It was interesting to watch, but it also deepened her sadness because this man before her would never be able to hold just one of those emotions for very long.

It wasn't fair, but it was what it was. And because his brain couldn't be fixed, and he could never be trusted to do the right thing, this was the only home he could ever have.

She looked around the room. At the block walls, the bars on the windows.

This was pointless. She'd hoped for strategies and tips on how to deal with her brother if he finally showed his face. No, not if. When. He would, she just needed to be mentally prepared for the meeting.

And she wouldn't be ready. She would never be ready. There would always be some part of her that would hope that he wasn't as bad as Aiden and Sun, and seemingly, everyone else feared.

Winter pushed to her feet. "I'll go now," she said softly. She felt his eyes on her as she walked toward the door.

"He'll only tell you what he thinks you'll want to hear."

She turned to face him. "Only?"

He smiled. And this smile appeared to be more genuine than any she'd ever seen on him. "Well, not only-only. He'll want to fuck with you, mess with your mind. He'll enjoy it. He's probably thinking about it right now, imagining ways to scare you, or worse, give you hope."

Winter couldn't help it, she shuddered. She didn't have to ask him what he meant.

Hope prolongs whatever torments us. Winter thought it might have been Nietzsche who had provided the world that quote.

Of course, hoping for something that *could* happen was smart. It was possible that she could win the lottery if she chose to ever buy a ticket. It was possible that she could rise in the ranks of the FBI if she worked hard enough.

But could she hope that her brother, who was tormenting her with emails and firecrackers, was emotionally stable? That was when hope became a torment, when it wasn't possible.

"What else, Cameron?" she asked, voice earnest. "What else can I expect? And how should I respond?"

He seemed to consider the question, and his face looked sincere when he answered. "Deep down, I think he wants to reach out to you, and he thinks that you can save him."

Hope rose inside her chest, swelled like a balloon inside her heart. "Really?"

Silence stretched and lengthened between them, then Cameron tossed his head back and laughed. "No, you stupid bitch. He's going to try to kill you."

Winter turned, pressed her thumb on the buzzer to have a guard let her out.

Cameron continued to laugh. "He's waiting and watching, just deciding how best to get the job done."

She continued to press the buzzer, and through the little window, a guard appeared and the sound of keys turning in the lock.

"He'll fuck you first," Cameron screamed, sounding on the edge of hysterical now. "He'll want a piece of you. He'll make you suck his dick."

Two guards rushed inside, and Winter fled into the hallway.

"He'll shove it in your ass." There were sounds of fists on flesh. "He'll cut a hole in your belly button and fuck you there too." His voice was breathless now, but it still carried down the hall. "He'll—"

The door slammed shut behind her with a loud *clank*, and she mercifully heard no more.

She didn't need to.

Shoulders ramrod straight, Winter walked to her car, mentally stomping hope into the ground with every single step she took. But the moment she was safely inside and the doors were locked, she wasn't able to stop the tears that flowed.

36

This was my favorite part.

The hunt.

The kill was fun too, but it didn't give me the rush that stalking my prey always provided.

It was the anticipation, I knew. I could feel it in my belly and my balls. It made me feel alive in a way I'd never known. The feeling was so powerful, observing those who didn't know they were being observed.

Just like God observed His peasants. Like a hawk observed the rabbits as it soared through the sky. Waiting to strike. To kill. To devour. To move on as it continued the circle of life, eliminating the weak.

I blended in perfectly. My black hair was a neutral brown now, thanks to a temporary color, and contacts made my blue eyes just a shade darker than milk chocolate. The artfully applied beard made me appear to be years older. The brown suit was as boring as the wall of the church in which I sat.

The little old lady beside me clutched a Bible in her lap, dabbing at tears as the preacher man spoke in front of the two coffins. The elderly woman was part of my disguise. That part was always simple. I just waited near the handicap parking area, waiting for someone who looked feeble to drive up. I offered a gallant, helpful arm, and almost like magic, I was no longer a single man walking into a building by himself. I was the son of a sweet old lady.

I reached over and squeezed her hand, and she gave me an appreciative look in return. People were so simpleminded. This was almost too easy, eliminating most of the fun.

My grandfather would be so pissed right about now. The minister was talking about celebrating life, not warning of fire and brimstone to the people in the congregation.

"Preachers these days need them a lesson or two too, sonny," he'd say. "They actually need more, because they're a part of the problem. Instead of leading the flock to Jesus, they're leading them astray. The heathens."

I believed him. I believed it all.

"Your journey will be difficult, young man," he told me once. "There will be those who rise to fight against you just as they rose to fight Jesus's message. They'll try to hang you on the cross, drive stakes into your hands. Expect it."

He was right. I knew there were those waiting to take me down.

"And when the day comes and I'm gone and you're strong, you'll step into my shoes and finish what I started."

Well, Grandfather was just a little off that time. Sure, I did step into his shoes, but I wasn't finishing what he started, I was expanding it. Multiplying it. Grandfather didn't have the vision I had. Couldn't see all the possibilities like I did.

He would be proud of that, though.

"I pray that Dana's and little Sadie's memory will be an inspiration to each and every one of us and that their deaths will stand to remind us that not a single one of us knows when it will be our time to leave this sin-filled world."

I almost snickered but managed just in time to keep the sound in my throat. I coughed to clear it.

Not a single one of us? The preacher was wrong. I knew, almost to the second, the time two people in this church would leave this sin-filled world.

My gaze strayed to the front pew, and to the man and little girl who sat there, both of their shoulders shaking from the sobs tearing them apart. It was too bad the girl wasn't a boy. If she was a boy, she might make me a good protégé, just like I'd made a good protégé for my grandfather.

But she was a girl. Useless to me. Anger turned me to stone. It was an abomination that those two sinners continued to rob the air of the truly just. It offended me deeply to have stepped on the carpet where their feet had been allowed to step.

"Are you okay, dear?"

The old woman startled me back to the moment, and I realized my hands had tightened into fists. Sweat dripped down my back and from my armpits. I forced my entire body to relax, then smiled down into the concerned face.

"I'm sorry," I whispered, "but my stomach is wanting to embarrass me, and I was trying to hold it back." I gave her a conspiratorial wink. "Trust me, you'll want me to hold it back."

She tittered, raising her lily-white handkerchief to cover her mouth. Then she dug in her purse and pulled out a damn anti-farting pill bottle and tapped two giant white tablets into her palm. "Chew these, dear. It'll help."

I could do nothing else besides pop the chalky medicine into my mouth and try not to gag at the flavor. I couldn't leave the service early because that would call attention to me. That wouldn't do.

"Thanks," I whispered around the mush in my mouth. "I feel better already."

She seemed pleased and returned her attention to the service. I did too, mentally correcting the preacher as he droned on and on about coming together to say goodbye to the faithful pair.

Blah. Blah. Blah.

I was careful to keep my gaze away from the father and sister. It upset me too much.

But I would get my revenge. I'd delivered a bug to Tim Young's smartphone by pretending to be a charity that just needed him to tap a link to accept the donation made in his wife and daughter's name. Easy peasy.

The bug gave me total control of the device. I listened to his calls, read his messages, watched him and the girl through the little camera.

Tim Young had many good friends, and one had offered to let him and little Mariah stay at their cabin on Westhampton Lake. The location was remote, the friend had promised, and "very secure." Not a soul would know where they would be staying.

The friend was wrong.

I knew. And I'd already been there, walked every inch of the place.

Tonight, I would finish what Will Hoult had failed to do.

"This afternoon," the preacher was saying, "I want to remind you of the day when Jesus hung on the cross. He didn't hang there alone. No, two others hung beside him. One of them mocked Jesus, but the other one believed. When the believer asked Jesus, "Will you remember me?" our Jesus responded with this." The preacher threw up his hands. "Today, you will be with me in paradise. You will be with me in heaven."

Finally, something this preacher man and I could agree on.

Tim and Mariah Young would be meeting Jesus today.

37

Noah stifled a yawn with the back of his hand. As he and Miguel neared the end of their bumpy journey down the narrow gravel road, Noah spotted the rear fender of a forest green pickup. From all the time he'd spent reading and rereading interview notes and information collected from Kent Strickland and his father, Noah knew right away that the pickup belonged to George Strickland.

Glancing to Miguel in the driver's seat, Noah raised a hand to gesture to the truck. "That's his vehicle. He's home."

Miguel nodded as they slowed to a stop in front of a hulking, two-story farmhouse. "Here's hoping he's not going to be as obstinate as his kid."

Noah almost groaned. Interviewing Kent Strickland had been about as helpful as consulting with a literal rock. For a man who was quite clearly guilty of the crime for which he'd been charged, Strickland sure liked to pretend there was a chance he was innocent.

His lawyer had filed one motion right after another to delay the trial, and Strickland was being kept in protective custody—right alongside the snitches and dirty cops that otherwise would be eaten alive by the general prison population. It pissed Noah off.

Flakes of black paint fell from the front door as Noah knocked on it a little harder than was absolutely necessary. He knocked a second time, then a third. Where was the man?

"I'm coming. Hold your horses."

George Strickland was tucking his shirt into his pants as he opened the door. His hair was freshly combed and still wet from a shower. He glared at them as he adjusted his belt. "You're early."

Noah checked his watch. They were, by three whole minutes. "My apologies. Sorry to rush you, but we appreciate you taking the time to see us."

Strickland held the door open. "Don't know why you're here. I've told you people everything I could possibly know about every little detail of my and Kent's life. I can't see how I'll have anything else to add."

Noah tapped a folder in his hand. "Is there a place where we can sit? We won't take much of your time. We have a different line of questions for you, and I'm hoping you can help us with a different case we're working on."

Strickland looked confused. "I don't see how, but come on, we can sit at the kitchen table. Got lemonade and sweet tea. Choose your poison."

Miguel chose tea, as did Noah and Strickland himself. It was actually really good. Most people made it too syrupy sweet or left it too bitter. Strickland scored a point for getting it just right.

"Thank you. This is very good."

The older man seemed pleased. "My mother's recipe. Calls for sugar mixed with honey. Glad you like it."

"I do, very much." He took another long swallow. "As I was saying at the door, we have another case that we hope you can help us with."

"And as I said at the door, I doubt I'll be able to help you, but shoot."

Noah pulled out the high school photo of Jaime Peterson. "Do you know this person?"

Strickland squinted at the picture, then pulled a pair of bifocals from his shirt pocket and slipped them on his face. "Oh yeah. That's Jaime Patterson." He frowned. "No, that ain't right. Richardson? No. Peterson." He snapped his fingers. "That's right. Jaime Peterson. Why are you asking?"

Noah ignored the question. "Can you tell me what you know about him? How you got to know him? The timeline."

Strickland scratched his temple. "Well, the boys were in high school and they'd all come out to the farm together to shoot guns and work on tactical kind of training. Told me they were going to join the service when they got old enough and they were practicing now so they'd be standouts." Strickland frowned, his eyes growing sad. "I guess they stood out in a different way."

Noah felt sympathy for the man, but he still wasn't convinced that he was completely ignorant to what the boys had been up to.

"They were all good friends?"

"Oh, yeah. The best. They had a club and code names and everything."

Noah leaned forward. "What were the names?"

Strickland scratched his temple again, before remembering that his glasses were still on and placing them on the table. "Let's see…it was something about ghosts, I remember that much."

Noah was afraid to breathe. Beside him, Miguel's pencil had stopped writing.

"Kent was Black Ghost, and I believe Jaime was Gray Ghost, or was that Tyler?" Another temple scratch later, and he snapped his fingers. "White Ghost was Jaime. I remember that now because I thought it was funny that the one with black hair would be the white ghost, but..." he shrugged, "kids. They're gonna do what they're gonna do."

That was the truth.

As a teenager, Noah had been a fairly good kid, but he'd also done some things that would've given his mother a heart attack if she had known anything about them. Now, even at over thirty, he'd never admit to how often he'd slipped out of the house or how much alcohol he'd drunk. He'd never let her know how many drag races he'd won. Or lost. Or what the prize had been, or the punishment.

If he and Winter ever had kids, he was locking them in the house.

They talked a little more, nailed down the timeline a bit tighter, but when George could do no more than scratch his temple, it was time for them to leave. It was getting late, and they still had a good two-hour drive back to the bureau. Parrish had scheduled a freaking eight p.m. briefing, so he needed to sit through that before he could go home and tug Winter's ponytail just once.

If she would let him.

As exciting as it was to know that Jaime Peterson was most likely the third person in the manifesto, he knew it would hit Winter hard.

He needed to call her on the way, give her a heads-up about what he'd learned. The last thing he wanted to do was have her hearing this news surrounded by her peers.

Miguel drove, and Noah dialed Winter's number. Straight to voicemail. Dammit.

"Hey, it's me," he said after the tone. "I'm two hours out, and we'll be going straight to the bureau for the briefing. Call me first. There's something I need to tell you."

For good measure, he texted her basically the same thing.

An hour later, he called again. Texted again.

As they crossed over the Richmond city line, they got stuck in a long line of traffic, and Noah knew they wouldn't make it back by eight o'clock.

He texted and called a third time. Where was she? He was ready to punch his fist through the windshield by the time the building was in view. As they pulled into the parking lot, he texted one last time.

Do not go into that meeting! Wait for me in the hall!!!
Urgent.

Heart pounding in his chest, he jumped out of the car before Miguel could even get the transmission into park. He ran into the building. He needed to find Winter.

THERE WERE STILL a few key members missing when Aiden started the briefing. He liked to be on time, and Max Osbourne expected it.

Everyone in the room looked tired, but that couldn't be helped. Too much was happening too fast, and they each needed to report any new findings.

SAC Osbourne went first, reminding each agent in no uncertain terms just how vital it was that they close this case and close it now. He was getting pressure from the governor and every world leader known to man. Or at least, that was how he made it sound.

After Max had finished his spiel, he went around the room, asking for updates. Unfortunately, there weren't many.

Will Hoult had been a breakthrough, but the man was no help to them since he was dead. Forensics had been over every inch of that hotel with a magnifying glass and had come up with exactly nada other than the cross and "Judas" spelled out in his blood on the wall. Whoever killed Hoult was a formidable opponent, and Aiden was deeply worried that he knew exactly who that opponent was.

Justin Black.

Douglas Kilroy's protégé?

All roads seemed to be leading back to Winter's brother, and Aiden was the one who was about to tell her that. He dreaded it immensely, almost as much as he was looking forward to getting that weight off his shoulders.

She was still pissed at him, that much was obvious. She hadn't even looked in his direction since she'd walked into the room. Not that he could blame her. He had behaved badly. He'd let his fatigue and his genuine concern for her blur the line between personal and professional.

Just as Sun Ming was finishing her report, Noah Dalton burst into the room. He seemed scared, then immediately relieved when his eyes landed on Winter. He swiped his arm over his face to wipe away the sweat.

What was that all about?

"Good of you to join us, Dalton," he said as the big guy took the empty seat to Winter's right. He began speaking to her in a low voice, and she waved her hand toward the door. There was something said about messages and phones and dead batteries and something getting charged. It didn't take a genius to put the story together.

Aiden loudly cleared his throat. "If you could please continue this lovers' spat later, the rest of the team would appreciate it." He immediately regretted his choice of words when Winter's vivid blue eyes flashed death daggers at him.

"Dalton, do you have anything to report?" Miguel came through the door, much more calmly than his partner, and took a seat in the back of the room. "Or should I ask Vasquez, since he's decided to join us too?"

Dalton gave Winter a "sorry" look, and Winter stiffened, as if bracing for what was to come. So did Aiden.

"I think we've found the third person in the manifesto," Dalton said. "Miquel and I questioned Kent Strickland and got exactly shit. Then we questioned his father, George Strickland." He pulled out the picture of Jaime Peterson, giving Winter another "sorry" look. "He recognized Jaime Peterson as a good friend of his son and Tyler Haldane. They all practiced shooting and played live war games."

Winter paled with every word as Noah continued to talk about what the father had said.

When Dalton was finished, Aiden cleared his throat. "Stay on that and learn everything you can. Good work."

Shit. He might as well make his report now too. Since the bandage had been ripped off, he might as well pour on the alcohol, getting the pain over all at once.

"I agree with your assessment of Jaime Peterson being the third person in the manifesto."

Aiden watched Winter closely as he spelled out the details regarding his conversation with Phil Rossway and the subsequent murder of his father.

Noah was actively holding Winter up by the time he was finished, and no one in the room seemed to care.

Aiden's phone buzzed on the table in front of him, and he glanced at the screen. The message line screamed: *URGENT!*

"Excuse me a moment."

Max picked up the meeting, instructing Bree to write the new information on the whiteboard. He heard them talking but their words faded away as he opened the email.

No. This couldn't be right.

But it was.

The world tilted to the side, and he put his hand on the table to steady himself.

"What is it?" Max barked. When Aiden didn't answer, Max took the phone from his hand and looked at the screen. "Son of a bitch."

The roomful of agents began to stir, the buzz of their questions and curiosity causing a hiss in the room.

"What is it?" Sun Ming asked, making the question seem more like an order.

Aiden didn't know if he could answer, so he nodded to Max, letting the SAC take the lead.

"We have a new case. Double homicide." Osbourne took in a deep breath, blew it out. "Timothy and Mariah Young were murdered this evening. Preacher style."

The End
To be continued...

Find all of the Winter Black Series books on Amazon.

ACKNOWLEDGMENTS

How does one properly thank everyone involved in taking a dream and making it a reality? Let me try.

In addition to my family, whose unending support provided the foundation for me to find the time and energy to put these thoughts on paper, I want to thank the editors who polished my words and made them shine.

Many thanks to my publisher for risking taking on a newbie and giving me the confidence to become a bona fide author.

More than anyone, I want to thank you, my reader, for clicking on a nobody and sharing your most important asset, your time, with this book. I hope with all my heart I made it worthwhile.

Much love,
Mary

ABOUT THE AUTHOR

Mary Stone lives among the majestic Blue Ridge Mountains of East Tennessee with her two dogs, four cats, a couple of energetic boys, and a very patient husband.

As a young girl, she would go to bed every night, wondering what type of creature might be lurking underneath. It wasn't until she was older that she learned that the creatures she needed to most fear were human.

Today, she creates vivid stories with courageous, strong heroines and dastardly villains. She invites you to enter her world of serial killers, FBI agents but never damsels in distress. Her female characters can handle themselves, going toe-to-toe with any male character, protagonist or antagonist.

Discover more about Mary Stone on her website.
www.authormarystone.com

facebook.com/authormarystone

goodreads.com/AuthorMaryStone

bookbub.com/profile/3378576590

pinterest.com/MaryStoneAuthor

instagram.com/marystone_author

Made in the USA
Columbia, SC
30 November 2022

72426774R00170